2/23

D1569541

HAYNER PLD/LARGE PRINT
Alton, Illinois
OVERDUES .10 PER DAY.
MAXIMUM FINE COST OF ITEMS.

KISS
THE
GIRL

Center Point
Large Print

Also by Melanie Jacobson and available from Center Point Large Print:

Kiss Me Now

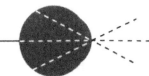

This Large Print Book carries the Seal of Approval of N.A.V.H.

KISS THE GIRL

MELANIE JACOBSON

CENTER POINT LARGE PRINT
THORNDIKE, MAINE

For Mom,
who was kind enough to have me
on Christmas Eve

CHAPTER ONE
GRACE

Hanging upside down in a bridal garden with a dress over your head is not the best time to regret your underwear choices. But here I was.

I meant to go to the rehearsal dinner. I did. I even turned to follow Brooke out of the bridal garden when she went to find her groom. But . . . if hiding out here would prolong the awkward setup Brooke was trying to trick me into then I'd pitch a freaking tent and call it home.

I paused for a final moment to admire the arbor. It looked good. I'd built it myself and installed it yesterday. The florist had filled it today with hundreds of flowers from Miss Lily's garden right here on the grounds. Fitting, since it was Miss Lily's grandson who Brooke was marrying. The blossoms spilled over the top of the arbor, twining with the sheer swathes of fabric swagged from the—

Ah, dang it. Like it knew I was thinking about it, the fabric pinned dead-center to the arbor's peak came loose and fluttered down, drooping sadly.

I walked up the aisle to examine the problem. It was sunset and not quite enough light to see by. Even squinting didn't help, so I slid off my shoes—a pair of platform wedge sandals I was only wearing because Brooke vetoed my flip-flops—and dragged a chair beneath the arch. Now I could see the problem. The florist had secured the gauzy fabric with tape, but that wasn't going to stick well to the wood. This would work better if—

I reached up to hook the fabric to a piece of vine, but since I was 5'3, it was like Jackie trying to climb the beanstalk.

In fact, climbing was the only thing that would work. I hopped down and studied the arbor again. I'd built it super sturdy with latticework up the sides. The cross pieces would support me without any trouble. I could zip up the side, secure the tulle, and shimmy down, easy.

Except I was wearing a dress. It was a floaty blue dress that Brooke had loaned me for the rehearsal dinner. I eyeballed the distance to the house. The flower garden was in the side yard, out of the direct line of sight of the people mingling on Miss Lily's back terrace. I could be up, fix the tulle, and down without anyone noticing. It would be one less thing for Brooke to worry about in the morning.

I climbed up the side of the arbor in no time flat, but when I drew even with the top, I couldn't reach the tulle hanging in the center despite stretching as far in as I could. "Great. Why did Brooke have to marry someone so tall?" It answered with a small flutter that I took personally.

I climbed on top of the frame, careful to keep my weight on the arches on either side while I scooched to the center. I reached down for the tulle, but it was a few inches too low.

I glared down at it. "I'll get you, my pretty, and your little bow too," I growled.

It took careful maneuvering, but I made a quarter turn so instead of a hand and knee on each side of the arbor arch, my knees rested on two of the cross slats, my feet on the frame behind me, my hands braced on the frame in front of me. Now all I had to do was lean down and . . .

My knee slipped and pitched me forward. I squeaked, but six years of gymnastics kicked in and I grabbed the frame in front of me tight with both hands. A second later, I was upside down but steady, my hips resting against the wood like they used to do on the uneven bars. Unfortunately, my dress was hanging upside down too, blocking out everything but a small patch of grass below me and flashing my panties to all the crickets hanging out in the garden.

I gave big, huge thanks that the garden was out of sight of the terrace and batted at the dress, feeling as lost as I used to when Tabitha and I had played hide-and-seek in the living room curtains when we were little. What underwear was I even wearing? I winced. Brooke's borrowed dress was so pretty that I'd almost grabbed my one pair of fancy underwear—a lacy thong—from the bottom of my drawer. Then I'd remembered I hated thongs and that was why I only owned one. Instead, I'd grabbed the ones on top, a bikini cut pair with frosted donuts printed all over them. Hanging upside down in a thong was the only thing that could have made this whole situation worse.

"Whoa."

I froze at the sound of a male voice. It turned out there were *two* things that could make this situation worse.

"Are you okay?"

I didn't recognize it, but it didn't matter. There wasn't a single soul on the whole entire earth who I wanted to see me hanging upside down in a garden with my dress around my ears. "I'm fine."

There was a long pause. "Are you sure?"

"I'm sure. Just fixing something." I thought about pushing the dress up to cover my butt, but honestly, I didn't want to lose my curtain and have to look this person in the face. I left it.

"Can I help?" Whoever it was sounded like he was trying not to laugh.

"Nope. I have it totally under control. Just fixing the arbor."

"Fixing the arbor," the voice repeated in a skeptical tone.

"Yes. Fixing. The. Arbor." *Go away, whoever you are. Far, far away.*

"Right. Okay." Another long pause. "I might come out here again in ten minutes to check on you." He still sounded like he was trying not to laugh.

I wanted to groan in frustration. "Are you some kind of creeper?"

"No. I mean, I don't usually expect to find women hanging upside down in gardens. Do you usually flash people?"

Fair point. "Only when I'm trying to fix an arbor."

"Do you want me to get a ladder or something?"

"No need. I've got it." *Just go AWAY.*

"If you're sure . . ."

"OH MY GOSH."

"Right." The man cleared his throat. "I'll go now."

"Bye."

I counted to twenty to make sure he was gone. "Hello?" No answer. Sounded like the coast was clear, and it was a good thing too, because the blood was rushing to my head. I reached behind me and tucked the hem of the dress into the waistband of my underwear then the front hem into my bodice so I could see what I was doing. With the dress out of my way, I could get to the tulle and had it secured and properly swoopy in thirty seconds flat.

I curled my hands around the frame and did a kick over, dangling for a second then dropping softly to the ground, Black Widow style. There was no one to admire my pose, thank goodness. I untucked the dress and let it fall down around my knees, smoothed my hair, and headed straight for the driveway instead of the rehearsal dinner. No way was I going to risk bumping into whoever I'd flashed.

Halfway to my car, I stopped, my fists curling tight. This night was not about me. This was about Brooke, the only friend I'd allowed myself to make since coming back to Creekville. And I was nothing if not loyal.

To a freaking fault.

I turned and headed back to the house to join the rest of the party. I'd have to hope the garden creeper was gentleman enough to never, ever mention what he'd seen to me or anyone else. I would paste on a smile and show up for Brooke, then slink away and try not to think about how many times I was going to relive this humiliation.

But right now, it was about running interference for Brooke with her mom and being there in case Brooke needed anything else. As her maid of honor, it was the least I could do.

I smoothed my dress one last time and headed around the house to the party.

It was late dusk, and gold light already spilled through Miss Lily's windows onto the flagstone terrace behind her house. A few people stood outside, enjoying the warmth of the late spring night, the soft clink of ice in their cocktails striking the perfect note against the harmony of the season's first crickets.

Crowds weren't my favorite. I wasn't much of a small talker. Give me someone who wanted to get deep and nerdy about finite element structural analysis and I could listen for hours. But chit chat about the weather? I'd rather hammer every one of my fingers like old Mr. Merlton did at least once on every project.

I climbed the shallow steps to the low terrace and smiled as I spotted Brooke tucked beneath Ian's arm.

"Hello, Gracie Winters," said Miss Lily's amused voice. She was studying me from her seat at a garden table several feet away.

"Hello, Miss Lily." It was a relief to run into her first. Miss Lily didn't expect small talk from me. Or maybe it was the way she asked the same questions everyone else did except that she made me believe she cared about the answers.

"Come sit a minute, honey."

I obeyed her as if she were my own grandmother, sliding out the chair across from her. "How are you holding up with all this wedding madness, Miss Lily?"

"I'm not holding up; I'm *thriving*."

"I hope I have half your energy when I'm your

age," I said. "Actually, I'd love even half your energy now."

"Would you like to know the secret?" she asked, leaning closer.

"Of course," I said, leaning too.

"Get married, have kids and grandkids, then retire, get widowed, and spend your considerable talents and intelligence in meddling with your grandchildren's lives." She grinned and smacked the table. "Keeps me young. Let's get you started. My other grandson Landon is here, and *he's* not married."

I laughed. "Landon had a thing for Tabitha, and I could never take her leavings."

Miss Lily scowled at me. "All right. I accept that." Then her face smoothed out. "How's your sister doing, anyway?"

"Great. Her show got picked up by the Food Channel, and it's keeping her crazy busy."

"And your parents?" Her voice grew softer, as if she were trying not to press on a bruise.

"My mom's hanging in there. We think my dad might qualify for a medical trial that's had good results for people with his form of lymphoma."

"Good to hear." Miss Lily settled into her chair as if a burden really had been lifted from her shoulders. "I miss seeing him around the hardware store. Not that you aren't as capable as he is. And better-looking too. Maybe I'll send Landon over there to buy me some . . ."

"Some what?" I asked when she trailed off. "What could Landon possibly come in to get that you couldn't pick out more easily yourself?"

"I don't know, but I'm going to think of something that's obscure enough to keep you both looking for at least a half an hour. *Together.*"

She was teasing me. Probably? But she'd tricked Ian into investigating Brooke to get her oldest grandson married off, and I didn't want to take any chances. I glanced around for an escape, something that would convince her not to sic Landon on me. I spotted him chatting with a guy I didn't recognize.

Hmmm. The best defense was a good offense.

Time to flip the script on Miss Lily.

"You're right," I said.

Her eyebrow rose. "I usually am." She cleared her throat. "Er, what am I right about?"

"I think I'm going to go catch up with Landon."

"That's an excellent idea."

I excused myself and slid back from the table, striding over to her younger grandson.

"Hey, Landon."

"Hey, Grace. Long-time, no see."

"Hey," I said to the guy he was talking to. I didn't recognize him, but I definitely would have known if I'd met him before. He had the wholesome good looks that meant he'd probably been captain of his high school baseball team and homecoming king. He'd be exactly what I would go for if I weren't hellbent on getting out of this town as soon as my dad could take back over the store. And if he didn't have a blank look on his face, like he'd already checked out.

"Head's up," I said, as I slid my arm through Landon's, his eyebrows shooting up like his grandmother's had. "Your gran has decided to fix us up, so I told her I was going to beat her to it, but I don't want to go out with you, so now I'm standing here faking."

The cute guy choked on his drink. Landon rolled his eyes. "Grace, let me introduce you to the third coolest guy at this party. Noah Redmond, meet Grace Winters, queen of the hardware store. Grace, this is—"

"Noah, Brooke's friend." I gave him a polite smile, but inwardly, I groaned. I'd just foiled Miss Lily's attempted matchmaking only to fall right into Brooke's. She'd tried twice to talk me into a setup with Noah, the PE teacher at her high school.

"Hi, Grace. Nice to meet you." His face wasn't blank now. In fact, he looked like he was fighting hard to keep it straight and losing.

And for the second time that night, I froze. I recognized that voice laced with laughter. I'd just heard it in the garden.

CHAPTER TWO
NOAH

I stifled a laugh when a woman in a familiar-looking blue dress sidled over to Landon. I didn't recognize her face, but there was a fair chance I knew what underwear she was wearing.

By the red flush creeping up her neck, it was clear she knew my voice, but how did she know my name already? I would remember meeting her. She was petite—not much over five foot—with dark, medium-length hair and a butt I would definitely have noticed if our paths had crossed.

Oh, wait . . . Landon had called her Grace. Maybe Brooke had mentioned setting me up with a friend named Grace a while back? But she'd dropped it, and I'd forgotten until now. Dang. I should have taken Brooke up on it, even if her friend's eyes were drilling holes through me.

"Nice to meet you too," she said.

Grace was a very bad faker. Even Landon picked up on a vibe.

"Is something wrong?" he asked.

"No."

"Not at all."

Grace and I both rushed to speak at the same time, and it made us sound like we were trying too hard to convince him.

"Landon," Miss Lily called from the other side of the terrace.

"Excuse me, I need to see what Gran needs. We'll catch up later, Grace?" She nodded. "Nice to talk to you, Noah."

Silence fell between us when Landon left.

"It was you in the garden," she said. It was an accusation.

I nodded. No use denying it. "Get everything, um, fixed?"

She cleared her throat and shifted from foot to foot. Her eyes wouldn't meet mine. "Yeah. It's all fixed."

Did she even realize she kept smoothing the skirt of her dress like she was checking to make sure it was still in place?

"That's good," I said. "I'm sure you saved the wedding."

Her eyes flickered to mine and she gave me a pinched smile. "Yes, I've saved the wedding, and no one will ever know. Just your average undercover superhero. Wouldn't want anyone to suffer a rogue tulle attack."

"Tulle? Is that what you call the—" I waved my hands in the air, trying to figure out how to describe the fabric on the arbor—"fairy stuff?"

"Fairy stuff?"

"It looks like fairy dress material."

She eyed me, the color in her cheeks returning to normal. "I have questions."

"About?"

"About why you know what fairies wear."

"I have a five-year-old niece."

She paused then nodded as if that explained everything. If she knew Evie, it would.

"So." I cleared my throat. I was not a ladies' man or player or whatever it was guys who were smooth were called these days, but I had *some* game. But the advice about picturing people in their underwear to make yourself less nervous was one hundred percent backfiring at the moment. "Uh, you're friends with Brooke?"

"Yeah. Helped her with some remodeling. We hang out."

I risked studying her more closely. "You seem familiar to me." It wasn't a line. She did, but I couldn't put my finger on it. When she looked wary for a second, I flinched. "Not because of the garden. I mean your *face* looks familiar." *Oh, nice one, Noah. Way to make it even worse.*

"Probably seen me in the hardware store. I run it for my dad."

"I'm not very handy. If anything goes wrong at my place, I call the apartment manager."

She shrugged. "I'm not sure, then."

Her face got the closed look I saw on students every day. It was the look of someone deeply uncomfortable but pretending not to be.

With my students, I tried jokes or distraction to nudge them out of it. It was worth a shot here if it meant she wouldn't look like she was scoping the terrace for easy exits. I didn't want her to walk away. Not that I wouldn't enjoy the view as she did.

"I think I need to even the score," I said.

Her gaze shot up, a spark of curiosity in her eyes. "What does that mean?"

"Let's make a deal. I'll embarrass myself in front of you, then we can be chill around each other."

"How would you do that? I'm curious to see how embarrassed you think you need to be to equal the show I gave you."

Oops. Hadn't looked at it that way. This suddenly felt like I'd asked myself a trick question, only I didn't know the answer. I scrambled to think of something. "Um, pretend to be drunk, stagger around, crash into the dessert table, and knock everything over?"

"Like every comedy with a wedding ever?"

"No. I'm offended that you'd question my creativity. Those always ruin the wedding cake. This is just the rehearsal dinner. Totally different."

"Right. Got it. And you'd do this in front of everyone?"

"Obviously."

"Wow. So I guess on that scale, me flashing an almost empty garden while trying to do my friend a solid should be humiliating."

You couldn't win at trick questions.

Time to backtrack. "I'm only spitballing."

She smiled at me, the first smile from her that had felt real. Real and warm. "I appreciate the offers, but no deal. Here's what would help: forget the garden thing ever happened. Forget what you saw, maybe even forget me. And on that note, I need to go check on Brooke."

She turned with a sexy swish of her dress that sent it flaring out from her knees enough for me to get a glimpse of the legs I wasn't going to forget.

Not those legs. Not her hanging upside down in the garden.

And definitely not her.

CHAPTER THREE
GRACE

It was a killer exit. I couldn't believe that for once in my life, I'd come up with the right comeback at the right time. Normally I didn't think of the right thing to say until the next time I was in the shower or stuck at a long red light.

I floated on that victory for about six steps until my stupid shoe hit wrong on the uneven terrace pavers and my ankle bent in like I was trying to do a Monty Python funny walk.

Once again, my gymnastics reflexes saved me, and I regained my balance with some wind-milling and core strength. I had to freeze for a second to make sure I wasn't going down the aisle on crutches tomorrow.

I gave my ankle a tiny wiggle and let out my breath when it felt okay. Then I froze again. Noah had probably seen that. Did I want to know? Could I stand it if he had? Because right now, it was fifty-fifty as to whether I would brush it off or leave town, family obligations be damned. This was potentially catastrophic ego damage, no repairs possible.

I wanted to know. I risked a quick glance over my shoulder toward Noah who was staring into the bottom of his cocktail glass like it was revealing the secrets of the universe. I snorted and walked off toward the pool house with the guest bathroom. That was the worst "I didn't see a thing" acting job I'd ever seen in my life.

I slipped inside and splashed cold water over my face, careful to avoid my mascara. Once again, I had the overwhelming urge to drive home and be done with this whole ridiculous night, but I sighed, splashed my face again, reapplied my nude pink lipstick, and headed back out to the terrace to run interference between Brooke and her parents so she could enjoy her rehearsal dinner. Heaven knew I understood high maintenance moms.

I made a slight detour to the table first, scanning the place cards to make sure I wasn't next to Noah. Knowing Brooke, she'd have seated us next to each other, but I'd had all the Noah-adjacent humiliation I could stand, even to appease her on her pre-wedding night.

She had. She'd put her mom on one side of me and Noah on the other. I rolled my eyes and snatched up the name card, hunting until I found the one that belonged to Izzy, Ian's sister, and made the switch. I could handle that. I liked Izzy, who was the only other bridesmaid.

I found Brooke with her parents and smiled at Brooke, who smiled back, slightly strained around the edges. It was the look Brooke wore when her mom was trying to tweak wedding details. "Hey, Miss Lily was asking for you," I said. She wasn't, but it didn't matter. Brooke needed a rescue.

"We'd better go see what she needs," Ian said, familiar with the maneuvers needed to escape Mrs. Spencer when she wanted to make yet another of her infinitesimal wedding adjustments.

"How are you liking Creekville?" I asked the Spencers as Ian led Brooke away. "Aren't Miss Lily's grounds so perfect for a wedding?" A courteous but long litany from Mrs. Spencer about why they should have had the wedding in McClean followed, so I fixed a polite smile on my face and made sympathetic noises while I didn't listen.

At last, one of the servers approached our group to let us know that dinner would begin soon, so I gently herded the Spencers toward the table, resigning myself to listening to more of the same when we took our seats.

Except when we reached the table, Noah was in the chair next to mine.

I frowned at him. "That's Izzy's spot."

He picked up his place card and flicked it a casual glance before turning it toward me. "I don't think so."

The rat. He'd switched places, but I couldn't call him out on it without making it clear that I'd changed it in the first place.

I took my seat and put my napkin in my lap,

determined to make the best of a bad seating situation. Mrs. Spencer still wasn't done so I listened to more of her wedding grievances. The catering crew had served our salads before Mr. Spencer drew his wife into a different conversation and I could take my first bite.

"I see why Brooke has you running interference with her mom," Noah said.

I pretended to be composed and glanced over at him. "So you're obligated to do the rehearsal dinner because you're ushering tomorrow?"

He flashed me a big smile. "I am. King of the ushers."

A big old piece of arugula was stuck to his front tooth, right up against his gumline.

"Oh, uh . . ." I'd have told Brooke if it was her, but how did you politely tell a brand-new acquaintance they had food stuck? I couldn't think of anything smooth, so I went for it. "You have some food caught on your tooth."

"Whoa, thanks." He closed his lips, ran his tongue over his teeth and bared them again. "Did I get it?" he asked through his clenched jaw.

"You got it."

"Thanks."

"No problem." It made me feel a tiny bit better about falling off my own shoes. "So what does king of the ushers do?"

We chatted for several minutes like any strangers at a dinner party might. At some point, the reverend sitting on his other side asked him a question, and Noah turned to talk to him. Mrs. Spencer reclaimed my attention, and I listened to her over the musical lilt of silverware on fine china and the murmur of conversations happening up and down the table.

The servers collected our salad plates and replaced them with salmon, lemon pasta, and sautéed bok choy.

"Oh man, this is good," Noah said. He cut off another piece of his salmon. "Do you like fish?"

"Yeah, salmon especially." I was going to ask if he'd tried the bok choy when I noticed a cowlick had formed since the last time we spoke. A tuft poked out near his part. His hair product must be failing although it didn't look like he used much. His medium-brown hair was the kind of short where he probably had to get it cut every four weeks exactly or it would get shaggy. But unlike the lettuce in his teeth, there was nothing he could do to fix the cowlick, so I didn't say anything.

It looked ridiculous, and I did appreciate the universe trying to tip the scales between us again.

"I know I already said this, but seriously, you do look familiar. It's bugging me that I can't put my finger on it." He studied my face, not in an intrusive way, but my eyes still skittered to his cowlick. "You're from here?" he asked.

"Yeah, Creekville born and bred. Graduated from Lincoln. You?"

"I'm not from Creekville."

I refrained from rolling my eyes. "I know that. If you'd gone to high school here, I would know you."

"Right. I'm from Mineral."

It was only two towns over. "So you went to Lone Valley?"

"Yeah."

"I went to a homecoming dance there once."

His gaze sharpened. "Wait, did you go with Blake Garner?"

My eyes widened. "How'd you know that?"

He started laughing. "We double-dated. That's why you look familiar."

I blinked a couple times. "Seriously?"

"Yeah. My date was Serena, the redhead? And I was a lot shorter. I grew eight inches the summer before my junior year, after that dance."

"You were my height at that homecoming." I couldn't process it. "You were so puny. I was taller than you in my heels. And now you're not puny. You did all that in one summer?" I waved my hand to encompass him head to toe. If he was under six feet, it wasn't by much.

"I'm 5'11 now, but I got it all at once. It was an uncomfortable summer."

"I can imagine. Or maybe not. I never got my growth spurt."

He looked like he was about to say something but then the tips of his ears turned slightly pink, and he reached for his wine glass instead. "A toast to the old days and our shorter selves."

"I'm still the same height," I said, smiling in spite of myself, "but I'll toast the old days."

Our glasses made a pretty clinking noise because Miss Lily, of course, had actual crystal stemware. It was a light, fruity red wine and I took a small sip, needing to keep a clear head for the drive home. Noah took a sip of his too, but then made a small choking sound and suddenly, a splotch of red wine bloomed on the crisp blue fabric of his button-down shirt.

"Dang," he said, picking up his napkin to dab at it. "Went down the wrong pipe."

He was having a rough night. Food in his teeth, a cowlick sticking out, spilling wine down his shirt—

Wait.

"Noah." My voice was stern enough for his head to shoot up.

"Yes?"

"Did you spill that wine on purpose?"

"What? No."

"You did." I leaned closer so I could watch his eyes. "And you made your hair stick up and you put lettuce in your teeth."

"No, I didn't." His eyes flickered the tiniest bit. I wouldn't have seen it if I hadn't been looking.

"You're busted."

"I don't know what you're talking about." But he dabbed at his shirt instead of meeting my eyes.

"Noah?"

"Yeah?" He kept dabbing.

"The memory of you in high school made us even. It's like seeing someone's bad yearbook photo."

Now he darted a look my way. "We're even?"

I nodded. "We're even."

He threw his napkin on the table. "Thank goodness. I was running out of ideas."

I laughed. "I see why Brooke is friends with you. You're all right, Noah." He was cute with his big brown eyes and easy smile, and if I were sticking around, I'd be doing some flirting. But I was counting down the days until I could leave Creekville. Small town guys were all about roots, and I had no time or energy for entanglements before I left. But I could for sure sit here and enjoy some friendly—*not* flirtatious—dinner conversation now that we'd gotten the awkwardness out of the way.

"I really am all right," he said, his expression serious. "The all rightest. Maybe even all right enough to take you out for dinner like I should have when Brooke suggested it weeks ago?"

When his grin flashed at me again, I wanted to say yes. My mouth almost formed the word. I had a feeling he was probably more than all right.

Instead, I pursed my lips and gave him a head shake. "Tempting, even after the garden thing. But I'm not dating right now."

He gave me an easy smile. "My loss."

But I had a sneaking suspicion it might be mine.

CHAPTER FOUR
NOAH

Grace may not have grown in height, but she'd filled out. So nicely. I was a smart enough man not to say it though. I wouldn't risk shoving us back into awkward territory again. Whether it was spilling the wine or the mental image of my scrawny high school self, the energy between us had changed. I wanted to keep it going, and that meant backing off the flirting.

"So, Creekville. Do you like it here?" she asked.

"I do."

"Why?"

There was something blunt about the way she phrased the question, like she didn't believe me. "You sound surprised."

"I don't see Creekville as the kind of place people want to grow up and move to. More like grow up and move away from."

"You didn't like growing up here?"

"I did." She gave a restless flick of her hand, and I wasn't sure what the gesture meant. Impatience? Dismissal? "It's great if you like small towns. I've gotten used to cities. I prefer them."

"Why?" I turned the question around on her with the same bluntness.

"You first," she said. "You haven't explained why Creekville."

"That's not really a conversation for dinner."

She cocked her head. "Sounds like a story."

A long, painful one. I gave her a sanitized version of it. "I'm not in Creekville, actually. I only work here. I liked Mineral. I like small towns. I like knowing the families and the community. But it started to feel too small." *So many people in my business. So. Many.* "I talked my sister into moving to Granger so I'd have a shorter drive to work in Creekville. Similar vibe, but . . ."

"But fewer people who've known everything about you including your weight at birth?"

"Right." I studied her, watching the slight lines in her face. "Which is why I don't live here. Didn't want to bump into students when I'm on a grocery run, you know? Granger is a good compromise. Is there a reason you can't leave though?" She had to be close to my age, maybe 26 or 27. Maybe college and a career hadn't been in her cards. Brooke had told me about Grace's personality, but not a lot about her background. "Are you looking for a career change? You can't throw a rock without hitting a college in Virginia. Maybe you could do night classes, or—" I broke off as a smile curved her lips. "I said something dumb, didn't I?"

"I resigned from a position at Boeing on their

aerospace design team to come home and help out my parents." She smirked at me. No other way to describe that smile.

"Not just dumb. Condescending and possibly sexist too." I lifted the tablecloth and tried to peer beneath it. "You think I can fit under there until dinner is over?"

"The sexism is super weird because I definitely don't deal with that every single day as a woman running a hardware store." She would have had every right to sound bitter about it, but her tone only held weary amusement.

"I think Brooke was being a better friend to me than she was to you when she suggested setting us up."

Grace outright laughed. "Don't be so hard on yourself. Her instincts weren't terrible. If I were sticking around, it might have been a good idea."

That statement was to a compliment what sparkling water was to soda—a pale imitation of the real thing—but it somehow made me want to strut off and high five the first bro-looking dude I saw. I tried to play it cool. "You leaving Creekville soon?"

She sighed, her smile fading, and I wanted to find a way to put it back on her face. "Maybe. I don't know. I hope so. It depends on my dad's health. There are a lot of variables."

It definitely didn't seem like the time to ask her to explain further, so I tried for a lighter subject.

"Would it be such a bad idea to hang out between now and whenever you leave?"

The corner of her mouth twitched. "Do we really need to? I don't remember how the bases go, but I think we've already gotten to second."

I'd just taken a casual swig of my wine, and I choked on it. It was the second time I'd done that in front of her. "That was an actual accident," I promised with a slight gasp.

"You got a drinking problem?" she asked, eyeing me.

I grabbed a napkin and blotted at my chin. "You should see me at a water fountain. A disaster."

She rested her chin in her palm and her lips curved into a sexy smile, the late spring breeze playing with strands of her hair. "You seem like a cool guy. If I were a fling kind of girl, I'd say yes. You'd be a cute distraction. But I'm not. And since I'm eventually going back to Charleston and Boeing, I'm going to concentrate on the hardware store and my dad. I'll tell Brooke she guessed right, though."

It stung. It was the second time she'd rejected me, and I had to respect that, even if I could see how easy it would be to fall for a woman like her. Pretty, smart, *and* funny. Maybe it was for the best. I'd probably be dead meat if we dated because that was a lethal combination for me. I smiled at her. "This is me, slightly disappointed but accepting your verdict."

Her gaze flickered past me to Brooke. "She's starting to look stressed. I'd better go run interference like I promised."

And I watched her extremely cute behind walk away.

I unlocked my apartment door and slipped inside. I'd been dreading the rehearsal dinner, but it had been fine. Maybe Brooke was finally desensitizing me to my wedding-related PTSD with her constant chatter on our lunch breaks, or maybe it was because my ex, Lauren, and I hadn't made it quite as far as the rehearsal dinner before she called off our wedding. But either way, it hadn't been as triggering as I'd expected it to be.

I slid off my shoes and collapsed on the couch to stare at the ceiling. I could respect Grace's reasons for not dating. It was a bummer for sure, but it would be fun to hang out with her at the wedding tomorrow anyway.

I reached for the remote to watch the NBA finals game, but my front doorknob rattled, and a very angry woman walked in.

"I'm going to kill you!"

I straightened back up on the sofa. "Something wrong, Paige?"

"Only that you're the worst brother ever." She charged toward me but on instinct, I batted away the pillow she threw at me. I knew Paige's go-to moves.

"What did I do this time?" Outbursts from Paige were the norm. She got mad at me a lot and lived across the hall, so it made it easier for her to charge in . . . uh, constantly, really.

"The rent?"

I blinked at her. "I need to buy a vowel."

She smacked me with a pillow I didn't see coming. "You switched our rents."

"Oh. That." Leave it to Paige to get mad about paying less rent.

"You have *got* to stop treating me like I'm a kid. I'm twenty-freaking-four. And a mom. And this whole time I've been so proud of putting a roof over Evie's head even if it's kind of a crappy apartment, and it turns out that *you* have been paying the two-bedroom rent, and I've been paying for *one.*"

She didn't need to explain the situation. I was the one who'd set it up that way with the office when we'd signed leases here. "It's not a big deal. You could be paying even less if you'd let me lease a house for all of us. Evie would love it."

"Gah!" She slashed her hand across her throat in a "cut it" motion. "What do I have to do to convince you that I don't need you parenting me? I've got this. Move to Creekville so you don't have to commute. Evie and I are fine."

"Yeah, that's not going to happen." I headed to the fridge. I grabbed a Gatorade and handed her one. She took it almost on reflex. "I can afford it. You know this is what Mom and Dad would have wanted." This was mostly true. The first part was stretching it. A fifth-year teacher's salary only went so far. My stipend for coaching wrestling only helped so much. It was maybe a month's worth of rent for the whole season, and I was using that to supplement Evie's daycare costs, which would definitely result in my murder if Paige found out.

"Then at the very least, quit smothering me. You've been so much worse since Lauren dumped you."

I flinched but said nothing, and she slammed her bottle down and stormed back out of the apartment.

Good old Hurricane Paige.

I leaned against the counter and drank my Gatorade, counting slowly in my mind. She was back before I got to twenty.

"Sorry," she mumbled. She kept her eyes on the floor.

"It's okay."

"No, it's not. That was a low blow. I never liked Lauren anyway." She picked up her drink and cracked it open.

"What's going on, Paige?" Spend enough time around teenagers all day, and you started to figure out that eruptions were rarely about whatever had set them off. There was always something under it. Same with Paige. "Something happen at work?"

"The usual. Marvin is the literal worst. He was nitpicking everything I did today, from the way I carried the trays to the way I filled the condiment bottles." She slumped against the counter and took a long swallow from her bottle.

"Sorry." I had to be careful about what to say here, or she'd get defensive. I'd told her a hundred times to quit and go to school, but she wouldn't do it because it would mean depending on me even more. "Marvin's a jerk."

"Yeah." She drank again then sighed, some of the fight draining out of her. "Look, I'm sorry I barged in here. But you can't keep paying my rent like that."

"I'm barely paying any of it."

"Any is too much. Seriously, I can afford it."

She couldn't. Her car was twenty years old and running on pure cussedness, I couldn't remember the last time she'd bought herself anything new, and she was working several double shifts a week to make her bills. I didn't mind watching Evie on the nights she worked; I liked it, actually. But I hated that she had to work so hard at a job that wasn't going to get her anywhere.

If Paige could get a job at a nicer restaurant so she'd make better tips, it would make a huge difference, but the nearest fine dining place was ten miles away, and she couldn't count on her car to get her there dependably. The heap worked when it wanted to, but at least at the diner she could ride my bike if the car wouldn't start.

"Okay. I'll quit paying your rent."

"Good. It makes me feel guilty." The expression on her face wavered between satisfaction and stress since it meant a $250 monthly increase for her. I'd figure out a different way to subsidize her. "And don't try to find a different way to subsidize me."

"Fine." I didn't mean it. Our parents had died in a car accident when she was halfway through her senior year of high school. We'd each gotten a $100,000 life insurance payout, but she'd blown through hers in a year on partying, a loser boyfriend, drugs, and gambling, at the end of which she was broke, four months pregnant, and on the verge of a nervous breakdown. A real one.

She sighed and kicked her foot out to lightly knock mine. "You need to get a woman to smother with all this pent-up caretaking. A way better one than Lauren."

A quick image of Grace flashed through my mind, but I shoved it away. She was leaving, and I wanted someone who would stick around, tolerate a teacher's salary—which Lauren wouldn't—and be okay with how much Paige and Evie were part of my life. Tall order, and I might be single forever based on how quickly my last couple of potential relationships had fizzled out. Or until Evie was in college.

I nudged Paige back. "Get out of here. I want to go to bed."

"Liar. You're going to stay up watching basketball."

"Yeah. By myself. Bye."

"Bye, love you," she called on her way out the door.

And as infuriating as she could be, I loved her like crazy too. Which is why I pulled out my phone to compose a letter to the principal letting her know I'd be willing to teach summer school after all. Evie had grown an inch every two months this spring, and she was going to need all new school clothes this fall.

CHAPTER FIVE
GRACE

"Fancy meeting you here," Noah said as he walked up to me.

"Weird that the maid of honor and an usher for the same wedding would both be at the reception, right?"

"*King* usher."

He looked good. The night air was balmy, perfect weather for Brooke's outdoor festivities. Strings of soft outdoor lights ringed the portable dance floor, and people laughed and visited at the surrounding tables. Noah had shed the dark gray coat from his suit, and his well-muscled chest made his white dress shirt look like it had been tailor-made for him. Nice.

"You look pretty," he said. I liked that he said it so simply, no hint of flirtiness.

"Brooke was merciful with her dress choice." She'd picked a midi-length spaghetti strap gown, pale yellow, delicate chiffon. "The joke is that brides always say you can wear it again, and you never can. Not enough events call for satin ballgowns with giant butt bows. But I think I actually could wear this one again." Maybe. If I were ever invited to a garden party. But I'd never gone to a garden party in my whole life, so

41

maybe it was doomed to stay in my closet forever.

"She looks so happy." He smiled at the dance floor where Brooke was dancing with Ian's sister, Izzy, and a couple of the teachers from school.

"They're a good fit. I wish they had more time before Ian has to report to Quantico, but I'm happy for them both that he got in." Her brand-new husband had quit his high-paying job as the lead investigator for a big Washington DC law firm after being accepted into the FBI.

"She probably told you she's worried about being a work widow, right?" he asked.

"Yeah. I figure I'll talk her into another reno-vation project in her house and drop by a few nights a week to help her with it."

"Sneaky checkups." He raised his glass in salute. "Good thinking."

A small cheer rose from the crowd as the deejay transitioned into "The Hustle."

"Should we go dance?" I asked.

Noah eyed the dance floor. "Do you want to?"

"Not really." Thank goodness it wasn't a slow dance. I wouldn't have been able to say no to him, and swaying with him under fairy lights on a balmy spring night sounded like such a good idea that it could only be bad news for my dating ban.

He looked relieved. "Then let's not dance. What should we do instead?"

"Um, make up back stories for the wedding

guests?" I didn't know most of them. I recognized a couple dozen from Creekville, but the rest seemed to be Ian and Brooke's friends from DC.

"I'm in." He glanced around the tables, then nodded to an older gentleman sitting by himself, reading his phone, his face pinched. "That guy just found out he got outbid to buy a bidet company."

I glanced at him. "Good guess but wrong. That guy is actually a five-star general who just found out he's getting reassigned to Greenland to oversee US caribou interests."

"Wow. I didn't know that we had a caribou supply problem."

"And you never will if this guy does his job right. It should be a peaceful transition of power."

"What about that lady?" He pointed to a middle-aged woman dancing like I only wished I could.

"Soccer mom by day, TikTok dance star also by day because she's too tired at night after making dinner and helping the kids with homework. But she has eleven billion likes on her last TikTok."

"It definitely explains her moves. Impressive. But wait until you hear about that guy." He pointed to a guy at the dessert table. "Russian spy. He's here to recruit Ian and flip him so they can infiltrate the FBI."

"That's bad," I said. "What should we do?"

"I have a plan. I'm going to go get us cake,

and I'll start up a conversation with him that will convince him not to recruit Ian."

I didn't know how Noah brought out the kid in me, but I didn't want to resist. I rested my chin on my fist. "Brilliant. How will you do that?"

"I'm going to pretend I'm injured and tell him Ian judo-flipped me when I told him I think the stars on our flag are tacky."

"This ends with you coming back with cake?"

"Yeah."

"I approve. You should go do it."

"On it." He walked toward the dessert table, and when he developed a sudden, exaggerated limp halfway there, I burst out laughing. I'd laughed more in two nights with Noah than I had in a long time. He chatted with the guy for a minute while they waited to be served then came back with two plates of cake.

"You forgot to limp back. You might have blown your cover."

"It's okay. I gave him a deadeye stare, and he knew without words that his mission would fail. But all that matters is that I have your cake."

"My hero." He set a plate down in front of me and took a bite of his own. It left a big white smear of frosting next to his mouth.

"You, uh . . ." I pointed at my mouth to help him out.

"Do I have something on my face?" he asked. He didn't look remotely flustered.

"Some frosting." It was a sizable blob.

"It would be pretty embarrassing if I had to sit here with a blob of frosting on my face, and maybe you saw that and felt kind of bad for me."

My mouth twitched as I realized what he was up to. "We're even, remember?" I held up a hand to indicate his high school height. "Shrimpy Redmond. Now let me get that." I reached over to wipe away the frosting, but I only smeared it more. "I don't think I'm helping."

"You should probably keep trying," he said, smiling. There was the slightest challenge in his eyes. And much like the rogue piece of tulle taunting me on the arbor last night, I couldn't back down.

I reached up and cupped his jaw to hold it in place while I went to work. He was clean-shaven, but the faint rasp of his evening whiskers against my fingertips raised goosebumps on my arms. He kept his eyes locked on mine, the faintest smile curving the corner of his lips. I slowed down, almost without realizing it, and forgot what I was doing for a minute.

"Got it?" he asked quietly.

I let go of him, and sat back, a hitch in my breathing. "Mostly." I handed him a fresh napkin. "You can get the rest pretty easily."

He took the offered napkin, our fingers brushing, and I almost cursed as I felt the spark from his touch race up my arm. This was *not* what I needed right now.

I sat back, and he dabbed the rest of the frosting away, his eyes still on me. I needed to break the mood fast. "What about that girl?" I subtly pointed to a pretty woman Brooke had introduced to me as a college friend. She'd come without a date. Let Noah's attention wander there, to someone who might be an option for him. I thought it worked until he gave a low whistle.

"Interesting case, that one," he said. "She's under investigation. Lawyer for the mob."

"That's unfortunate," I said. "She looks pretty young for that job."

"That's what happens when you make a deal with the devil. She's sixty, but when you sell your soul . . ." He trailed off with a meaningful look.

"Good to know. I'll steer clear."

The rest of the night was like that, us hanging out and cracking jokes. But I was careful not to touch him again, and when Brooke tossed her bouquet, I nearly sprained six different muscles going out of my way not to catch it. But I cheered for the mob lawyer when she did. Better her than me.

When I got home around ten, I expected my parents to be in bed already. I lived in the "mother-in-law" apartment upstairs that I'd helped my dad build when I was in high school, but if a light was on when I came home, I still didn't always make it past my parents' living room. I liked extra time with my dad whenever possible, and a light shone now. I walked in to find my mom reading on the couch.

"Hey. What are you still doing up?"

She'd cropped the dark hair I'd inherited from her into a flattering cap of springy curls, but at the moment it was looking wild and slightly frizzy, like she'd been running her fingers through it a lot. That meant she was stressed.

"I wanted to hear about the wedding." She set her book aside, a self-help book on personal finances. If ever a book could put someone to sleep . . .

"It went great. Brooke and Ian look really happy. Lily Greene's garden was gorgeous. The food was good."

"Sounds lovely."

"You're looking . . ." I hesitated, trying to find the right word. "Ruffled?"

"Ruffled?" she repeated. "Am I a doily?"

"Is something going on, Mom?"

She sighed and rubbed her eyes with one hand, but when she dropped it, she was smiling. "Your dad worked in the yard with me today. For an hour."

My jaw dropped. "You're kidding." He hadn't had the energy to do that in over a year. His chemo treatments for non-Hodgkin's lymphoma had drained the energy from him.

"I'm not. He really did." She leaned over and took my hands. "We didn't want to say anything until we were sure, but he started that experimental drug trial six weeks ago. He's been feeling better each day, and on Monday, he's going in for new scans to see what kind of progress he's made, but we're pretty sure there *is* progress."

"Oh, Mom. That's amazing."

"Yes, well." She let go of my hands and sat back to wring them instead. "It's meant everything to have you here, honey, but we'll get you out of here soon. I promise."

"I'll be here as long as you need. Don't worry. Now go to bed."

She hugged me back and headed upstairs to her bedroom.

Most nights, I barely avoided crashing on the couch, tired from working all day, then heading over to Brooke's a few nights a week to help her with something or another.

I guess that was why we'd grown so close so fast. We'd been hanging out for hours each week, working on different parts of her house. My mom had complained once that I spent more time with Brooke than with her and my dad, but my dad had shut her down quick.

"She didn't come here to take care of me. She came here to take care of the store," he'd said. "We've already asked too much of her. Let her have a life outside of us."

Tonight, though, I didn't have the same exhaustion, not even after working all morning and doing bridesmaid duty the rest of the day. We had a part-timer, Gary, a retired plumber who helped out twenty hours a week so I could take lunch breaks and have an extra cashier on our busy weekends, but I couldn't leave him to handle the Saturday rush on his own. We'd given customers plenty of notice all week that we'd close at lunch, and then I'd left the store and driven straight over to Brooke's house, ready to help her dress then get my game face on to socialize.

And socializing was ten times more exhausting than renovating.

So why wasn't I tired?

I hopped up from the sofa and drifted toward the kitchen, stopping halfway to the fridge when I realized I was humming the song that had been playing when Noah first came over to my table tonight.

"No, Grace Winters. Definitely not. No Noah. No Noah-related songs. No Noah-related anything."

Maybe this improvement with my dad was something, maybe it wasn't. But I wouldn't be staying in Creekville long-term, and Noah Redmond, high school teacher and small-town guy, was definitely a long-term kind of man.

CHAPTER SIX
NOAH

The first days back at school are a weird energy. A good energy, but odd. Teachers came in two days before the students did, officially. Unofficially, most of us got started even earlier than that. Otherwise, you didn't have a prayer of being ready. Most of those two days were spent in boring in-service meetings and left little time for getting our classrooms set up.

Even PE teachers had stuff to get ready, which was why I reported to Lincoln High three days before I had to. I had to pull out the equipment for the first unit of the semester and figure out what we had enough unbroken or complete sets of to use with the kids. I had to go over the wrestling schedule and figure out a recruiting strategy and practice schedule.

I liked those details. That was the good part of coming back on campus. The weird part was that even though this would be my fifth year of teaching, somehow I still felt like I was doing something slightly transgressive by being in the teacher's lounge or copy room, like maybe one of the real grownups was going to tell me to scram.

This always went away after my first freshman PE class of the year. Watching them reminded me who was the grownup in the room. If anything, I felt more like a zookeeper trying to organize the monkey house.

At lunch, I took a break and headed across campus to Brooke's classroom. I had no doubt she'd come in early too. Sure enough, she was up on a desk, working on a bulletin board display.

"Knock, knock," I said, stepping into her room. "How's married life treating you?"

She turned from the bulletin board and came over to greet me with a hug. "Right now, pretty much like engaged life. Ian reported to Quantico. So basically, it's like the last year when I only saw him on weekends and holidays, except now I won't see him at all for fifteen more weeks."

"Did you guys have a good summer together, at least?"

"Yeah. It was so great. I was able to spend June with him at his apartment in DC, then he put in his notice at the firm, and we spent July at our house."

"Miss Lily must have been in heaven." Brooke's house was right next door to hers.

"Of course she was. It's the whole reason she tricked me into dating Ian in the first place."

I grinned. The story was already legendary. "Remind me never to get in her crosshairs."

"You're not her neighbor or her grandchild. You should be safe. You ready for the school year to start?"

"Kind of. Is that crazy?"

"No, I get it. I like the kids, even when I want to kill them."

I held out my hand for a fist bump. "I hear that. You have to like them if you're going to do this job. And there's something about the beginning of school that feels more like the new year than actual New Year's."

"Fresh starts, new opportunities, all of that?"

"Exactly."

"I'm also glad for something to keep me busy and distracted while I wait for Ian to finish his training. Speaking of which, I need to keep busy out of school too. I was thinking of doing a regular game night, maybe on Thursdays? Would you come? I promise to have a small handful of fun people there, keep it chill, and have good snacks."

"Sure, if it works with Paige's babysitting schedule, but I think that would be okay. But why Thursdays? Wouldn't the weekend be better?"

"I don't want to tie up your date nights. You need a woman. But also, Thursday is when I would start looking forward to seeing Ian the next day, so that's when I'll need the distraction, since, you know . . ."

"You'll have nothing to look forward to. Got it. And I don't need a woman. I like them, I go out with them often, but I'm a full-grown man, and I can take care of myself."

"And your sister. And your niece. I know.

That's not what I meant. I meant you need a life outside of them and work."

I would have argued that I liked my life fine as it was. But this was an old conversation, so I let it drop. "About this game night?"

"Do you need to know anything besides the snacks will be good?"

"Not really."

"That's what I thought."

I almost asked if Grace would be there but kept my mouth shut. It would make Brooke think I was interested, which would make her relentless, and Grace had made it clear she wasn't looking for a relationship. I'd already tried—and failed, miserably—to talk Lauren into being with me, and I was barely recovering my dignity. I was never doing that again.

"This Thursday, then," Brooke said, breaking into my self-pitying thoughts. "See you at seven."

I nodded and left, off to pop in on some of my other teacher friends. It really did feel good to be back.

I found myself looking forward to game night for the next couple of days, but every time I caught myself wondering if Grace would be there, I forced myself to think of other things instead. The health curriculum. The Nationals stats. The wrestling schedule.

But Thursday night when I got ready to head over to Brooke's, I switched out of my track pants and golf shirt and put on my nice jeans and a casual button-down shirt Paige had given me for Christmas because she said it made my eyes look more green than hazel.

I knocked on Brooke's door at five after seven. My college roommate had convinced me that only nerds were on time, but I couldn't bring myself to be any later.

"Hey," Brooke said, opening the door with a smile. "Come on in."

I followed her into the living room where Grace was already sitting on the couch, a glass of wine on the coffee table in front of her.

"Hey, Noah." She gave me a normal smile, probably exactly like the ones she gave Brooke.

"Good to see you again." *Wow, Noah. Remember when you used to have* some *game?*

"Even if it's just my face?" Grace asked, quirking an eyebrow at me as she reached for her wineglass.

"Wait, what?" Brooke said. "What does that mean?"

"Nothing," I muttered.

"There was an incident at the rehearsal dinner." Grace took a sip of her wine.

"What kind of incident?"

"I can't comment," I said. "I don't want to expose Grace further than she's already exposed herself."

Grace snorted, and Brooke's forehead wrinkled

54

even more. "Grace?" she said, in an I'm-waiting-young-lady teacher voice.

"No grace," Grace answered. "Opposite of grace. Noah here found me hanging upside down on the arbor in your dress, flashing the world."

"Wow," Brooke said, her voice dry. "I didn't realize you made a habit of that, Noah."

"Ha, ha," I said.

"Now I feel like I'm missing something," Grace said. "Noah regularly goes around checking out women's underwear?"

"It's not my fault you two insisted on showing me yours," I said, not in the least embarrassed. Because it absolutely *wasn't* my fault.

"Brooke?" Grace said, her tone demanding an explanation.

"First week of teaching last year. Noah came to my classroom for lunch. I went to the restroom. I tucked the back of my skirt into my underwear. Noah was the one who had to let me know why all the kids in the hall had laughed at me."

"Whoa, Noah," Grace said. "You get around."

They were revving up. I'd never spent time with them together, but I could tell I was about to get tag-teamed. "Can we stop talking about y'all's underwear? You both need to develop new interests beyond flashing innocent bystanders. Like—" I flicked a glance at the box on the table. "Scrabble? Really, Spencer? That's your idea of a good time?"

"It's Greene now," Brooke said, plopping down in the only armchair in the room. "And yes. Scrabble."

The only other place to sit was next to Grace on the sofa. I had a feeling that wasn't an accident on Brooke's part, and I didn't mind one bit. I hoped Grace didn't either. "Scrabble isn't a great team game," I said, reaching for the box.

"Who said anything about teams?" Brooke asked.

Grace looked from me to Brooke. "It's just the three of us tonight?"

"Of course," said Brooke, and then she jumped to her feet again. "Oh, I almost forgot to offer you a drink, Noah. What can I get for you?"

"A beer is fine. Also, I was promised snacks. Good snacks."

"Coming right up."

She disappeared into the kitchen, and Grace glanced over at me, smiling. "The funny thing is that she thinks she's subtle."

"As long as you know I didn't put her up to this."

"Don't worry. I'm aware of Miss Brooke's misguided ideas."

"For what it's worth, I used to be a Boy Scout." I held up my fingers in the Boy Scout sign. "I promise not to date you, Grace."

She held up her wineglass in salute. "I accept your solemn vow."

"So this means we can have a non-awkward game night?"

"Hundred percent."

And we did. Brooke came back with a cold beer, a tray of chips and salsa made from the garden she and Miss Lily shared, and a bowl of Muddy Buddies Chex mix.

"Greatest party food in the history of American junk food," Grace said, reaching for a handful of Muddy Buddies.

"Co-signed," I said, reaching for some too.

"My snack game is strong," Brooke said.

"The question is how is your Scrabble game? Because I will destroy you."

"That's a bold claim, Grace," I said. "Are you going to be embarrassed when you lose?"

"I won't."

And she didn't. "Eat it, losers," she said, laying down her final word. There was no way either of us could catch her at that point.

"I could have won if I hadn't drawn the Q and Z on the second to last round," I said, laying out the tiles that would now count against me.

She looked from my letters to the board, then picked them up and spelled Q-U-I-Z with the Z landing on a triple letter score. "You could have won anyway if you'd been paying attention."

"Burrrrrrn," said Brooke, tallying the scores. "Grace wins by thirty-seven."

Grace stood and did a gymnastics salute. It

57

popped her chest and booty out for a second. I would throw all the games if that was going to happen every time she won. I wasn't a pig, but I appreciate art when I see it, and her butt qualified.

"All right, trash talkers. Go again," I said, already sweeping tiles off the board into the draw bag.

We played two more rounds, Brooke taking the next game and the final game going to me because my competitive side called BS on my art appreciation side.

"Finally," Grace said as Brooke announced my winning score.

"You guys talk more smack than sophomore boys during the football unit," I said.

"We backed it up," Grace said, unruffled.

"Then why did I just win?" I stood up and did an end zone dance, which made Brooke laugh and Grace shake her head.

"Boy, sit down before you embarrass yourself," Brooke ordered, climbing to her feet. "Now I'm going to make some brownies, and we'll play for tiebreaker while they bake. Then we'll see who gets final bragging rights."

She disappeared into the kitchen again.

"You know she's going to stay in there an extra-long time because she's the most obvious matchmaker in the world, right?" Grace asked.

"Yeah. But seriously, don't worry about it. I know you're not into it."

She cocked her head to study me. "That's not the way I would put it. It's more that I'm not into the idea of dating anyone at all. I'm leaving soon."

"Soon, huh?"

A smile stretched over her face, the biggest one I'd seen yet. "I came home last year to help my parents. My dad was diagnosed with non-Hodgkin's lymphoma, and the doctor warned him that the treatments were going to wipe him out too much to run the store. Our part-timer is retired, and it was too much to ask him to do it."

"So it was up to you?" I wondered what her family situation was like. Maybe she didn't have siblings.

"Yeah. My mom is a real estate agent, and she earns more than the store does, so they couldn't afford for her to give up her income to run the store instead. And my sister has a big deal career in New York, so she couldn't do it either."

I frowned. "It sounded like you had a big deal career too."

"I did. I do," she corrected herself. "Probably. But she had a YouTube cooking show that blew up, and now she has a cable show, and she can't leave because of the taping schedule."

"So you had to quit your job."

She shrugged. "Yes and no. I could have said no, but . . ."

She didn't have to finish this sentence. I could

59

have left Paige to figure it out on her own too, claimed that being twenty-two with college graduation two months away exempted me from stepping in to help. "But you don't say no to family," I finished for her.

"That." She sighed and grabbed some more Muddy Buddies, then her smile returned. "Anyway, they started my dad on a drug trial that's having good results so far. He has another scan in three months, and if it's still clear, he's officially in remission and I'm out of Creekville."

"That's awesome about your dad."

"Yeah. We're pretty thrilled. My dad and I are, anyway. My mom's a pessimist and she's trying not to get too excited, but even she can't help it, I don't think. She might even get all the way excited if it meant I'd stay around here."

"She misses you, huh?"

"She spends all her time when we're not here trying to convince my sister and me to move back. Now that Tabitha has her show, my mom has backed off some, but with me, every other day she's trying to convince me that running the hardware store with my dad would be the best thing ever."

"Would it be so bad?"

She shrugged. "It would be great if I wanted to stay in Creekville. Or it would even be great if Creekville had a big aerospace company nearby where I could work. Then I'd be happy to stay. I like Creekville, but I have bigger goals than I can meet here."

"I can respect that."

"What about you? Small-town guy through and through?"

"I guess so. I was happy in Mineral until I wasn't."

Her eyebrow went up. "Sounds like a story."

"Not one you'd get without way more liquor in me. But I do like small towns. I don't mind bigger ones. I taught in Charlottesville for three years, and I liked that. I think my ideal place is something smaller than a suburb but close enough to a big city that I can still go in for the perks. Restaurants. New movies. Stuff like that."

"Why leave Charlottesville?"

I gave her a wry smile. "Again, a long story. But I like teaching in Creekville, and it allows me to live by my sister and my niece, so it all worked out."

"You probably have other family around too, right?"

I nodded. "Extended family. Cousins, aunts and uncles." I braced for the next question and the inevitable awkwardness that always followed the answer.

"Your parents don't live here?"

I shook my head. "They died a few years ago in a car accident." People rarely knew what to say to that. It was always some version of "I'm sorry." What else could they say, really? But I always wondered exactly what the apology was for. Then again, it wasn't like I knew what they should say instead.

Grace frowned at me. "That sucks."

Oh. That. That was the right response. I gave a short almost-laugh. "Yeah, it does. Thanks."

She held up her wineglass for a toast. "To big cities and small towns."

I clinked it with my beer bottle. "Cheers." Inside, I felt anything *but* cheerful. I couldn't remember the last time I'd been this attracted to someone *and* this comfortable in a conversation with them. And so explicitly friend-zoned.

She glanced toward the kitchen. "Not sure why we need brownies when we haven't finished the snacks we already have."

"How else was Brooke going to throw us together? I guess she could have said she needed to go bake a squash or weed the garden at ten o'clock at night, but we might have gotten suspicious."

"So how do we stop her?"

I shrugged. "Boycott game nights?"

She shook her head. "Not unless you want to. Tonight was fun."

"I agree. So then what?"

She studied me over the rim of her wineglass. "A friendship pact."

"A friendship pact?" I made a face like, *Yikes*.

"Last time I made a pact with a friend, we spit in our hands and shook. And before you said your no-dating thing, I had a different idea for swapping spit." She blushed slightly and blinked at me, the tiniest bit wine-muddled, I was guessing. "I'm fine with that being off the table, but I'm not doing the other spit thing either. The word pact makes me nervous."

Grace set her glass down and slapped her thighs. "All right, so it's blood then."

"Uh . . ."

"Or maybe just a handshake without spit?"

"Deal," I said, holding mine out. She took it. Her hand was warm and small with light calluses on the palm. I tried not to notice how good hers felt in mine.

"Deal," she said as Brooke walked back out.

Her eyebrow went up, and she gave us a pleased smile. "Holding hands already? I knew you were a good fit."

Grace rolled her eyes and slid her hand from mine. "Do you not know what a handshake looks like? We made a deal not to get trapped in any more of your matchmaking."

"So no more game nights?" Brooke asked, her face falling.

"Yes to game nights," I said. "And maybe we can switch it up with movie nights sometimes. I make killer stovetop popcorn. But I only do that for my *friends*."

"All right, all right," Brooke said. "I just came out to tell you that the brownies are taking longer than I expected, so I'll be a few more minutes." Then she was off to the kitchen.

Grace shook her head. "Unless she's back there growing the cacao beans herself, I think this is still more matchmaking."

"Why do we put up with her?" I asked.

"I ask myself that every day."

"Because you love me," Brooke said, returning. "Now save your smack talk for the game. It's time for me to prove I'm the Scrabble master once and for all."

I won but only because Grace had a J left on her tray and it counted against her.

"You're supposed to let me win because it's my house," Brooke informed us.

"Uh, you're playing with two former athletes," Grace said. "We always play to win. You're out of luck, so you're going to have to depend on skill, which means you're *still* out of luck."

"Nice." I high-fived her. "But how did you know I was an athlete?"

"You're built like one." And then, as if embarrassed she'd commented on my body, she fish-mouthed a couple of times. Slightly buzzed Grace was cute. "Plus, you're a coach. Aren't coaches always former athletes?"

"That wasn't a *grace*-ful recovery, but I'll allow it," I said.

Her eyes narrowed and a throw pillow sailed toward me. Tossing pillows at me like Paige? Yeah, I'd been friend-zoned. And that was for the best. I admired her drive, but it was taking her the opposite direction of my own obligations.

"What was your sport?" I asked.

She stood up and held her hand on top of her head to indicate her height. "I'll give you one guess."

"Gymnastics."

"Bingo. And then cheer."

Brooke and I exchanged looks.

"What?" Grace asked.

"Well . . ." Brooke said, and I could tell she was looking for diplomatic words. I kept my mouth shut because I'd already been hit with a pillow once. "I wouldn't have pegged you for a cheerleader."

Grace vaulted herself over the back of the sofa. She gave a sharp clap and broke into an aggressively happy smile. A *cheer*ful one. "Go, Bulldogs! B-U-L-L-D-O-G-S." Kicking and sharp arm movements happened.

Brooke's jaw dropped slightly. "I take it back. I fully believe you."

Grace vaulted back onto the couch and slouched down again like she'd never moved. "It looks good on college applications."

"Did you cheer in college too?" I asked.

She glanced at me like I'd asked if the moon

was cheese. "Ain't nobody got time for cheer practice *and* astrophysics."

"Fair." A text buzzed on my phone. This late, it could only be Paige.

Paige: Evie running fever. Children's Tylenol expired. Can u get some?

I winced. It sounded like an easy request, but it wasn't. At this hour, the small grocery stores would be closed which meant driving a half hour to the Charlottesville Super Walmart that stayed open 24-hours.

"Something wrong?" Brooke asked.

"My sister needs me to get Evie some children's Tylenol."

"Are you sober enough to drive?"

"Definitely. That bottle has been empty for an hour, but I think the only place open is going to be the Walmart in Charlottesville."

Brooke was already climbing to her feet. "No, I just made an emergency kit, and I'm pretty sure I put some in there."

"*Children's* Tylenol?" Grace asked.

Brooke paused halfway to her mudroom. "Do only adults have emergencies?"

"Guess not," Grace muttered, picking up her nearly empty wineglass.

"You going to be okay to drive?" I asked. She wasn't drunk, but a little wine went a long way

66

in someone her size. She shouldn't be behind a wheel.

"Of course not," she said. "I'll crash in Brooke's guest room until I feel better. Or maybe until morning. Wine makes me sleepy."

Brooke came back with a box in her hand. "Got it. Will this work?"

I took it and glanced at the label. "It'll work. Thanks, Brooke. Sorry to pass on the brownies, but I'd better get this home to my sister."

"See you tomorrow," she said.

"See you tomorrow," Grace mumbled. She looked and sounded half-asleep, curling up to rest her head on the sofa arm.

And as I drove home, I tried hard not to think about how much I wished her words were true. But Grace would have to be an occasional habit. A *very* occasional habit.

CHAPTER SEVEN
GRACE

I woke up with a crick in my neck, cringing as Brooke threw open her living room curtains to let the sun in.

"Good morning," she practically sang.

"It shouldn't surprise me that you're a morning person," I grumbled.

"Are you hungover?"

"No. Just allergic to cheerfulness before I've had coffee."

"Coming up."

I swung my legs down to the ground. "Don't make any on my account. I'll stop by the café and get some on the way home. You need to get to school, right?"

"Yep. Big official faculty meeting today, and I get my class rosters too."

"I'll get out of your hair." I stood and stretched.

"You're never in my hair. It was fun to have you and Noah over last night."

I froze mid-stretch and eyed her. "Stop trying to fix us up, by the way, or we'll stop coming over."

She held up her hands in surrender. "I will, I promise."

I dropped my arms too. "That was too easy. Why are you giving up?"

"Probably because my work here is already done." She shot me with finger guns and headed for the kitchen.

"No, it's not!" I called after her. "We're not fixed up, and we're not going to be!"

"Okay," she called back. I didn't know how she could make that single word sound like she didn't believe me even a little, but she did.

"I'm leaving!"

"Bye!"

I stopped by the café and got a coffee, then popped in at the house to change into my work uniform, a pair of jeans and polo shirt with my name stitched on the chest. My mom had handed me a stack of five of them with a big smile when I moved back, like I should be so thrilled I got to wear a uniform like my dad.

I was not thrilled.

My parents weren't home, and I wondered where they were, but they would let me know if there was a problem, so I showered, changed, and headed out to Handy's.

The nice thing about the hardware store was that it didn't open until 10:00. Gary came in to get things ready at 9:30, then stayed until 1:00 so I could get a lunch break in. Then I closed the place down at 6:00. I made it in with ten minutes to spare and set to work doing the ordering while Gary organized the paint chip display, complaining as usual about people who didn't put the danged things back where they got 'em.

The morning was fairly slow for a Friday. Usually people came in all day to get their supplies for weekend projects, but we'd definitely be busy this afternoon while I ran the place by myself, and I mean *ran*. That was what I'd be doing until closing, zipping all over the place between answering customer questions, ringing up purchases, and listening to a bunch of dudes who hadn't grown up working in their dad's hardware store tell me why my recommendations were wrong.

A half-hour after opening, the front door chimed as I finishing ringing up a customer, and my dad walked in.

He wore a big grin on his face, one I hadn't seen in far too long. He was young as dads go, in his early fifties, his blond hair starting to fade to silver at the temples, but still handsome, even if his face had lost its color over the last year. It squeezed my heart to remember how ruddy his cheeks used to get after spending early mornings working in the yard before he'd leave to open the store.

"Hey, kiddo."

"What are you doing here? I didn't see you this morning, and I assumed you had a doctor's appointment."

"I did," he said. "We drove over to Charlottesville, and I wanted to tell you the good news myself." Going the forty-five minutes into Charlottesville meant they'd been to the oncologist. I tried not to let my hopes get too high.

He leaned on the counter and took my hands in his. "All my bloodwork looks normal. I know my next scan isn't until November, but Dr. Pearson was optimistic today, and I should be back to full strength pretty soon."

I let go of his hands to throw my arms around him in a hug. "Oh, Dad. I'm so happy to hear that." I held him tight and listened to the steady thump of his heart even though the counter was digging into the bottom of my ribcage.

He patted my back and let me go. "You know what that means, don't you, honey?"

"That you don't have to do any more chemo?"

"Yes, actually. We're skipping my last infusion. But it also means you get your life back. I can take over the store soon."

"I wasn't even thinking about that. I'm just so glad you're getting better." I had refused to consider what it might mean if he didn't, mainly because the weight of those what-ifs would have crushed me.

"I think about it all the time, though. I'm still not a hundred percent back, but I feel better each day. It won't be too long until I'm in here running things. But until then, I figured I ought to at least go over the holiday ordering with you so it's ready."

"Sure, Dad." We usually did this at home, and I'd log in from my laptop to do all the ordering at his direction, but he looked giddy as a pup in a park full of hydrants to be back in the store, so I didn't object. Instead, I followed him up and down the aisles and made notes as he told me what to stock up on for Christmas.

"The decorating season starts early," he said. "You'll want to have Gary put up the artificial trees the day after Labor Day. He'll know where to find them in the storeroom. You only need to order two of each to sell. People around here mostly like to go out and cut their own. And order a bunch of big yard stuff. Inflatables. Big plastic light up displays. But only one of each because people get mad at me if someone else buys the same thing. And don't choose anything you see offered on the websites for the big box stores. Our customers will pay more to have something unique."

I watched him for signs that he was tiring, but if anything, he seemed energized as his mind raced to catalog everything we'd need for the holiday. He wasn't cruising the aisles as fast as he used to, but he kept up a steady pace to match his instructions. "Where you want to stock up is lights," he said, walking down the seed aisles. "This'll be the best place to put them. We'll go over which brands and kinds of bulbs to buy."

"Am I doing our house too?" My dad had

always gone to Clark Griswold lengths when decorating for Christmas. He said we had to be an advertisement for the Christmas goodies in the store, but he not-so-secretly loved the holiday, hauling down our decorations well before Thanksgiving. Last year he'd been too sick to care, and I'd only had time and energy to put up a single strand of colored lights around the first-floor eaves.

"I'll do it," he said, stopping at a shelf displaying weedkiller. "Might have to start earlier this year so I can pace myself. You worry about the store."

"Sounds good, Dad." I didn't comment on how tightly he gripped the shelf for support, or how he went off on a tangent about snow shovels to give himself more time to recover.

The front bell chimed again, and I was glad for the excuse to give him time alone where he didn't have to act healthier than he felt. "I'd better go take care of that, see if they need something."

A few minutes later, my dad came up to the register, no longer sagging. "I better head home and let you get back to running things, honey." He was quiet for a second, seeming to be looking for words. "I sure appreciate you. I know you gave up a lot to come do this."

A lump formed in my throat. "You gave up plenty over the years so we could get our schooling in. It's the least I can do." That was the argument Tabitha had made to convince me to come out here, but while I had resented her for it then, I meant every word of it to my dad now.

"Still, it's time you start thinking about real life again."

"What do you mean?"

"Start looking for a job building rockets."

I smiled. "It was satellites."

"Satellites, then."

"There's no rush."

He gripped the edge of the counter and leaned forward, like he wanted me to understand how serious he was. "You didn't see Dr. Pearson's face, honey. I've got this beat. I know I do. I'm starting to think about getting back to normal life. And for you, that's out there." He waved in the direction of the door.

"Main Street?" I said, teasing him.

"Charleston. Seattle. The moon. Whatever you want, Gracie."

"We'll see."

"No, start now. It's almost September. My scan is November. If it's clean, and I keep feeling better, there'll be no reason for you to stay. It takes time to get a job like this, doesn't it? Applications, interviews, security checks. All of that. So hop to it."

"Okay, Dad." I wouldn't be posting a profile on any of the job sites until I was sure we were looking at remission, but I'd at least start looking to see what jobs were out there.

He cleared his throat. "Don't stay too late. It's Friday. That means—"

"Meatloaf, I know." I would never understand his obsession with my mom's meatloaf.

"See you at home."

He walked out, a touch slower than he would have a year ago but better than I'd seen him in months. He was still wearing out easily, but him even having the energy to come in and boss me around today had been a major improvement.

It kept a smile on my face for the rest of the morning, and even cranky Cheryl Biggle couldn't get me down when she came in with her Pomeranian tucked in her giant purse to demand a refund on a pair of garden gloves. She tried to return at least one item every week because her puffball—Captain Braveheart—chewed on everything his devilish teeth could get to. Today I handed her cash without even pointing out that the "defect" in the gloves clearly showed teeth marks.

My dad was getting better, and not even Creekville's most ill-mannered dog could get me down.

No, it took a call from my sister on the way home to do that.

I eyed her number in the call display of my Audi dashboard—a car bought when I was making Boeing money—and frowned. I didn't want to talk to Tabitha, but I hadn't returned either of her last two messages. I groaned and hit answer.

"Hey, Tabitha. How's New York?"

"What? Oh. Busy. Crazy. Crazy busy." She sounded distracted, and sure enough, she said, "Hang on a sec," then covered the phone up while I listened to her give muffled directions to someone involving the word "chiffonade." "Sorry about that," she said coming back on the line.

"It's dinner time there too. Are you still at work?"

"Yeah. We're shooting our Thanksgiving epi-sodes next week and this week has been full of late nights testing recipes in the studio kitchen."

"Got it."

"Mom called," she started, and already I wanted to grit my teeth.

"Did she?"

"She said Dad's feeling better, and you're already packing your bags to leave."

"Not exactly. If anything, she's trying to pack my bags for me." She'd been hellbent on "launching" us out of Creekville since we were kids.

She paused.

"What, Tabitha?"

"Is that a good idea? Is Dad ready to go back to work?"

I shouldn't be irritated with Tabitha when she was only being concerned, but I couldn't help it. I hadn't been able to help it since Tabitha had made it clear that it would be me who would have to quit my job to take care of Dad.

I was honestly glad that I'd been here to help. But I resented having her micromanage me from New York and showing no faith in my judgment. "I'll stay until we're sure he's in remission and he's strong enough to take over. That's at least a month."

"You're going to leave before Christmas Town?"

I cursed.

"You forgot Christmas Town? How do you forget Christmas Town?"

It was a reasonable question, but I didn't like the accusation in her tone. "I don't know. I guess I overlooked it in my excitement that Dad is getting better. Can't we just focus on that?"

"Not better enough to be ready to take on Christmas Town by himself."

She was right. Christmas was the biggest season of the year for Handy's, not only because of the decorations, but because the town Christmas fundraiser and celebration poured so much money into the store as people built their displays. Even if Dad and Gary could handle all the extra business, Dad had always helped the high school build their booth. I had done it for him last year, spending several nights a week at the high school supervising in the two weeks before Christmas. Of course it would be too much for Dad on top of running the store.

"We'll hire holiday help," I said.

"Help that can build an elaborate booth?"

Christmas Town was exactly what it sounded like: a temporary town that sprang up in the Main Street square for two magical days on the weekend before Christmas. It was corny. I was not corny, but even I sort of liked it.

Fine. I liked it a lot.

"It'll be fine, Tabitha."

"You have to stay, Grace."

"I don't have to do anything, Tab." I had every intention of staying, but it wasn't Tabitha's place to tell me what I needed to do. Not when I was the one who'd been here for fifteen months, handling business. Literally. I was the whole reason Handy's had stayed in business, and she couldn't even give me credit for that.

"Then who's going to do it? Gary can't."

"Stay in your lane, Tabitha. Because this isn't it. You made it clear that it's mine, so you don't get to start butting in now."

"I'm not trying to tell you how to run the store. I'm only talking about what affects Dad."

"Again, I've been here for all of it. You were here for two days at Christmas last year when the store was closed, and Dad didn't have any appointments. Why do you act like you know what's going on here?" I knew why. It was the same reason she'd been doing it my whole life: she was two years older than me, and she'd always acted like it granted her the right to be my third parent. I'd been over it by the time I was five. "It's fine, I'm fine, Dad's fine. Make your chiffonade with a clear conscience. We've got it covered."

"But I—"

"Bye, Tab." I disconnected the call. She'd managed to dampen the high I'd been feeling ever since Dad had come in with his news. For over a year, I'd refused to consciously consider the worst. It wasn't until he'd told me that hope was finally in sight that I realized how much every molecule in my body had been bracing for the worst ever since coming back to Creekville.

I wouldn't let Tabitha steal that relief.

I would definitely go home and start looking at job postings with my availability date as January 2. If Tabitha had a problem with it, she could come supervise him herself. But Dad was getting healthy. I would be getting my life back soon.

And I smiled again because I finally had something to look forward to.

CHAPTER EIGHT
NOAH

I rolled into work short two hours of sleep but on time, if slightly bleary-eyed. Paige was working the breakfast shift, and that started at 6 AM. Evie's fever had broken about an hour after we'd given her the Tylenol, but I'd stayed and slept on the floor in her room so Paige wouldn't worry. Evie had been fine when I dropped her off to daycare, and the director had said it was fine if she kept a mask on. Evie promised she'd keep it on if she could stay in the reading corner and rest. It was a good solution all around.

I settled into my desk with a smile on my face, remembering one of Grace's attempted words in the final match last night. "Jackwad." Brooke had challenged it. When the online dictionary didn't list it, Grace had insisted it was a word if you could use it in a sentence. "I'll even speak your language," she'd said. "High school boys are jackwads."

"That is both true and also still not a legal Scrabble word," I'd ruled. And Grace had complained about it the rest of the game, especially when she got caught with the J after I laid down my last tiles.

High school boys were definitely jackwads,

and on Monday, this locker room would be full of them, but I enjoyed their dumb butts anyway. They had more good moments than bad. Well, except for . . .

With a sigh, I went to work on the outline for the second quarter health unit—AKA "the condom talk," the duty falling to me since I had the least seniority in the department and couldn't say no. It was not my favorite unit. Even saying the word "unit" made the boys lose it. "Sophomoric humor" is an insult for a reason.

A knock sounded on the door and saved me from trying to figure out which diagram I could use that wouldn't call down the wrath of every parent in the Lincoln High school district.

"Coach Redmond? You got a minute?"

I looked up and smiled. "Hey, Coach Dean. Come on in."

Frank Dean was the Lincoln football coach, a grizzled veteran who was in his mid-sixties, at least, and revered by his players. He'd coached a lot of their fathers too.

"Ready for this year?" he asked, taking the chair across the desk from me.

"I think so. I can always think of a dozen more things that need doing, but it always works out."

"You did a fine job coaching wrestling last year."

"Thanks. I hope we get past semi-finals this year."

"I'm sure you will, son."

It fell quiet, and while we had a cordial working relationship after a year of sharing the gym and locker room, we weren't sit-in-silence-together type friends. I shifted, looking for something to talk about. "How about you? You ready?"

He pushed his cap back and sighed. "I don't know. Mrs. Dean wants me to retire. She's been saying that for about five years, but I think this year, I might listen."

"Wow. Retirement is big. I've only been here a year, and you already feel like an institution."

He gave me a small smile. "Being an institution is overrated. And it's starting to be less fun. I found myself wanting to cut summer practices short because I don't like the heat, and it's taking longer for me to recover on Saturdays from Friday night games. I reckon the wife has a point. She usually does."

"Bulldogs football won't be the same without you."

He tilted his head and fixed me with a steady gaze, one I'd seen him use on his players when he wanted something out of them. "You said you coached football at your last high school?"

"Assistant," I said. "Defensive line."

"I should have made space for you on my staff last year, son."

It had stung when I'd been hired on at Lincoln and Coach Dean had politely declined my offer to help. He'd told me his coaching staff was full. But he'd made a point of staying friendly through the year, and I'd gotten over it.

"That's all right, coach. You didn't know me. I know how important it is to work with people you trust."

"You got that right. That's why I want to talk to you about coaching this year."

"You losing an assistant?"

He shook his head slowly. "No. But I can squeeze another stipend out of the boosters to bring you on for the season."

"Defensive coordinator?"

"No. He's solid. How would you feel about working with the offensive coordinator?"

"It's not my strength, coach."

"That's why I'd like you to consider it." He leaned forward. "In fact, I'd like you to consider taking over as head football coach next year."

I sat back, caught off guard.

"I've been watching you over the last year, Redmond. You've got a good head on your shoulders, and you're good with the kids. I think you'd make a fine coach. You should consider it."

"What about Leach and Jones?" I asked, naming his two assistants.

"They don't want it. This is a labor of love for them, and they're content in their jobs. Dr. Boone may want to open it up to an outside candidate search, but if you're up for it, I'll put in a good word for you and train you all season so you can hit the ground running next year. I'm only sorry I didn't make this decision before summer camp so you could see how we do that too, but Leach and Jones will help you out with that next year."

"I played two years in high school. I remember it well enough to know what to expect."

"Even better. Also, to sweeten the pot, the head coach stipend is generous. It still won't be close to covering the time you put in, but it's about five times the stipend you get for coaching wrestling."

My eyes bugged out. I could feel them.

He pushed back from the desk and rose with a smile. "If you're interested, let Dr. Boone know soon. I told her my retirement plans this morning, and the sooner you get on her radar, the better your chances."

"I'll keep that in mind, coach. Thank you."

"Sure, son." He headed to his office on the other side of the locker room.

I did some quick math in my head. Five times would be . . . an extra $8,000 a year. And yes, I'd be working far more hours, but that was real money, in the bank, that could help Paige and Evie.

I couldn't say no. I'd been thinking about getting a second job anyway, but it would limit how much babysitting I could do for Paige. If I was coaching football, I could bring Evie with me. She'd love helping, and if push came to shove, I could always turn practices over to my assistants if I ever needed to take her home.

I knew it was a huge commitment. It had been a big commitment when I was a player, but if I was going to step in as an assistant, I needed to start yesterday. The season was already underway. The first game was next week.

It wasn't a hard choice. I grabbed my Bulldogs cap and headed for Dr. Boone's office. Might as well throw my figurative hat in the ring for the job right now, and it wouldn't hurt to be showing some extra school spirit when I did.

"On my way to Dr. Boone's to tell her I want the job," I told Coach Dean on my way out.

"Go get 'em, kid."

"Hey, Nancy," I said, walking into the front office. "Is Dr. Boone available?"

"She's in a meeting." The secretary nodded toward the principal's closed door right as it opened. "Or else you lucked out and caught her at the tail end of it."

The department chairs filed out, talking and ribbing each other as they headed back to their classrooms.

"You have a minute, Dr. Boone?" I asked.

"I have about five, Coach Redmond. What can I do for you?"

"I wanted to talk to you about the football job."

Nancy's eyes sharpened, and I could practically see her antennae go up.

"Step into my office, coach. How can I help you?" she asked as she closed the door behind us.

"I'd like to be considered for the head football coach position," I said as she settled behind her desk.

She paused before lowering herself all the way into her chair. "I'm not sure that's the right fit."

Whatever I had expected, it wasn't an outright rejection. "Can I ask why not?"

"You haven't even been on the coaching staff this year, and you want to take over? That's a big leap."

"Coach Dean thinks I can do it. And he says neither of his assistants want the job. I do. I think I did a good job with wrestling last year, and I'm confident I can bring that same energy to the football program."

"Program," she repeated. "That's the thing. It's much more than just a team. People around here take football seriously. On a Friday night at the football field, you'd think you were in the heart of Texas. There's more than the coaching. You have to run a larger staff, work more closely with facilities, manage a larger budget, and maybe most significantly, you have to deal with the boosters."

"I know, Dr. Boone. I served as the defensive coordinator for a year at my last school."

"But that's one year in a part-time capacity. And you left at the end of it."

Because I'd needed a clean break from Lauren, but I wasn't about to lay out the dusty old bones of my personal drama for my boss. "I'm a fast learner. I've experienced high school football as both a player and a coach, and I understand the Lincoln High school culture. I'll learn from Coach Dean, and I promise that you'll feel good about me running the program when he retires."

She removed her glasses and rubbed her eyes with the type of exhaustion I usually didn't feel until November when the kids started whining about doing outside sports in the crisp weather.

"First bookworms, now this."

"Pardon? Did you say bookworms?" Why would that be a problem? I thought we wanted to improve literacy.

"Yes. Literal bookworms worked through about a quarter of the textbooks stored in the library, and now we've got to figure out what to do in several of our classes while we place an emergency order. But there's no such thing as 'fast' when it comes to requisitioning new materials."

"That . . . sucks." It didn't feel like the most professional thing to say, but it was the best way I could sum up the situation.

She gave a short laugh. "Yes, it does. I'd better get on it."

"So just to be clear, you'll consider me for the coaching job?"

She sighed. "Legally, I have to. But if we're

being honest, I wouldn't bank on it if I were you. We need someone more seasoned. It's a beast with many heads, and it takes an experienced wrangler to make it all work."

She rose, and I did too. "I'll find a way to win your confidence on this, Dr. Boone. You'll see."

"I admire your enthusiasm, Coach Redmond. I wish I could give you more encouragement, but I try to be as transparent as possible."

"I appreciate that. It shows me what to shoot for."

She gave me a polite smile. "I'll see you this afternoon at the faculty meeting."

I spent my entire lunch break running the pros and cons. Brooke even texted to see where I was since I usually made it over to her classroom at some point during lunch. I told her to save me a seat at the faculty meeting.

By the end of lunch, I was convinced. No matter which way I looked at it, getting the head coaching gig would be a major help financially. Besides, it came with an extra prep period so I could get a lot of administrative work done. "Mentoring young men" didn't even factor in; I already got to do that in wrestling, so the football job was a lateral move in that sense. And really, I could work full-time at a drive-thru window all summer and still not make what I would with the coaching stipend, even if it paid less than it should for the time it would demand.

If Paige and I could work out the babysitting, I would do everything I could to convince Dr. Boone that I was the man for the job.

The bell rang to signal the end of lunch, and that meant I had ten minutes until the faculty meeting started. I made it to the multi-purpose room with five to spare and took a seat next to Brooke.

"Everything okay?" she asked.

"Yeah." It was too much to get into right now, but I'd catch her up later. "How's it going over in science land?"

"It's nice to be more excited than scared, like I was last year."

"That's what a year of experience will do for you."

"I don't feel as clueless, but I'm still nervous," she admitted. "When does that go away?"

"Not your fifth year," I said. "I still have first-week nerves too. Although last year they cleared up by day three. Maybe this year it'll be day two."

We chatted about our class rosters for a few minutes before Dr. Boone called everyone to order. It took a few times because even though she was well-respected by the faculty, teachers are the *worst* about talking in meetings.

"Settle down," she called for a third time, more sternly. "I'm glad you're all excited for school to start. Now let's get down to business." She moved through the agenda on the screen at a good clip, knowing that she had a short window of time before the side conversations started up again. Within fifteen minutes, she'd gone through the procedural updates for the new year, and the agenda on screen was replaced by a picture of a megaphone overlaid with the words, "Exciting Announcement."

A low murmur ran through the audience.

"We getting a vending machine in the lounge?" the drama teacher called. It earned a couple of whistles.

"Mr. Ritzau and the ASB have declined to do the Christmas Town booth this year," she said. The murmur in the crowd grew louder. "That means one lucky campus organization will have the opportunity to do an amazing fundraiser. This will be awarded on a first come, first serve basis, so hurry if you want the chance."

I waited for a flurry of hands to shoot up, but while the rumbling got even louder, not a hand went up. "I thought people would jump on that," I said to Brooke. "Clubs and teams are always grubbing for money."

"No one's that dumb," said a veteran English teacher sitting behind us. "There's a reason Ritzau quit. It's a pain. You have to raise funds, manage kids, get donations, battle with the Christmas Town fascists, and you lose a year of your life for every year you do the booth."

"Huh." It sounded like the conversation I'd had with Dr. Boone that morning.

"Don't everyone volunteer at once now," Dr. Boone called from the front of the room. The goading didn't work. "Seriously? No one? It's the most wonderful time of the year and all of that?" Still no hands went up. Even from eight rows back, I could see the look of desperation creeping into her eyes. "The whole town looks forward to seeing the Lincoln High apple cider donut booth every year," she said. "We can't break with tradition."

The only sound was shuffling feet and creaking chairs as people shifted to avoid eye contact with her.

"I'll do it." I raised my hand to make sure she knew it was me.

I had just figured out how to prove to her that I was head coach material.

CHAPTER NINE
GRACE

The bell rang to announce another customer late Saturday morning as I straightened the display of straw bales and pumpkins at the front of the store. A frazzled young mom with two toddlers had stopped by for childproof doorknob covers, and her toddlers had knocked over all the mini pumpkins while I rang her up.

I glanced over to see Noah walking in. "Well, Noah Redmond, as I live and breathe," I said in my best Scarlett O'Hara impersonation to hide that his appearance had set my stomach fluttering. "Whatever brings you in today?"

He smiled and scratched his head. "I haven't even spent enough time in hardware stores to fake a good answer to that."

Which meant he was here to see me. I tried not to let it show on my face how much I liked his answer. "You'd better think of something so we don't stand here awkwardly."

He nodded. "Good point. Um, okay. Do you know what Christmas Town is?"

I blinked at him.

"Oh, right. You grew up here."

"Ding, ding, ding."

"I'm in charge of the Lincoln booth."

I blinked again. "What about Bob?"

His mouth twitched. "Good movie."

"What?"

"That's a movie. *What About Bob*. You've seen it? Tell me you've seen it."

I could not tell him I'd seen it.

"You know. 'Baby steps out the front door. Baby steps down the hall'?"

"You can keep quoting it, but I still won't have gone back in time to see it before having this conversation."

"Guess I know what I'm picking for the first movie night. Anyway, Bob Ritzau is refusing to do the Christmas Town booth this year on account of some drama with the ASB kids last year. I didn't ask too many questions because it looked like he might cry."

I sucked in a breath. "That's not good. I heard something about a food fight between the ASB treasurer and the junior class president. I remember the cider donuts ran out early. Maybe that had something to do with it?"

"Apparently, they ruined so many donuts that the booth made negative money and they had to skip the DJ for the midwinter formal."

"Tragic."

"Like I said, he looked like he was going to cry."

"How'd you get stuck with the job?"

A slightly sheepish look crossed his face. "I volunteered."

I leaned over and patted his arm. "It's okay. You're still new. Tell them you take it back. They'll understand. You didn't know what you were signing up for."

"The thing is, I did."

I dropped my hand. "Uh."

"That's pretty much what Brooke said. But I had to."

"Why?"

"The football coach is retiring. I talked to Dr. Boone about applying for the job, but she doesn't think I have the experience to do it. I'm sucking up to her by taking on the booth while also proving that I can wrangle a complicated project."

I tried to find a diplomatic response. I couldn't honestly say, "You'll do great!" because it was nearly impossible for anyone to do a good job. Exhibit A: weepy Mr. Ritzau, who'd tried for five years during which he'd barely kept it together before flaming out in a hail of cider donuts.

I cleared my throat, "Well, that is . . . something."

"Don't sound so excited."

"I don't know if anyone has adequately explained to you the minefield of Christmas Town politics."

"The word 'fascists' came up," he conceded.

"That's only scratching the surface."

"Great." He glanced around the store. "Is your dad here? I was told he's the guy who always helps with the high school booth."

"He is, usually. But I did it last year, and you're stuck with me this year."

His smile reappeared. "That's the first good news I've heard since I got the gig."

It was such a cute smile. He would be so easy to flirt with, drawing that smile out again and again. But after my dad's news yesterday, I now had an exit date: January 2. And that left no time for a romance with Noah.

I took another casual step away from him, like I needed to physically find the friend zone. I wasn't sure where it was, but at a minimum, it was two arm's length away from Noah. "I'll do my best to help, but the ASB needs to come up with a theme first."

"The football team is sponsoring it. ASB doesn't want to do it, so now it's ours, and we get to keep the proceeds."

Great. That meant we wouldn't even have the Type-A neurotic class officers who would work their fingers to the bone rather than turn out anything less than perfect for the booth.

"Most of those boys know how to swing a hammer, so that's good." It was the only encouragement I could offer at the moment.

"That's what I was thinking," he said. "I promise I won't make you do all the work, but I was hoping you could help me understand the Christmas Town experience."

"You saw it last year, right?"

He shook his head. "No. I didn't come into Creekville over Christmas break. No reason to when I'm not at work."

"Oh, boy." I glanced at my watch. "Gary? I'm going to take my lunch now. Can you handle the store?"

"Sure thing, Gracie," he said, emerging from the plumbing aisle with a U-joint.

"Come on," I said. "We'll go to the office and you can have the other half of my turkey sandwich. I can't be off the floor long on a Saturday, but you definitely need to understand Christmas Town."

He followed me back to the small office. There was only one office chair, but I pulled in a low step ladder. "Get comfy," I said, pulling my sandwich from the mini-fridge. I handed him half, but he waved it away. "Eat it or you'll hurt my feelings."

He took the sandwich.

"So Christmas Town has been happening for almost thirty years. Glynnis Hunsaker threw the first one, and she's run it every year since. It starts with a parade."

"In Creekville? Is it . . . small?"

I nodded. "Yes. Probably as many people in it as watching it, but you'd think it was the Rose Parade from the way the crowd goes nuts. You've got the fire truck and the sheriff, the cheer squad, the Cub Scouts, Miss Leslie's Tap Ladies, the

Girl Scouts, a half-dozen other groups, and then, of course, Santa."

"Of course," he said, like it was no big deal.

"No," I said, leaning forward and gripping his knees. He had nice quads—a thing I noticed against my will, but they were right there at my fingertips, so yeah. He stopped with his sandwich halfway to his mouth. "*Santa*. You cannot imagine the scale of the production. The parade starts at the end of Main, then goes up to the corner of Main and Fir. Then it stops, and the marching band comes, and behind them, Santa on a sleigh pulled by actual *reindeer*."

His eyes got big. I nodded. "Now you're getting the scope of this thing. When the marching band catches up to the rest of the parade, they all part, each group moving to their assigned side of the street, while the marching band passes through, escorting Santa into Christmas Town. Then the rest of the parade falls in behind them, and then"—I poked his knee to make sure he was paying attention—"the rest of the town falls in behind them and we all go to Christmas Town."

"Whoa," he breathed. "And you haven't gotten to the Christmas Town part."

"I know," I said, sitting back. "But you have to understand that the whole production is insane. Or at least, it feels that way when you're an adult getting ready for it. But when I was a kid, it really did feel like magic. And that's why everyone does it."

"So my job is the booth. What does that involve?"

"The Main Street square becomes Christmas Town. Did either of your grandmas have one of those ceramic Christmas villages they put out every year?"

"My Aunt Peggy did."

"It's that come to life. Except . . . more eclectic. You might see a Whoville booth next to something Moroccan themed in a vague salute to the Three Wise Men. The booth part itself is simple. It's a basic wooden frame, and that part is half built already. Ask the school custodian where to find it. It's the façade and costumes you have to worry about."

"Costumes?" A fleeting look of panic crossed his face. Good. It was sinking in.

"Yes. The booth is organized around a theme approved by Glynnis. She'll want to see design concepts for the façade and the costumes to approve your aesthetic. It should be an 'immersive' experience." I gave him air quotes for Glynnis's favorite word.

"Okay. Get Bruce the Custodian to take me to the booth. Come up with a theme for the booth and costumes. Give them to Glynnis."

"Oh no, you don't have to worry about taking

them to Glynnis. *She* finds *you*. That's a whole experience in itself."

"I'm beginning to understand why no one else volunteered. And our booth does apple cider donuts every year? How do you make a theme that goes with that?"

I shrugged. "A couple of years ago it was Snow White and the Apple Cider Donuts, and they made the façade look like the exterior of her cottage in the Disney movie, and all the dwarves became elves. And they had a bunch of stuffed woodland creatures in Christmas hats." I smiled, remembering it. "It was pretty adorable, actually."

"So they made one good theme one time with donuts."

"One year they did 'Oh, Baby,' and they dressed like babies to sell the donuts."

"Oh, no."

"That's the spirit," I said. "Just think of lots of phrases that use 'Oh' and then turn one into something."

"I meant oh, no, we are *not* doing that."

"Better think fast. I have a feeling Glynnis will track you down pretty soon."

He'd started chewing on his bottom lip, his gaze far away. "What about, 'Uh-Oh'?"

"What about it?"

He blinked back to the present. "As a theme. I've been reading *The Cat in the Hat* to my niece at night, and that's one big book of uh-oh. So a *Cat in the Hat* theme."

I considered it, the picture already taking shape in my head. "You may have something there."

A look of relief crossed his face, and I laughed. "Don't relax yet. You have to get your team on board with your choices, and there's always some drama there."

He rested his elbows on his knees and dropped his head into his hands. "Do you have *any* words of encouragement?"

"Sure, Redmond. We give the high school the materials at cost, and I'll come over to supervise after I close up the store. You'll do fine."

"Even if I barely know a wingnut from a washer?"

"Even then. And hey, at least you know what wingnuts and washers are. That's not nothing."

"It's half of nothing, because I lied. I don't know what a wingnut is."

I watched him eat his final bite of sandwich in amusement. "Don't worry. Handy Hardware has its name on this project too. We'll make something cool."

"Good. No pressure, but it's pretty much on you to save Christmas Town."

I knew it was a joke, but for over a year, the pressure had been on me to save everything. I felt my smile try to slip but I kept it in place.

"Christmas Town. My dad. This store. I'm Super Grace. I got this."

His eyes softened. "Grace, I didn't—"

I held up a hand to stop whatever consoling thing he was going to say. "It's fine. And now I need to get out there and hustle. I'm half-afraid Gary will fall over and crumble to dust if he gets too many questions at once."

I stood, and he did too, following me back out to the floor. Gary was at the register with a line of three people waiting while he cursed and mumbled about starting the transaction over again. "Not a minute too soon," I said.

"Good luck. I'm going to go Google wingnuts. And Christmas Town ideas."

"You've got this, Redmond."

"Noah," he said.

"Redmond," I repeated. I needed the fraternal vibe of using his last name.

"All right, Winters," he sighed.

"Let me know when your team gets a theme together," I said. He gave me a thumbs up as he walked out, and I tried not to think about how much I was already looking forward to that call.

CHAPTER TEN
NOAH

"Nah, coach."

I stared at DeShawn Jones, our starting tight end. I'd hit the ground running with the team, jumping into practices at the beginning of the week. I thought I'd developed a good rapport quickly with these guys. Maybe not?

"Did you just say, 'Nah'?" I asked.

"Yeah."

"Why did you say nah?"

"How are we supposed to practice all week, game on Fridays, keep our grades up, *and* come in at nights to work on this float? And some of these cats got part-time jobs too. So nah."

"There is no 'nah,' " I told him. "We have to make a Christmas Town booth."

"Can't we march in the parade or something?" one of the offensive linemen asked. "Those booths are a lot of work."

"They're also a lot of money. Based on what the ASB has made the last few years, we could buy two more tackling sleds."

"Ask J.J.'s dad to buy them. That's how we usually get stuff," another kid called out, and the team laughed.

I'd seen J.J. pulling into the school parking

lot in a shiny Wrangler. No doubt his dad could afford the tackling sleds. But that wasn't the point.

"It builds character for you to earn what you have," I said.

"Bruh," DeShawn said. "It was supposed to build character just to play football. I'm already keeping a 3.5, putting in fifteen hours a week at football, and another twenty stocking shelves at the grocery store. I don't know how much more character I need, but for dang sure I don't need to get it by paying for tackling sleds. I ain't even on the D-line."

The rest of the team laughed again, and I could feel them slipping away. If I couldn't convince them they needed to participate in the fundraiser, there was no way Dr. Boone would consider me for the head coaching job, and in all honesty, I wouldn't deserve it.

"I can understand that. But what if the fundraiser benefitted each of you more directly? What if we got something other than tackling sleds?"

"Like what?" DeShawn asked.

"What if it offset the cost of uniforms? However much we earn would be divided up and applied as a discount, so that could knock down your costs for next year. And for those of you who are graduating, that might not feel like much of an incentive, but think about what it does for your team. You leave that as a legacy."

This was met by murmurs instead of grumbles, which sounded more like interest than complaining.

"I like it," said Grant, a graduating captain. "I could have used a break like that this year."

"No kidding," said DeShawn. "That's a five-hour shift at the grocery store I could spend studying instead."

"You've got a head for economics, DeShawn. Hope you're thinking about that as a major in college."

"I wasn't, but maybe I will," he said with a small smile.

"Let's make it as easy as possible to work on this booth. Christmas Town isn't until right before Christmas—"

"That's how it got its name, coach." DeShawn smirked.

"Thanks, DeShawn. Anyway, even if we get to state—"

"When," said Grant.

"Even *after* we get to state," I corrected myself to a couple of cheers, "that still gives us three weeks to work on this thing. How about you give me two hours every Saturday"—more grumbling—"but we don't start until October, and we rotate offense, defense, and special teams, so everyone doesn't have to show up every Saturday."

The grumbles settled down. Grant scanned the

faces of the team. "You've got a deal, coach."

I tried not to show my immense relief. I had to play it as if we'd negotiated as men. "That's settled. Now we have to think of a theme."

Everything went promptly off the rails again. Zero surprise with a bunch of teenage boys. They shouted out suggestions from violent video games, rap videos even I wasn't old enough to watch, NFL teams they couldn't agree on, and memes no one over the age of eighteen would understand.

Cat in the Hat wasn't going to go over great, but I tried anyway after giving them a minute to holler out a dozen less appropriate options. "It needs to go with cider donuts, so something O-shaped, like the word 'oh.' "

"Cider donuts? We're selling cider donuts?" the kicker asked.

"You don't like cider donuts?" I asked.

"They're fine," another player said. "But if we did Doom Eternal, we could sell plastic doom blades."

"Buddy, think about that for a second. What little kid's mom is going to let them buy that? And if they did, can you imagine them running around and causing mayhem all night?"

"Yeah," the kicker said. "I can. That's why it would be awesome."

That got a bunch of agreement. I was back to negotiating with boys. "Let's think strategically,"

I said. "Practice some of those economics like DeShawn was talking about. We need to do apple cider donuts because that's what people expect from a booth at Lincoln High, and we don't want to mess with tradition, or we risk cutting into our profits. So how do we make apple cider donuts cool?"

Several of them exchanged glances.

"That's not a thing, coach," Grant said.

"That's the challenge. We figure out how to make it a thing. If you guys get on board, the customers will get on board. Someone who thinks they don't even want one apple cider donut will suddenly buy a dozen if you sell them right."

Doubtful looks.

"Think of the uniforms," I said. "Every donut you sell, that's money saved next season."

More doubtful looks.

"Think about it over the next week, guys. We'll make a decision and get some ideas going." Like *Cat in the Hat*. But it was dead in the water if I brought it up now. "Try to focus on what little kids would love. You know football players are heroes to them, so think about what would make them beg their parents to come to our booth. That's it for today, boys. Dismissed."

They headed for their lockers with a clatter of cleats, and I headed into my office, drawing the blinds before I collapsed into my chair and let out a deep breath. Whew. I had almost lost them, but so far, my plan to impress Dr. Boone was still in effect.

I made sure Saturday mornings were okay with Grace. When she agreed to it, I spent the rest of the week figuring out how to make the team think *The Cat in the Hat* was their own idea. And also resisting the urge to text her every day with made up reasons to talk to her.

"So what are your theme suggestions?" I asked the team as they piled into the locker room at the end of practice. "What would little kids go for?"

"Star Wars?" said one player.

"Star Wars is corny," objected another one.

"I hear what you're saying, but what if it's not corny enough?" I asked.

"What does that mean?" Grant asked. "How can it not be corny enough?"

"I mean that sometimes if you try to do something too cool, it falls flat, but if you take something really dorky, you can make it cool just because you're football players."

This argument made perfect sense to them. They saw it happen every time they did the dance routine the cheer squad choreographed for them at the homecoming pep rally.

"You got any ideas, coach?" DeShawn asked.

This was the part I'd have to navigate like that giant ship in the Suez Canal—no margin for error. I'd placed my props carefully. "Let's see, something nerdy you can make cool." I rubbed my chin and began to pace in front of the bench where I'd set my messenger bag. "Let's brainstorm. What about Snoopy and Charlie Brown?" I asked.

"The elementary school does that every year."

"Oh, right. Woody Woodpecker?"

"Who?"

"Bugs Bunny." Meh. "Paw Patrol?" No. "Mickey Mouse?" No. "SpongeBob?" Maaaayb . . . No.

Good. They weren't supposed to like any of those ideas. I paced behind the bench, turned, and accidentally "bumped" into it, knocking my messenger bag to the floor. The top contents spilled out: an empty water bottle, my whistle, and . . . a copy of *The Cat in the Hat*.

"I got it, coach," Grant said. I'd made sure it would fall over in front of him specifically. He hopped up to pick up my stuff and set it on the bench, but when he straightened, he still had the book in his hands. "Why are you carrying around *The Cat in the Hat*?"

"My niece wants it for her bedtime story every night, so I've been reading it aloud a lot. 'I know some new tricks, I will show them to you. Your mother will not mind at all if I do.' I probably have it memorized by now."

"*The Cat in the Hat*," DeShawn said.

"Yeah. That's the book." I took it from Grant and started to slide it into my bag.

"No, I mean, we could do *Cat in the Hat*,"

DeShawn said. "He's the right kind of corny."

Grant gave a slow nod. "I could see that."

"We could dress like those crazy kids, what are they called?" the kicker asked.

"Thing One and Thing Two," another player supplied.

"Yeah, I mean, we all got red warm up sweats. We just make a paper label for our shirts, spray our hair blue, and boom, you got a costume," Grant said.

I'd been banking on the red sweats to sell the idea. I pretended to consider it. "That's not bad. Cheap costume. But how do we tie it to donuts?"

"Man, do we have to think of everything for you, coach?" DeShawn asked.

The rest of the players laughed.

"Fair enough. Maybe . . ." I rubbed my chin again. "Oh. Oh. Huh. What about 'uh-oh,' like the mess the Things make? And O, like the donut shape."

"Seniors get to be Cat in the Hat," DeShawn said. "Everybody else has to be the Things."

"That's dope," another player said. "I want to be a Thing, anyway."

I let my eyebrows rise in surprise as I looked over the team. "Gentlemen, do we have ourselves a theme?"

"I think we do, coach," Grant said, going back to his seat.

"All right, then. Practice dismissed."

I went to my office to grade quizzes from the freshman health unit while they got changed. A few minutes later, a knock sounded and DeShawn poked his head in. "You're a pretty good actor, coach, but you're not that good."

I glanced up at him, keeping my face neutral. "Not sure I know what you mean."

"You played us. And that's fine. *Cat in the Hat* is cool. Bye, coach."

I smiled when he left. One big hurdle out of the way. That only left a million more.

I finished up my grading, and it was nearly six o'clock when I headed to my car. "Coach," a voice called as I unlocked the door.

I looked up to see Dr. Boone heading for her own car. "Need something, ma'am?"

"I heard you got the football team on board with doing the booth and even picked a theme."

"Wow. News travels fast."

"DeShawn Jones is my nephew."

Ah. Now she'd have an inside source to report on how I was doing.

"He stops by my office sometimes on his way out after practice. He doesn't like to talk to me during school because he says it ruins his credibility with the other players."

"He's a good kid," I said.

"He is that. Have a good one, coach. We're almost to Friday. Get the football game out of the way, and you can enjoy your weekend."

"Sure thing, Dr. Boone." But I didn't have my usual end-of-the-week tiredness, because Thursday was game night, and I was hosting so I could babysit Evie while Paige worked. And that meant Grace was coming over.

I had some prepping to do.

CHAPTER ELEVEN
GRACE

"I have good news," I announced when Noah answered his door.

"I can always use some of that." He stepped back to let me in.

I glanced around as I shrugged out of my hoodie. The late September evenings were beginning to acquire a slight chill. "Glynnis came into the store today."

"I thought you said Glynnis would be the most stressful part of doing Christmas Town."

"She would be if she were still doing it. But she's retiring. Said she's getting too old. So that's one less thing to worry about." His apartment was small but cozy with a comfortable-looking corduroy sectional and a couple of framed prints of the Blue Ridge mountains on his walls.

"Nice place. Is that a guy requirement?" I nodded at the giant TV. "Get a degree, a job, then a huge television?"

"Yes. How else are we going to watch all of our manly and violent sports?"

A cute little girl with blonde hair in two braids walked out from the short hallway that probably led to his bedroom. She was in unicorn pajamas, and she climbed on the sofa and clicked on the remote like she'd done it a hundred times. *Mickey Mouse Clubhouse* blinked into life.

"Manly and violent sports, huh?"

He grinned at me and shrugged. "Evie gets what Evie wants. Can you say hi to Miss Grace, pumpkin?"

Evie rose to her knees and twisted around to study me over the back of the sofa. "Hi to Miss Grace, pumpkin."

"Hi, Evie. What are you watching?"

"Mickey Mouse." She waved me over. "Come."

Noah smiled at me. "Better watch while you can. After I finish getting the snacks ready, I'm putting her to bed. She has a cot in my room, and it'll take me about fifteen minutes, but Brooke should be here any minute for you to entertain each other."

"Sounds good." I walked around to take a seat on the sofa at a respectable distance from Evie so I didn't make her nervous.

"I'm five," she said. "How old are you?"

"Twenty-six," I answered.

"Is that big?"

"I think so."

"Okay." Then she popped her thumb into her mouth and scooted over and curled into my side. "Toolbox," she said around her thumb as Mickey called for something named Toodles. An animated toolbox popped up on the screen.

"My kind of show," I said, settling in. I hadn't

spent a lot of time around kids, but Evie was so laidback that she made it easy.

I heard the sound of the oven door opening and a warm wave of something delicious-smelling wafted through the apartment. "Smells good," I called.

"Potato skins," he answered. "My specialty."

A text chimed on my phone, and I checked it and snorted. "Hey, did you see this text from Brooke?"

"No. Do I need to?"

"She can't make it tonight after all."

"Did she say why?"

"Nope. She didn't even have the decency to think of a pretend excuse."

A baking sheet clattered on the stove top, then Noah walked back into the living room. "It's night-night, Evie," he said, leaning down to scoop her up. She held her arms up without objection. "And don't worry," he said to me over her head as he straightened. "This is still not a date."

"What's a date, Noah?" Evie asked.

"Not this," he said, and whisked her down the hall. "Help yourself to some food," he called over his shoulder as he went. "It'll be a few minutes."

I responded to Brooke's group text.

Grace: You're the worst and you're not fooling anyone.

I heard Noah laugh from the end of the hall as Brooke responded with a halo emoji.

Yeah, right.

I investigated the kitchen, which led me to some potato skins and a condiment bar of crumbled bacon, chopped green onions, and bleu cheese dressing for dipping. There was also a heaping bowl of popcorn. That more than covered the savory, but I didn't see anything to cover the sweet. Which was fine. He was playing to his strengths, obviously, because the baked potato skins looked good.

I served myself two with some topping and dip, then went back to the sofa, surfing the channels while I waited for Noah.

He was back in ten minutes. "How was everything?" he asked, eyeing my empty plate.

"Delicious."

"I told you I was good at popcorn."

"I didn't try it. The potato skins covered the savory."

He rolled his eyes. "Hang on." He was back in a minute with the popcorn. "Try a bite."

I did to be polite. "Oh," I said, as the sweetness hit my tongue. "Kettle corn."

"Uh huh. Popped in coconut oil for extra sweetness."

"Awesome." I took another handful and munched. "What are we playing?"

"A movie," he said. "That's why I popped pop-corn."

"The Bob one?"

"Definitely the Bob one. Friends don't neglect friends' cultural educations." He pulled up the movie and we settled in to watch.

Maybe it should have felt weird to suddenly be alone with him without Brooke as a buffer. But it wasn't. I curled up in the corner of the sectional and he stretched out on his end, his feet up on the coffee table.

"You were right about this movie," I conceded a half hour in when I'd laughed for at least the tenth time.

"It's good, right?" He sounded smug, so I gave a lazy kick in his direction that failed to connect.

"It's good."

We watched the rest of it, but when it got to the escalating absurdity of the last fifteen minutes, I didn't hear an answering laugh from Noah, and I glanced over to see that he'd fallen asleep. Within a couple of minutes, he was snoring softly. So softly that it was kind of cute.

I left him alone and finished the movie, then muted the volume as the credits rolled. I leaned back against the cushions and watched him in the light of the TV, his face relaxed as he slept.

I should probably have woken him up, but I wasn't in a hurry. The couch was comfortable, and I had nowhere to be. And I wanted the opportunity to study him openly in a way I hadn't been able to since we'd met.

He was definitely my type, looks-wise. But I liked his personality too. He was easy-going and kind, two things I'd learned to value from my dad. And he was so cute with his niece. It was clear he'd be a good dad too. It was too bad I wasn't staying, because if I were, I'd be into him. Or maybe it was a very good thing I was leaving in a couple of months, because I was a little bit into him already.

How often had I been in a guy's apartment and felt comfortable enough to lean my head back and rest for a minute without worrying about the message I was sending? Or how my hair looked? Or what he was thinking? Maybe never?

"Grace."

Something tickled my toes and I wiggled them.

"Grace." A male voice, a little louder, definitely more amused.

I blinked my eyes open. I'd fallen asleep, stretched out, and apparently had decided that the most comfortable place for my feet was in Noah's lap. His hand was resting across my shins, his thigh warm and firm against my Achilles.

"You fell asleep."

I shook my head to clear it.

"I also fell asleep. I have to say I'm surprised, Grace. You're blowing my image of wholesome small-town girls."

I rubbed my eyes and didn't bother sitting up straighter. I liked my feet right where they were. "What are you talking about?" I asked around a yawn.

"We got to second base before we even met, and now we've slept together without even going on a date."

I took advantage of my position to hit him with my heel. "If you want me to help you with Christmas Town, you better stop talking."

His hand tightened for a second around my leg. "If I have to."

"You have to." But I still didn't make any effort to move away. "How's it going with all the booth planning, anyway?"

"It's good," he said. "Especially now that I don't have to deal with Glynnis. It feels anti-climactic, to be honest. Who's going to be in charge instead?"

"Taylor Bixby."

"As in Bixby Café?"

She nodded. "I like her. She graduated with Tabitha. I don't remember her as being one of those take-charge types, but she must be if she can start and run her own café."

"So do I wait for orders from her?"

"Yeah. Get the donut recipe from Ritzau, order your stuff so you have the nonperishables here in plenty of time, order the perishable stuff for delivery closer to Christmas, and then work on

118

the booth. I'm sure it'll make Taylor's life easier if she's not having to micromanage everyone the way Glynnis did. Taylor seems more mellow. Did you get the team to buy in?"

He picked up my foot and set to work massaging it, almost absent-mindedly, like his hands always needed to be busy while he thought.

It was definitely not absent-minded for me. He kneaded the tendon in my arch that always got sore at the end of a day on my feet in Handy's, and I bit back a moan that would have embarrassed us both when he hit it just right.

"The team went for it," he said. "I got them on board, and they're willing to come back to campus on Saturdays next month in shifts to work on the basics."

It was hard to concentrate on his words when he was working such magic on my feet, and maybe that was why I made my next offer. "Instead of working on it at school, we can do it at my parents' place. Dad has a shop out back, and he'll enjoy supervising."

"You don't have to do that," he protested. "You're already doing too much."

"It's fine. My dad will honestly enjoy it. He feels better every week. He's not ready to come back to work full-time, but he's getting restless."

His hands stilled, and I opened my eyes to see what was wrong. He was staring at me. "You're amazing," he said.

I closed my eyes, unnerved by the directness of his words and his expression. It felt . . . intimate, with my feet nestled in his lap.

"No big deal. It's about time we started hiring a couple of seasonal workers, and they can cover for me on Saturday mornings while I help the boys with the booth."

"I'll have Evie with me most Saturdays so Paige can work. Saturday and Sunday brunch mean big tips for her at the diner."

"That's no problem," I said. "Evie seems like a cool kid."

"She's the best."

There was no twenty-six-year-old on the planet who would not fall under the spell of a foot rub from a hot guy who was good with kids. Not even one like me who was ready to leave Creekville behind as soon as the holidays were over. No one could blame me for sitting there longer than I should have, picturing for a minute what it would be like to stay and hang out with Noah and Evie.

When I realized where my mind was drifting, I slipped my feet from Noah's lap and climbed off the couch. "I should go. Good call on the movie." I sounded weird. Stilted, like I'd rehearsed the words.

He looked startled but got to his feet too. "It's only ten. I have plenty of potato skins left. And we could . . ." He glanced around the room.

"Watch another movie?" But a yawn caught him at the end.

"Don't you have to be at school early tomorrow?"

He sighed. "Yeah. I do."

"Then I'll help you clean up before I take off."

He was shaking his head before I finished the sentence. "I'll clean up. You've got a drive ahead of you. You should go."

"It's only twenty minutes."

"Twenty-five," he said, smiling. "I make that drive every morning, remember?"

"Right. Okay, well, see you around. Let me know when you're ready to start on the booth."

"I will. Would it work if I came by your place this Saturday morning to get a feel for the setup? I can stop by before you go to work."

"Sure," I said, trying to ignore the tummy flutter at the idea of him coming to my house.

"Great. Let me walk you out."

For Noah, that meant walking me all the way down to my car in the complex's parking lot. "Thanks for driving out," he said, as I pulled my keys from my purse. I fidgeted with them then stopped as Noah's hazel eyes grew a shade darker. The scene from *Hitch* flashed through my head where Hitch tells Albert that fiddling with keys was a girl's sign that she wanted a goodnight kiss.

"No problem. See you on Saturday morning."

I wanted to turn slightly so he could pull me into a goodnight hug. I wanted it like Seuss's Cat wanted chaos. I fumbled for my door handle to get out of temptation's way. I climbed into the car and pulled the door closed with a wave through the window.

Noah had a small smile on his face, like he knew exactly why I was escaping, but he only waved back and slid his hands into his pockets, watching as I pulled out. His eyes were still on me when I checked the rearview mirror before pulling out of the parking lot.

It should not have been so hard to drive away.

Dang it, Noah Redmond. There wasn't time for this.

But I declined to define to myself what "this" was.

CHAPTER TWELVE
NOAH

"Where we going, Mama?"

I glanced at Evie in the rearview mirror, comfortably buckled into her car seat, then over to Paige in the passenger seat.

"We're going to see Uncle Noah's friend," she said.

"Toodles," said Evie, satisfied.

Toodles was the name of Mickey's magic toolbox on her favorite show, and when I'd tried to explain Grace's job at the hardware store, Evie had listened carefully and then announced, "She is Toodles." It was close enough.

She went back to playing with her stuffed kitty, showing it the passing scenery.

"This can't be how you want to spend your morning off," I said to Paige.

"If Evie is going to be hanging out a lot with your new friend, then I want to meet her."

"Don't say it like that."

"Say what?"

"Don't say 'new friend' like it's code. Grace is my friend. That's all it is."

"Uh huh. You always wear your best cologne for your new friends?"

"Shut up," I grumbled.

"Unc! You said the S-word," Evie called from the back seat. "That's a no-no word. He needs a timeout, Mama."

"Yes, Evie. Unc will do a timeout when we get home, but he has to drive right now." Paige pinched my arm when Evie wasn't looking. I scowled at her.

"Grace is cool," I told her. "Don't make it weird when we get there."

"Who me?" she asked in a tone so innocent it raised the fine hairs on my nape.

"Paige . . ."

"Relax. I just want to meet her. It's important to me to know people spending a lot of time around my kid."

I nodded. "I get it." I slid a quick glance her way. "You're a good mom."

"Thanks." She cleared her throat and turned to look out her window. We stayed quiet except for Evie's make-believe chatter for the remaining ten minutes to Creekville.

When I pulled into the parking lot behind Handy Hardware, I cut the engine and took a deep breath, but Paige jumped in before I could speak. "Seriously, don't sweat. It'll be fine."

She hopped out and unbuckled Evie, and we headed into the store.

"Help you?" asked the old man at the register as we walked in. I recognized him from the first time I'd come in.

"We're looking for Grace, actually."

"Check the yard aisle."

"Uh . . ."

"Aisle seven," he grunted.

"Thanks."

Evie slipped her hand into Paige's, and we walked down to aisle seven. Sure enough, there was Grace, crouched over the bottom shelf, fixing a price sticker.

"Hi, Toodles," Evie said.

Grace turned and smiled when she saw us. "Hey, Evie," she said, as she straightened. "Good to see you."

"Hope it's okay that we dropped in," I said. "Paige wanted to meet you."

Paige strode forward and held her hand out for a shake. "Sorry, I nagged him into bringing us. Don't think he's weird. I mean, he is, but not because of this. It's a me thing. Or maybe a single mother thing. I wanted to know who Evie would be spending her Saturday mornings with."

Grace shook Paige's hand without looking remotely thrown by my sister's flood of words. "Of course, makes perfect sense. Nice to meet you."

"You too," Paige said, stepping back.

"Unc says you'll teach me to build," Evie announced.

"That's not exactly what I said," I hurried

to explain. I crouched to meet Evie's eyes. "Remember, I said she's going to help the football team build something, and you and I are going to supervise."

"No building?" Evie asked, her face falling.

"Of course building," Grace said. "My dad taught me to build when I was your age. Want to build something right now?"

"You don't have to do that," Paige told her.

Grace smiled. "I grew up working in this store, and when I was a teenager, my dad had me running Builder Buddy workshops for kids on Tuesday mornings during the summer. I have the perfect project for you guys, if you want."

"If you're sure it's no trouble," Paige said, smiling.

"I'm sure. Evie, do we want to hammer stuff or glue stuff?"

"Hammer!" she shouted.

I winced, but Grace only grinned. "My kind of girl. Follow me."

She led us to the lumber section. "First, we're going to need some wood." She grabbed a sheet of plywood and set it on a table with a locked table saw, pulled the pencil from behind her ear, and dug a measuring tape from her toolbelt. It was sexy as hell.

"First rule of construction, Evie: measure twice, cut once."

"What's that mean?" Evie asked.

"It'll make sense when you're eight," Grace promised.

I hid a smile at the easy way Grace answered her. Paige looked utterly charmed. I got it. Grace did that to me too.

"I'm making the measurements for a box, then I'll cut it up, and it's going to be your job to hammer it. Think you can handle that?"

"Yeah!" shouted Evie.

"All right, then. Here we go." If I thought the toolbelt was sexy, it was nothing compared to when Grace unlocked the table saw and fired it up, feeding the plywood through its teeth in deft turns while Evie held her hands over her ears to block the noise.

Paige glanced over at me and mimed wiping away slobber. I snapped my jaw shut and reminded myself that Grace was my friend and I shouldn't be panting after her in the lumber aisle of her father's store.

Paige looked like she was trying not to laugh.

A minute later, Grace cut off the saw and relocked it, handing Evie several pieces of wood. "Can you help me carry these to your workbench?"

Evie clutched the wood to her chest and trotted after Grace, who headed toward the back of the store. Paige hung back long enough to say, "I love her," out of the side of her mouth.

"Move it," I said, nudging her ahead of me.

Grace stopped at a door marked "Employees Only" at the back of the store. "Wait here a minute, okay? It's tricky to get around back there right now, but I'll be back with the tools you need."

Evie nodded. "Okay, Toodles."

"Her name is Grace," I reminded her.

"I don't mind," Grace said. "It'll take me a minute to find what I'm looking for, but I think I know where it is."

"Sounds good."

"Sounds amazing, is more like it," Paige said when Grace disappeared through the swinging door. "Is she for real?"

I smiled. "She's for really real."

"So why are you sleeping on that? If you don't date her, I will, and I'm straight!"

"We're just friends, Paige. Don't make it weird."

"The only thing that's weird is that you're just friends," she said, but she dropped it when Evie dropped her wood, and Paige bent to help her gather it all back up.

A few minutes later, Grace popped her head through the door. "Noah, you want to help me with this?"

"Sure." I stepped into the back room, which was bigger than I would expect from the outside, but even more crowded than she'd hinted, an explosion of tinsel and ornaments everywhere. "Wow. I think I found Christmas Town."

"I know," she said. "We'll get this stuff on the floor soon, and it won't be so bad back here." She handed me a sturdy canvas tote full of tools and hefted a small, kid-height portable workbench. "We'll set these up in the back corner near the fishing tackle. That won't get much traffic today."

I would have offered to carry the workbench, but I had a feeling it would offend her, so we all trooped dutifully behind her to the fishing corner, where she set up the workbench and brought out a couple of chairs for Paige and Evie.

"Would you guys mind if I borrow Noah after I teach you how to build the box?" she asked.

"Not at all," Paige said.

"If you give him back," Evie said and looked confused when we all laughed.

Grace demonstrated how to nail the four sides of the box together, showing Evie how to hammer, and more importantly, showing Paige how to hold the nail for Evie with a pair of pliers so she didn't have to worry about her fingers if Evie missed.

"Smart," I said, as they got to work.

"Told you, it's not my first time turning kids loose with a hammer. Should we head up front?"

I followed her away from Evie's enthusiastic pounding. "I'm going to work on this Halloween display while you tell me how the booth plans are going," she said.

"Can I help?"

"Sure. We're making a mini graveyard to show off the new tombstones."

"That's a weird sentence." But I grabbed one of the decorative tombstones she indicated that read "RIP I.M. Wormfood." "This is awesome," I said, hefting it. Like most of the things in Handy's, it was better quality than the cheap stuff we used to buy online for our frat house decorations. Those had been made of Styrofoam that chipped away and showed white chunks through the cheap spray paint if you even looked at them wrong. This had a real stone veneer on the front, and a sturdy plastic stake to keep it anchored in the ground.

"You *would* think that," she said, wryly.

"What's that supposed to mean?"

"It means you like dumb dad jokes as much as my actual dad does."

I couldn't deny it.

I followed her orders for a few minutes, but customer after customer set off the front bell, and before long, there was a grumpy call from the direction of the register. "Getting backed up here, Gracie."

She straightened. "I really gotta hire some holiday help. Come on, you're about to get some register training."

I followed her to the cash register. "You'll do any cash purchases," she said. "Just scan the tags, press total, punch in the amount they give you, and it'll tell you how much change to give back. Can you handle it?"

"It sounds like a monkey could handle it."

"You're not wrong," she said. "That's why you get the job."

"Ha ha."

"Now watch me a couple of times, then you take over while I go answer questions on the floor."

It was as easy as promised, and I rang up customers for the next twenty minutes until the line was down to one again.

"You're off the hook," the old man said. Gary. That was the name stitched on his shirt. "Go find the girl."

I listened for a second. "You're right. The hammering stopped. It usually means trouble when she gets quiet."

"I meant Gracie."

"Right." I went to look for her at the graveyard display but instead I found Paige and Evie moving an Evie-sized skeleton around. "Uh, guys? What are you doing?"

"Grace needed help," Paige said. "So I told her I'd take over the display."

I stepped back to look at it. She'd rearranged some of what Grace had set up, but it looked good. Not a surprise. Paige had always had a good eye. "Do you know where she is?"

Paige shook her head. "Store's not that big. I think your chances of finding her are good."

I shook my head and went looking for her. She was in the yard aisle, talking to an older man about leaf blowers. I couldn't hear the conversation, but her face was a polite mask, and I wondered if this guy had any idea how close he was to getting punched.

She nodded a few times, tried to talk twice, but he cut her off both times, until finally she slid her hands into her back pockets and pressed her lips tight. I interpreted it to mean he was wrong, but she was done arguing. He walked past me toward the exit.

"What was that all about?" I asked her.

She shook her head. "Happens at least once a day. He thinks this leaf blower is overpriced. Says he can get a cheaper one on Amazon. I told him to go ahead. He'll get what he pays for, and when it breaks in a month, he'll be back to buy this one anyway. A lot of dudes don't like to listen to me."

"That must be irritating."

"It's been happening my whole life. Sometimes my dad sets them straight when he's in here, but he can't correct all the dummies."

"Excuse me, miss," a middle-aged woman called from the other end of the aisle.

Grace shot me an apologetic look. "Sorry. Saturdays are crazy around here."

"Don't apologize. We crashed without an invitation. I'm going to check on Paige and Evie."

She walked off toward the customer, muttering again about hiring holiday help.

Paige immediately began ordering me around. For the next half hour, I rearranged all kinds of Halloween stuff. Grace would zoom by occasionally as she moved from one customer to the next, and at one point Paige called, "Can I rearrange your window display?"

Gracie cast a quick glance at Paige's Halloween display and said, "Go for it," before zipping off again.

We spent another hour working in the front window while Evie entertained passersby on the sidewalk by tapping on the window and waving at them. Paige would send me down the aisles in search of random stuff. "Get me a pitchfork," or "Now go find a gas can." Grace and I would cross paths a few times, and every now and then she'd glance at me in total confusion—especially when Paige sent me after the black stuff that went under the bark in landscaping beds—but she didn't say anything.

It was about an hour after lunch before the steady stream of customers slowed to a trickle.

"This looks awesome," Grace called, and we climbed out of the window where Paige had been putting her finishing touches. We joined Grace at the Halloween display, which Paige had managed to turn from a collection of corny tombstones into the corner of an eerie cemetery with the help of peat moss, a tipped over camping lantern, and a few creatively placed skeletons.

"Glad you like it. You want to make sure you're okay with the way I changed your front window display?"

"Let me go check it out."

Grace hurried out to the sidewalk, and we stood inside behind the display to watch her reaction through the window. Her eyes widened and her jaw dropped before she broke into a huge grin.

"This is *awesome,*" she yelled through the glass.

I nudged Paige with my elbow. "She doesn't smile like that very often. Good job."

"Interesting you know that," she said.

I ignored her as we waited for Grace to join us.

"Do you want a job?" she asked Paige. "I need to hire some seasonal workers, and I could desperately use you on the weekends."

Paige laughed. "That's sweet of you, but I normally work the brunch shifts at the diner. That's when I make my best tips."

"Tell me what you make hourly, and I'll match it."

Paige shook her head. "Seriously, that's so nice, but it's good money. Like between $18 to $20 an hour some weekends."

"Done," Grace said. "You're worth two of the part-timers I usually hire. You're proactive, fast, creative, and you solve problems well. Ever thought about being an engineer?"

Paige laughed. "No. Interior decorator, maybe."

"So you'll do it?"

Paige's smile was replaced by surprise. "You're serious?"

"Dead serious. I bet after two hours of training, I'll be able to leave you to run the store with Gary, and then I can help your brother with the Christmas Town stuff without worrying that this place is falling down without me."

"And you can drive in with me on Saturdays and borrow my car for Sundays," I added. "I'll watch Evie, same as usual."

Paige looked torn, so I threw in the clencher. "It's got to be better than working for Marvin."

She drew a deep breath. "I'll do it. For eighteen dollars an hour, as long as you know you're overpaying."

"Twenty," Grace said. "And I'm definitely not. Can you start tomorrow?"

Paige looked at me, and I grinned and nodded. "I was already planning to watch Evie anyway. Doesn't change my plans."

"Okay," Paige said. "If I can get someone to cover my shift, I'll start tomorrow."

"Great," Grace said. "I'll send you home with some paperwork. Just bring it with you, and we'll make it official. And thanks, Paige. You saved me about five hours of trying to post and fill this job later this week."

"Excuse me, miss, can I get some help over here?" a man's voice called from the paint aisle.

Grace rolled her eyes.

"We'll get out of your hair," I said.

I watched her go for a second, her butt looking even better in her worn jeans than it had in her fancy dress. But I was coming to like all of her bits. A lot. Her smile. Her brain. Her smart mouth.

That mouth . . .

I swallowed hard and looked away, catching Paige's eye as she watched me, clearly entertained.

"You are so into her," she said.

"Am not," I answered like I was seven instead of twenty-seven. "Let's go home."

I needed to get out of Grace's orbit, because it would be far too easy to get sucked into it. But she wasn't meant to stay on this trajectory forever. Soon she'd be launching out of Creekville, far away on a path I couldn't follow, no matter how closely I felt myself teetering on the edge of falling for her.

I had Paige and Evie to think of, and where Grace and I each needed to be was worlds apart.

CHAPTER THIRTEEN
GRACE

Brooke: Game night this week?

I stared at the text, suspicious.

Grace: Is this another trick?
Brooke: No. Learned my lesson. I promise.
Grace: Miss Lily is a bad influence on you.
Brooke: No tricks! I promise! Just Monopoly or something.
Grace: Monopoly is stupid.
Brooke: Trivial Pursuit?
Grace: Fine.

For someone who should be avoiding Noah, I was scheduled to spend more time with him than ever. Game night on Thursday now, on top of the first official team booth-building day coming up on Saturday morning.

I couldn't bring myself to object to any of it.

Whatever. It was fine. All friendly stuff.

Thursday night, I headed over to Brooke's after I closed the store, which meant beating Noah there by a half-hour. As if to prove she wasn't in the matchmaking business anymore, she didn't bring his name up once, instead catching me up on Ian's training at Quantico.

"He gets to come for Thanksgiving for two days," she said. "I can't wait. Gran does an amazing Thanksgiving. You should come this year."

"Gran" was Miss Lily, who I adored. Everyone did, really. But I smiled and shook my head. "We're having a family thing. Tabitha's coming from New York, and I can't wait. My dad feels so much better than last year, and it should feel like normal Thanksgiving again."

Last year he'd been too ill from chemo to want to eat. This year, he was coming into the store a couple of hours a day to help Gary while I took lunch and caught up on ordering. Every week, I saw signs of my dad returning to his old self. In fact, I'd finally posted my resume online this past Monday. Getting back to real life wasn't a hope anymore; it was a given.

Noah's name didn't come up until the man himself knocked on the door promptly at seven. A second armchair had magically reappeared since our last game night here, and I'd claimed it so she couldn't try to maneuver us into a cozy couch situation again.

"Hey, Noah. Come on in," Brooke said from her foyer. "Did you think about what we discussed at lunch?"

My ears perked up. This sounded code-like.

"Um, is Grace here?"

"Yeah, but she won't care. I've accepted you guys don't want to be set up with each other, but that doesn't mean I can't try to fix you up with someone else."

What was it with newly married people that they were always convinced all their single friends secretly wanted was to be married too? Ugh. But I leaned forward, like that was somehow going to let me hear the conversation at the front door better. I wanted to know what Noah thought about this.

"Sure," he said. "Give me your friend's number. What's her name again?"

"It's my hairdresser, Nikki. You'll love her." Then Brooke interrupted herself with a laugh. "Or at least like her. She's cute and fun."

I frowned. I was cute and fun.

I sat back and barely refrained from giving myself a face palm. I was also not at all on the market.

Brooke walked into the living room with Noah behind her. "Hey, Grace," he said with his usual easy smile. "I hear I'm about to deliver a trivia beatdown."

"You wish," I said. "When are you going to learn there's nothing I'm not good at?"

"I wish I had a comeback for that, but so far, that's been true."

My stomach did a flip at the words. *Good luck, Hairdresser Nikki. You're going to have to be good at everything if you want to beat me.*

Except it wasn't a competition. I gritted my teeth for a moment to remind myself that I didn't care who Noah went out with or how good she might be at anything. Noah looked slightly startled, and I realized I must look mad at his compliment. I forced myself to smile. "I'm bad at doing makeup. Does that make you feel better?"

"It would except, you don't need it. And it's not like I'm good at it. So, no. So far, you're still better at way more things."

Another compliment. I felt the beginnings of something, a feeling in my stomach or my head—I couldn't even tell—that was . . . what was that? An impending swoon?

OH MY GOSH.

Pull it together right now, Grace Winters. You are a ridiculous woman.

"Let the massacre begin," I said, reaching for my Trivial Pursuit pie.

In the end, Brooke beat us both. Noah dominated sports and leisure, and I had a good handle on geography and science, but Brooke was also a whiz on science plus she killed in entertainment.

At the end of the night, Noah and I had to endure her victory dance. We exchanged looks as she strutted back and forth beside the coffee table.

"Is this a seizure?" Noah asked.

"Maybe. Should we do something? Like first aid? Or call 911?"

"Funny, guys," Brooke said, but she didn't stop the dance.

"Why are we friends with her?" I asked Noah, and Brooke added arm motions.

"Good snacks?"

"Oh, yeah."

We helped her clean up, and Noah offered to walk me out to my car when I yawned. "I need to get going too," he said.

"You ready for Saturday?" he asked as I opened the car door with zero key fumbling. It would be our first day working with the boys on the booth.

"Yeah. My dad's excited to supervise."

"Evie too," he said. "She's pretty sure she's an expert after hammering her box together."

"Cool. Saturday will mostly be about making sure there's a clear plan and figuring out who has which skills. You have someone bringing over the booth frame from the school, right?"

"About half the team drive pickup trucks, so a couple of the guys already got it from the custodian, and they'll bring it Saturday morning." He tilted his head. "You weren't by any chance a project manager at your old job, were you?"

I gave him a small smile and slipped into the driver's seat, starting the car and lowering the window. "Not quite. But I had just gotten

141

promoted to team lead when I had to resign."

"If you're not running your own division in ten years, I'll . . ."

"You'll what?"

"I was going to say 'eat my hat' because that's what they say in movies a lot, but it didn't have the right ring to it. Besides, I definitely wouldn't eat my hat. How would you even do that?"

I don't know why that made me laugh, but it did. Hard.

"It's not that funny," he said, his lips twitching.

"But it is," I said between giggles. "I'm picturing you sitting there with your hat on a plate, a napkin tucked into your shirt—"

"Like I'm five?"

"Like you're five," I confirmed, "and then you've got ketchup and mustard and barbecue sauce and a look of total confusion."

He bent to meet my eyes through the open window. "Grace Winters, you are a total weirdo. I'll see you on Saturday."

I drove off, still grinning, something that seemed to happen every time I hung out with Noah.

I looked forward to Saturday morning way more than I should, right until Tabitha ruined it for me. She called right after breakfast, as usual. She always tried to fit us in between her morning run and getting ready for whatever fancy adventure she had going on that day. Soirees. Personal appearances. I didn't even know. It all sounded completely foreign to me. And kind of sucky. I never wanted to be as busy as she was.

"Hey, Gracie," she said when I answered. "Is Mom around?"

"Try her phone."

"No, I'm not trying to get hold of her right now. I want to make sure she doesn't overhear your side of the conversation."

"Uh, why? What is my side of the conversation going to be?" I already didn't like where it was going.

"I talked to Dad yesterday after dinner. He sounds good."

"He *is* good. He'll get another scan next month, but Dr. Pearson is optimistic. Way more than he usually is."

"That's good to hear. That means I only have Mom to worry about."

A tingle alerted me that trouble was coming. "What do you mean?"

"I'd break it to them myself, but you're right there, so I figure you can manage them better."

"Break what to them, Tabitha? You've been busted for running drugs? You're pregnant with a two-headed alien love child? What?"

She took a deep breath. "I'm not going to make it home for Thanksgiving."

"Oh, even worse, then."

"Come on, Grace. Don't be like that. I'd come home if I could."

"Would you, though?"

"Grace."

"Tabitha," I answered with no inflection. I was not helping her out of this one.

"It's work. I can't leave."

"Seriously? You're not taping on Thanksgiving Day."

"No, but I'm doing a big segment on the *Today* show the day before, and another one on New York One about leftovers the day after. It takes a full day of travel just to get out to Creekville, and there are no Thursday flights I can take to get me back by Friday morning."

"Then cancel Friday. It's just a local show."

"A local show in *New York*. That's eight million people."

"They don't all watch the morning news."

"But over a quarter million of them do, and with my cookbook coming out, I need to get my name out there and get preorders rolling in."

"This is lame, Tabitha. Mom and Dad are going to be so bummed."

"That's why I want you to handle it. Having you there will remind them that they won't be alone for Thanksgiving."

"How is it that you guilted me into quitting my job and coming here by telling me that family comes first but you can't even make it home for Thanksgiving because of a single TV appearance?" It was mean, meaner than I usually was, but I'd been handling my parents for eighteen months almost entirely by myself with the exception of a couple of holiday visits from Tabitha. And now she wasn't even going to do that much.

She was quiet, and I could hear her hurt in the silence. But I wasn't going to make her feel better about this.

"I know you don't get it," she finally said, "but this is how it is for me right now. I'd be there if I could, but I can't. I'll tell them myself. Consider this a head's up so you can distract them or something, maybe cushion the blow."

"Fine, Tabitha."

"Grace . . ."

"I said it's fine, Tab. I have to go."

Talented Tabitha. She could ruin Thanksgiving a month ahead of time from hundreds of miles away.

Talented Tabitha.

Frustrating freaking Tabitha.

Blerg.

CHAPTER FOURTEEN
NOAH

I checked my reflection in the mirror and was once again thankful that makeup wasn't a thing for dudes. All I had to do was make sure I didn't have any random hairs poking up and that I smelled okay, and I was ready to go.

"Noah?" Paige called from my living room.

"Hey." I walked out and presented myself for inspection.

"You look fine. Tell me again why this isn't a date with Grace?"

"I've explained it five times already."

"She's leaving and doesn't want to get involved. Right, I get that. Except I think you could change her mind pretty easily."

I'd wondered about this myself a couple of times, when I'd caught Grace looking at me when she thought I wasn't looking, or when we accidentally touched. I couldn't be the only one who felt those points of contact like they were supercharged.

Could I?

Maybe. But it didn't matter. "Even if that were true, I wouldn't try," I said. "Mr. Winters is getting better, and she has her first job interview lined up for next week. She'll totally get it too."

An employer would have to be an idiot not to hire someone as smart and capable as Grace. "I'm not a casual dating kind of guy, and she's leaving. Case closed."

"You are so stubborn," she said. "But at least you're going on a date. Are you excited? Is she hot?"

Brooke had shown me a picture of Nikki, my date, who was a striking blonde. "Very hot."

"Good for you, then."

"That's premature, P. We haven't even met yet."

"Maybe don't use the word 'premature' before a hot date."

"Leave."

"I kid, I kid."

"Leave anyway. I need to go meet her."

"What are you guys doing?"

"Bowling," I said. "And I'll give her the option of going out to eat first or eating at the bowling alley."

"Like a test to see if she's high or low maintenance?" she asked.

"No. Or at least it wasn't. I was thinking she might like options, but you just turned it into a test, so thanks for that."

"You are high strung tonight," she said. "What's got you so on edge? Are you nervous?"

"No." Which was true. It was more like I was cranky because I should be looking forward to a date with a hot woman, and instead it felt like a chore. "Now go."

Paige went back across the hall to her place, and I left for my date.

It did not get better.

It wasn't that it was a bad date. Nikki was nice. She had a nervous energy that made it hard to relax, but that wasn't a dealbreaker on a first date. And she definitely did her part to keep the conversation going.

But the whole night, I kept feeling like I was having to *work* at it. It wasn't easy, like hanging out with . . .

Bah.

BAH.

That was the whole problem. No matter how cute Nikki looked—and she looked cute—or how cheerful her conversation was—and it was cheerful—weirdly cheerful—I couldn't connect. Because it didn't feel easy like it did with Grace.

I almost didn't want to drop by Brooke's classroom on Monday for lunch, but she would hunt me down in the gym if I didn't, so I manned up and brought my roast beef sandwich and Fritos over and pulled up a chair at her desk.

"Hey. How did it go with Nikki?" she asked.

"You didn't talk to her yet?"

"I thought I'd hear your version of events first."

"She's cute but we didn't click."

"She put it stronger than that."

"Which is how?"

"That you were—" she made air quotes "—checked out."

"I don't even know what that means. We talked all night and bowled two games."

"She said your mind was on other things the whole time. Was something distracting you?" Brooke's question was soft, like she was genuinely concerned.

"No, I'm all good."

She leaned over and went in for the kill. "Then maybe I should ask if *someone* was distracting you?"

I knew where she was going with this. The best technique with Brooke—as with well-meaning puppies—was redirection.

"Nope, no one. How's that fifth period class of yours shaping up?"

She didn't look like she was going to take the bait, but her classroom phone rang, and she sighed and picked it up. "This is Mrs. Greene."

I smothered a smile at how delighted she looked at using her married name.

"Hi, Nancy. Yes, he's here. Sure, I'll let him know." She hung up. "Dr. Boone would like you to stop by during your prep period."

"Got it. Now, your fifth period class?" I made sure the conversation didn't drift toward blind dates or Grace for the rest of lunch.

• • •

"You wanted to see me, Dr. Boone?"

The principal looked up from her desk and smiled. "Come on in, coach. How's the booth coming?"

"Great," I said, relieved I could report that without lying. "The boys have a good concept, they've started laying out their design, and we shouldn't have any problems getting it ready in time."

"Glad to hear it. That's DeShawn's take on it too, but I wanted to hear it from you. He says you've got things well in hand, and it's nice to confirm it."

I shifted in my seat. "Are you getting more comfortable with the idea of me applying to the head coaching position?"

She leaned back in her chair and sighed. "I'm pleased with how well this fundraiser is going, and I like what I see of your management skills so far, but there are other things to consider."

"Like what?" I asked, trying not to get frustrated by more hoops.

"Do you know how long Coach Dean has been running the program here?"

"Almost thirty years."

"Yes. And he taught here for ten years before that and played for the Bulldogs when he was in high school."

"I'm aware." Where was she going with this?

"The point is that he's a man with roots in this community. He was born here and he'll die here. A program like ours needs that kind of longevity. Do you have that kind of longevity?"

"Of course." I almost smiled at the question. "I'm from Mineral, born and raised, and I only moved as far as Granger. I loved growing up here. If I wasn't a deep roots kind of guy, I would have left a long time ago."

"And yet you're already working at your second school district after only being at the first for three years. Do you know how long the average new teacher lasts in this profession?"

"I've heard the stats."

She supplied them anyway. "Four years. They leave for a number of reasons, but if they make it past that point, they'll stay in for the full length of their career."

"I've made it past that point."

"Barely," she said. "This is your fifth year, right? And you've still got big life stuff coming up that can change things."

"Like what?"

"Legally, I can't discuss any of that context in terms of why you might not be hired for a job."

I sat back and studied her. Was she going where I thought she was going?

She sighed. "I'm going to make some observations by way of conversation, okay?"

I nodded.

"Male married teachers tend to grow roots so deep that you couldn't yank them out with a backhoe. But single male teachers who get married often move away to where the wife wants to settle. If it's here, great. If it's not, great. And if a single male isn't already dating someone local, let's say, it's hard to guess which way that might go."

I leaned forward like it would help me read her body language better. "You're saying you would be more open to the idea of giving me the head coach job if I were married or at least dating someone local?"

"Of course not," she said, leaning forward and meeting my eyes directly. "That would be illegal for me to even consider as an employer."

Words began to come out of my mouth, words that came from a deep and devilish part of me, words I was ashamed of but couldn't stop. The coaching stipend could make a real difference for Paige and Evie. "I get that," I said. "And not that it has anything to do with the head coaching job, but I'm dating a local girl right now."

Dr. Boone leaned back in her chair. "Well, that's certainly an interesting thing that I just learned about you in the course of getting to know my faculty better that definitely doesn't have anything to do with your employment status. Do I know her?"

"Maybe. Grace Winters? She runs Handy Hardware." I had to hope that Dr. Boone wasn't wired into the community enough to know that Grace's situation was temporary.

"Is that the petite brunette you were with at Brooke's wedding?"

Holy cow. Coincidence was totally working in my favor. "That's her," I confirmed. "In fact, she's helping me with the booth."

"Oh, that's right. It's usually Bill Winters who supervises and provides materials. I should have made the connection faster."

As soon as I left Dr. Boone's office, I was going to have to run either straight to a priest or to Grace, but I owed *someone* a confession over this.

"Is it serious?" she continued. "I ask in a purely conversational, getting-to-know-my-staff way, of course."

"Of course. I would say it's going well." When Dr. Boone's expression grew a touch wary, I added, "Very, very well." That was true. Grace and I were doing this friend thing so well that we should be poster children for how to be friends with someone even when you spend a lot of time thinking about what it would be like to make out with them and whether the answer was "really great" or "awesome."

"I'm pleased to hear that," Dr. Boone said. "I see my next appointment out there, but this was an enlightening conversation, Coach Redmond. Thanks for stopping in."

"Glad to shed some light," I said. Which was an interesting way to say "lie my face off." I needed to go figure out how to balance the scales before karma came for me hard.

I'd have to start by coming clean to Grace, which felt like possible karma, because there was a good chance she would kill me.

CHAPTER FIFTEEN
GRACE

Noah would be dropping off Paige at work right about now and heading over here to get everything ready for the boys, so I spent too long fixing my ponytail and applying lip gloss for a morning of construction.

"You're ridiculous," I said to my reflection. But I tightened my ponytail again anyway and went outside to my dad's workshop.

My parents lived on two acres—cheap land being one of the perks of small-town living—and the workshop behind the house was a cross between a large shed and a small barn. When my dad had been healthy, it wasn't unusual to find him back here on a Sunday afternoon with an entire Boy Scout troop doing a woodworking merit badge.

I tried to focus on how having the yard full of boys would make it feel more like normal, one more step to my dad getting back into the swing of things. One more step for me getting back to my own life.

Evie would need her own work space so she didn't get underfoot with the team. I pulled out my old kid workbench just like the ones we kept at the store for Builder Buddy workshops. We'd grown up working at this bench next to my dad, who'd been saving it for grandkids neither Tab nor I were in a hurry to provide.

I was looking for extra hammers when Noah's Honda pulled in. Noah got out to unbuckle Evie from her car seat.

"Hi, Toodles!" she yelled.

"Hey, Evie," I called back.

Soon I had Evie settled at her workbench with paper and crayons so she could make her own "plans." She chattered and asked me lots of questions, which I tried to answer, but she had to repeat herself a few times when my mind wandered to the impending conversation with my parents about Tabitha canceling for Thanksgiving. I'd decided to make them a nice dinner tonight and break it to them then.

"Everything okay?" Noah asked, and I realized I'd missed something he'd said.

"Sure, it's fine." Except for stupid Thanksgiving being ruined.

"You don't seem fine. Is this a bad time? Should we reschedule?"

"No, it really is okay." I gestured for him to follow me to the work shed while I unlocked it. "My sister called to tell me she's not coming home for Thanksgiving, and that won't go over well with my parents. I'm in a mood, that's all. I'll be fine when the boys get here."

"Ah. That sucks." He looked as if he might

156

reach out to lay a hand on my shoulder, but he paused and ran it through his hair instead.

I clapped my hand over my mouth. "I wasn't even thinking, Noah. I'm annoyed she's not coming home, and you don't even have . . ." *Parents*. How could I be so insensitive?

Noah shook his head. "Don't worry about it. Paige and I are used to being orphans."

He said it without a trace of self-pity, but it was hard to believe it didn't hurt on some level. *Way to go, Grace.*

Like he was reading my mind, he smiled and said, "Seriously, vent if you want. I'm a good listener." He climbed onto the picnic table we used every Fourth of July and patted the spot next to him. "Is this a situation where your parents are going to be majorly depressed? Or only a little bummed? Will this cause drama?"

I hesitated, not sure if I would make it better or worse by getting into it. Would I make him feel more awkward if I changed the subject? He was looking at me with the same genuine interest he'd shown when he'd wanted to know about my life before Creekville, so I took him at his word and sat on the table beside him.

"My dad will be bummed, but he'll get over it. My mom will be the problem."

"Why?"

"She'll see it as a failure of her parenting that Tabitha didn't prioritize coming home."

He didn't say anything, just waited for the rest of the story.

"My mom was the super ambitious type. She wanted to be a museum curator but got pregnant with Tabitha right before she graduated in art history, and she never applied to grad school. But she wasn't going to waste all her brains and energy, so we became her career."

"She sounds . . . devoted?" Noah was clearly struggling to see how any of this was a bad thing.

"I know she just sounds like Super Mom, but it was more than that. Our grades were her grades. Our wins, her wins. Our losses, her losses. If you ever meet her, you'll see she's pretty intense. When I was fourteen, I won the district science fair, and my mom became . . . I don't know. She told everyone about how 'we' won first place. She spent our entire childhoods training us to grow beyond Creekville, to conquer the big, bad world."

"She must be happy to see you both so successful."

"Yes, but she also trained us that it's family over everything, so she's in conflict with herself a lot. Like, she wanted to sell the store rather than have me quit my job to come home to run it. But there's no way we'd let my dad give it up when he loves it so much. So now she feels guilty that I'm here while also stressing about what happens when I leave."

"It sounds like it's a no-win situation," he said. "For her, I mean."

"Exactly. She needs control over things, which makes her sound bad, but she's not. Just very invested in our futures playing out in a specific way because she wants us to be happy."

"And that means not in Creekville?"

I nodded. "Pretty much. I'd sum up her motto as family first but get out of Creekville."

"Isn't that contradictory if family is *in* Creekville?"

I shot him a quick smile. "Welcome to the paradox of Lisa Winters. Tabitha can't come home because work is going so well which will make my mom happy while also feeling like she failed in forging a family bond because Tabitha isn't coming home for Thanksgiving." I looked down at the bench between my feet and scuffed at a flaking piece of paint. "Did I mention my mom's intense?"

"Sounds like it."

"No matter what I do, she carries the weight of the world on her shoulders. But . . ."

He nudged me with his knee, like, *say it.*

"But I miss my job. A lot. And at least twenty percent of me being happy about my dad getting better is knowing I can go back to my career." I looked away, unable to meet his eyes. "That must sound selfish to a guy who's helping to raise his niece."

"I get it better than you might think." His voice was quiet, and I glanced over at him. "I'm happy teaching, but that wasn't the end goal. I'd love to be a principal someday, making a difference on a whole-school level. I'd always planned to be starting my masters right now and then a PhD. But . . ."

"But you can't because Paige needs help with Evie."

He nodded. "It would kill her if she knew, but this is the right thing, and I'm okay with it. Someday I'll do it," he said, with a small smile. "Also, FYI, super selfish people don't leave their jobs to come home and take care of their dads. So if I hear you saying that about my friend Grace again, we're going to have words."

My grandma used to say this expression about stuff "warming the cockles of her heart." I had no idea what a cockle was, but I knew he'd just warmed mine.

Why was I sitting on a picnic table trying to get crowned as the Queen of TMI? Time for an emergency bailout.

I cleared my throat. "So how was your date?"

He looked confused. "What?"

"The hairdresser? Brooke's friend? You went out with her the other night?"

"I know who I went out with."

He didn't add anything, and I might have traded Tabitha for a report on how it had gone. Honestly, right now, I'd probably trade Tabitha for a combo meal at the Dairy Keen. I currently had kinder feelings toward french fries than my sister.

"We can talk about dating. Friends would," I said.

"That a fact?"

"That's a fact."

"Good," he said, glancing over, "because I *do* want to talk to you about dating."

His hazel eyes were pretty. And he had long lashes. I hadn't noticed that before. And as I stared into them, I discovered I didn't want to hear about him dating anyone else at all, but I forced a fake interested expression. "Lay it on me."

"You might be sorry you said that in a minute," he muttered.

"Your date was that bad?"

"She was fine."

I did gymnastics inside. "Fine" was bad. *Yes!*

"But I don't want to talk about that date. I had an interesting conversation with Dr. Boone the other day."

"You want to date your boss?"

He put a hand over my mouth. "Hush or I won't get this out."

I licked his hand. It had always worked like a charm with Tabitha, but Noah gave me a half-smile and kept his hand where it was. "Careful."

Of what, I wanted to ask. But saying that would

have been a dare, and I was glad I couldn't talk. I raised my eyebrows, like, "Get on with it."

"So the thing is . . ." He removed his hand and stared down at it, cracking his knuckles before he got on with it. "Dr. Boone called me in yesterday to update her on the booth progress. I thought she'd be impressed. But she raised some other concerns. And I could pretty much feel the coaching job slipping out of my fingers, so I . . ."

That was it. He just stopped. My eyebrows went up again, this time in confusion. "So you what?"

"ItoldDr.Boonewe'redating."

I stared at him. Surely I'd misunderstood that jumble of words. "You told Dr. Boone *what* now?"

"I, um."

"So help me, Noah . . ." I pulled the hammer from my toolbelt and hefted it as a warning.

"I mentioned that we're dating." He looked deeply uncomfortable, like sudden-onset-hemorrhoids uncomfortable.

"Why would you do that?" I wasn't even sure what I thought about this other than that hemorrhoids would be the least he deserved if this was a true confession.

"Because she implied with all the subtlety of the Bulldogs play-by-play announcer that she thinks I'm a bad candidate for head coach because I'm likely to get married and run off to another town."

"So you decided to—" I glanced at Evie and dropped my voice "—*lie* to her?"

"I panicked. Please don't make me tell her I lied."

"Noah . . ."

"Grace. How does that mess anything up for you? It's not like it's going to screw up your love life here. Is it?"

He was working way too hard to sound casual on the last question.

"That's not the point. This is how rumors get started. She's going to mention it to someone thinking she's reporting facts, and it'll spread like lice at a summer camp." My voice was barely more than a heated whisper because of Evie.

"Okay, I get that, but honestly, do you think it's fair that she won't consider me for the job because I'm single?"

"No," I admitted grudgingly. I shot another glance at Evie. "You are definitely a grounded guy."

"Right? So I gave her a different lens to see me through because I need the job, Grace. Teacher's salaries don't become livable until year ten, and I'm doing my best to cover Paige."

I didn't love the idea of fielding questions about this from the entire town. I wasn't sure how I would explain this to my parents. I already dreaded Brooke's glee when she heard about this. And I was sure Handy's could expect a spike in business as people came in to sniff out the details under the guise of making random hardware purchases.

But I looked at Evie and knew what I was going to say. "Okay. I'll do it."

"Yeah?" The lines around his eyes softened.

"Dr. Boone doesn't come into Handy's, and I don't go to the high school. It's not like it changes a single thing about how we act around each other."

Noah didn't say anything. It was a very suspicious quiet.

"It's not like it changes a single thing about how we act around each other, *right, Noah?*"

"Well . . ."

"Noah . . ."

"Her nephew is on the team. DeShawn. I think he's a spy."

I waited, my lips pressed tight, knowing what was coming next. I would not make this easy for him.

"He'll be coming today, in fact. So."

I stayed silent and glared.

He cleared his throat. "So I was thinking maybe we could put on a show—a little one—when the team gets here."

Of course I would help Noah. I wasn't heartless. But I would make him pay. Right now. Big time. "Define little."

"Maybe, uh, flirting?"

"How do you imagine this flirting going?" It was fascinating to see Noah look awkward. He wasn't a cocky guy, but he always acted so comfortable in his own skin, so self-assured, that it was highly entertaining to watch him fumble.

"I'm thinking, like, touching?"

"Interesting. Where?"

His eyes narrowed. He was onto me. "I figured we could do the old, 'Oops, our fingers touched,' like this." He reached out to take the hammer from me, but his hand lingered over mine before slipping the hammer from my suddenly weak grasp.

I gave him a doubtful glance, which drifted down to his broad chest in spite of myself. I pulled my eyes back to his. "I don't know. That feels too subtle. We're dealing with high school boys here."

"You have other ideas?" he asked, a distinct challenge in his tone.

"Definitely. If we're going to fake date, I don't want people thinking you're not that into me. At a minimum, you need to be into my personal space." I patted the table beside me. He scooted over a couple of inches, looking wary. I shook my head and patted again. We did this a couple more times until only a few inches separated us, way closer than casual friends would ever sit. "You see how this sends a message without saying a word?"

He was close enough for me to see the twitch of his pulse in his throat. I swallowed hard.

"I'm getting it now," he said. "For example, if I wanted to borrow your measuring tape, I wouldn't ask for it. I'd reach out and take it."

"Right." My own pulse sped up. The measuring tape was hooked above my hip.

"Like this." He stood, hauled me to my feet, and looped his fingers into the front pockets of my tool belt. He pulled me until my hips were flush with his thighs. "Grace," he asked softly, "can I borrow the tape measure?"

"Sure." I barely had the breath to say it.

He slid it from my toolbelt and moved it to his jeans. "I can see how that's more convincing. Thanks for the tips. Now we better practice your moves."

"My moves?"

"I'm assuming you have some?" His voice was way too innocent.

"A few," I said, resting my hands on his arms then slowly sliding them up to his shoulders—the shoulders I'd admired from the first night I met him. "For example, as your friend, I might tell you that you have a piece of lint on your shirt. But if we were dating, I'd probably brush it off for you." I ran my hands across his shoulders, in slow, smooth brushstrokes. "You know, to help you out, like a good girlfriend."

"Very helpful," he murmured. "Did you get it?"

166

"Probably. Your turn. Unless we're limiting ourselves to borrowing tools all morning when the boys get here."

"The boys. Right." But he said it as if he weren't registering the idea of the team coming at all, and a small thrill of power ran through me. I'd distracted him with a simple touch.

And yet, it only underlined that I'd been right from the start about not getting involved with him. This kind of chemistry could easily ignite. I started to step away from him, but his hands tightened around my hips.

"You bring up a good point about clueless high school boys," he said. "Might need to paint them a picture, go for bolder moves. To make sure they don't miss it. I want DeShawn having something to report to Dr. Boone and all."

"Of course." I swallowed hard. I was losing control of the situation. It was a bad sign, I knew it, and I didn't care. "What are you thinking?"

"Something they can't miss. Maybe this." He leaned down and brushed his nose against the soft skin below my ear. "Mmm. You smell good," he said, his voice husky, and I couldn't tell if it was part of the game.

"Vanilla," I said. "It's my deodorant."

He gave a small laugh and shook his head, his cheek rasping every-so-slightly against the line of my jaw. "Just smells like Grace."

Suddenly Evie barreled into us, throwing

167

her arms around us both. "Puppy nuzzles!" she shouted.

I blinked down at her, still bemused by the spell Noah's warmth and words had woven around me. "Excuse me?"

"Puppy nuzzles," she repeated. "Me too, Unc!"

He let me go with a regretful smile and scooped up Evie to nuzzle against her neck too, shaking his head like a dopey golden retriever and making her giggle. She returned the favor by burying her head in his chest and shaking it hard. It had to be uncomfortable against his sternum, but he only laughed, tossed her once in the air, then set her on her feet and pointed her back toward the workbench. "Better finish those blueprints."

He turned back to me. "Should we try a couple more moves?"

"Pretty sure you've got it." I stepped out of reach. "Let's get everything ready so they can get right to work."

"Good idea."

The first truckful of boys pulled up, and I launched into action, directing them where to put the frame, sending them to find the right tools in the workshop.

"Lookin' good," my dad said, coming out of the house as more boys trickled in. "Nice to see you again, Evie."

She waved at him. "Hi, Mr. Winters." They'd

gotten to know each other at the hardware store.

"Dad, this is Noah Redmond. He's the assistant coach and the sucker who signed up to do Christmas Town."

"Nice to meet you," he said. "Your sister is doing a great job at Handy's."

"She's a hard worker," Noah answered with a smile. "She likes the customers more, too. Says they're nicer when they're not waiting for food."

My dad laughed. "I can understand. Should we get this started?"

Noah called the team to order, and we spent the next half hour listening to their ideas for the booth, my dad piping in a couple of times if he thought their imagination was exceeding the limits of physics and plywood. Pretty soon, with the help of paper and a crayon borrowed from Evie, we had a solid sketch of what they wanted to do.

"That looks good, coach," DeShawn the Spy said. "How do we make it?"

"Easy," I answered. "You have to build everything so it's simple to disassemble and transport, but so that it looks like you spent fifty years designing it and building it when it's all put together."

"Is that all?" the team captain asked, his voice dry. I liked these kids.

"Dude, I build satellites. Trust me, we got this." I went into an explanation, pointing to the relevant spots on the frame. "So basically,"

I concluded, "you want to do the façade in a series of panels that you can secure from behind with mending braces, and to the Christmas Town shoppers, it will look seamless."

Instead of seeming intimidated by the idea, the boys looked intrigued. "How do we do that, Miss Grace?" one of them asked.

"It's all about the plywood," I said. "Figure out who has the best art skills among you and start drawing out what you want. Don't worry about making mistakes. We can paint over anything. Right now, it's time to start figuring out what we need to cut."

The boys were all Christmas Town veterans, so they knew how extra it could get. Noah and I retreated to the patio, where my dad sat watching.

"You did good, Gracie," my dad said.

"Thanks, Dad. Time to give them the safety lecture."

He grinned. "I prefer to think of it as a sermon. Listen up, boys!"

"He's really good with them," Noah said a few minutes later.

"Yeah. He's patient. When Tabitha and I were teenagers, we helped him build our addition, and I don't think he raised his voice to us once even though we whined and bickered nonstop."

"Addition?" He turned to look at the house, and I smiled, proud that he'd never figure out where it was if I didn't point it out to him. That was how meticulous my dad was.

"The garage," I explained. "We converted the original garage into another family room, added a second story, and then added a new garage."

"Wow. I would have never guessed. And you helped with all that?"

I nodded. "From the foundation to the roofing. He wanted us to know what we were talking about when we worked in the store. And he liked spending time with us. I didn't love it so much while we were doing all this in the July heat and humidity, but it's pretty cool to think that I'm staying in an apartment I helped build."

When my dad wrapped up his safety lesson, we broke the boys into groups and set them to work, one group cutting the easiest pieces first and then moving it to other groups to sand and then prime.

Noah dropped his dating hints right away. Squeezing my shoulder any time he passed me, brushing hands, long looks that made me fumble tools. Twice. At one point, he physically picked me up and moved me out of his way. I hoped my dad wasn't noticing any of this. A few minutes later, he stood behind me and rested his chin on my shoulder to study the plans I was holding. It made it hard to concentrate, but I tried.

"Does that make sense?" I asked the kid in front of me, as I explained which part he was working on.

"Yeah, got it," he said, nodding.

"Hey, coach, that your girlfriend?" one of the players hollered from near the workshop. My dad looked up, interested in this question too.

"None of your business," Noah said, but he squeezed my hand before he walked off, leaving no doubt as to the "real" answer.

My dad raised his eyebrow at me, and I gave him a weak smile. I needed to explain this before he gave my mom a heart attack when he reported his version of events.

As the two hours neared an end, my nerves were stretched to the fraying point as we directed the boys to start packing up for the day. Not because of them—they'd been fine. My dad had even left after about an hour to head over to the store because the team was handling themselves so well.

No, it was Noah who was wearing me out, sending enough electrical zaps flying along my nerve endings that I could qualify as a circuit board.

As the last players climbed into a car and left, I took my first deep breath since Noah had dropped his fake dating bomb. We could quit the act. Based on the comments I'd overheard from the players, our show had worked.

Maybe too well. Even without an audience, I found myself anticipating his next touch, my body almost straining for it, looking for reasons to drift into his orbit.

But the show was over for now. What I *needed* was distance, not sparks.

The sliding doors to the house opened, and my mom stepped out. I'd expected her to hover much earlier—as soon as my dad inevitably told her that Noah and I might be dating. But she looked even more unhappy about me dating a Creekville guy than I'd expected.

"Tabitha called," she said. "She's not coming to Thanksgiving." Her voice wavered, and she looked so bummed.

I had a tiny moment of panic. I'd run out of time to figure out how to break it to my mom, and now all I wanted to do was cheer her up. "That's okay because we're going to have some fun company."

"Who?" she asked.

"Noah and Evie here, and Evie's mom. You've met her at the store a couple of times. Paige? The new holiday hire?" I'd warned Noah he was going to owe me big. I hoped he was okay with me hijacking his Thanksgiving.

She tried to arrange her expression into something resembling excitement, but I could still see disappointment in the lines around her eyes. It had been a hard year for her, trying to keep her real estate business going, holding it together for my dad. She was entitled to be sad that Tabitha wasn't coming.

"Mom, it'll be fine. We'll have a fun Thanksgiving, and Tab will be home for Christmas." I was desperate to find the words that would make this better.

"I'd wanted to . . ." She stopped, sniffed, swallowed hard. "I just wanted this to be a special Thanksgiving because I have more thanks than ever to give. I wanted it to be a celebration when your dad's scan comes back clear. A first Thanksgiving for the rest of our lives kind of thing."

"Mom . . ." I didn't know what to say. Dang it, Tabitha.

My mom straightened. "You're right, honey." She mustered a smile. "It'll be fun to have company for Thanksgiving. Do you like to cook, Evie? You can help me make some Thanksgiving pies," she said when Evie nodded enthusiastically. "Won't that be fun?"

"Yay, cooking!" Evie said.

"Tabitha learned to cook from me, you know," my mom informed Noah.

"I believe it. Looking forward to seeing where she got it from."

He was good at rolling with the punches. I'd give him that.

"I'll leave you to clean up," my mom said, turning back toward the house. "I need to start planning my menu."

When the door closed behind her, Noah cocked

his head at me. "She knows it's still almost a month until Thanksgiving, right?"

"Sorry I dragged you into that, but you can see how much it cheered her up."

"Fair is fair," he said. "But is she going to be bummed when we fake break up?"

"I'll tell her this is fake," I said. "It'll stress her out if she thinks it isn't. She'll worry about me staying in Creekville. Then she can enjoy Thanksgiving without brooding about that and have fun entertaining guests. She'll be in her element."

He nodded as he closed the clasp on the toolbox and hefted it up. I liked that he made it look easy. That toolbox was no joke.

But also, my dumb monkey brain did not need to be preoccupied with his biceps.

"Thanks for putting on a show for the team," he said. "For being basically honest people, are we way too good at this fake dating thing?"

"Speak for yourself. I was sweating bullets."

"You don't look sweaty." He ran his eyes over me, and it was enough to make the nape of my neck sweat for real.

"I'm sweaty inside where my conscience is." I headed for the garage. "This is a very dumb thing we're doing. You know that, right? Will it mess up your story with Dr. Boone when I leave?"

Noah shook his head. "I won't bring you up, and if she does, I'll explain that you moved to wherever you move to, but the fact that I'm still here proves I'm the kind of guy who sticks around. It'll work. Probably?" He watched Evie for a moment. "It has to."

I reached out and wrapped my hand around his wrist, a way to say, "I got you." "We'll make it work," I promised. "Just eight more weeks."

CHAPTER SIXTEEN
NOAH

"Have y'all lost your minds?" Brooke asked when we settled in for game night the following Thursday.

"I thought you'd be happy about this," Grace said. "You've been trying to hook us up for months."

"Hook you up for *real,*" Brooke said. "Not cast you in some Hallmark Christmas comedy."

"Dr. Boone isn't taking me seriously for the head coach job," I said. "She says changing districts once already is a red flag and being single is another one because I'm likely to up and move to wherever my future wife wants to live."

"She can't use that to keep from hiring you."

"Not officially, but you know how she can drop a strong hint."

Brooke sighed. "I do." She darted a glance between Grace and me. "I want to go on record as saying you two are idiots."

"But you'll play along when you have to?"

She rolled her eyes. "Yes. I'll pretend I'm learning to do deep cover ops like Ian is. Have I told you guys that—"

"—he's coming for Thanksgiving," Grace

and I said at the exact same time and busted up laughing.

"It's come up," Grace said.

Brooke flipped us both off. "You two deserve each other."

Grace pretended to be shocked. "Why, Mrs. Greene, I do believe you'll need to serve a detention for that."

"Then you can't have my snacks."

"All right, no detention. What are we playing tonight?"

We played Settlers of Catan over Grace's objection of it being deeply nerdy, and Brooke dropped the subject of our fake dating.

We only had to keep up the act for the next few Saturday mornings in front of her dad and the boys. But it made me wish that we had more reasons to keep it up, because I liked how we were together. By the second Saturday, we had the boys doing some obnoxious hooting and catcalling when DeShawn asked point-blank again if we were dating, and I told him it was none of his business but dropped a kiss on Grace's cheek.

Grace did a good job. An excellent job. She brushed against me often, sliding her arm around my waist casually and tucking herself against my side, where her head nestled perfectly beneath my shoulder. Or she'd brush my hair out of my eyes sometimes, even though I kept it too short to get in my way, like she was looking for an excuse to touch me. Other times, I'd catch her giving me long looks, even when no one else was paying attention to us.

I wished we weren't faking.

There was something about Grace and the way you had to win a smile from her like it meant something. About the way she smelled like vanilla. About how she was patient with the boys. How she fussed after her dad. How she didn't wear much makeup, but her hazel eyes always looked bright, and how her hair was so soft that I was always making up excuses to touch it, tucking in strays from her ponytails or messy buns.

It was torture, and I was thirstier for it with every single Saturday.

On the third Saturday, her mom came out midway through our booth-building session carrying a platter of donuts. Mr. Winters saw her and ducked his head but grinned.

I looked at Grace who shook her head at me, but she was smiling.

"Boys, gather in for a minute," Mrs. Winters ordered. "Now, most of you probably don't know this, but Mr. Winters here was diagnosed with cancer last year. Stage 3, which isn't great. But he's tough like Bulldog football, which he played, same as you boys. And he stuck it out, took a risk on a drug trial, and it paid off. We officially heard from the doctor on Thursday morning: Mr. Winters is cancer-free, and we're celebrating with donuts!"

I looked over at Grace, and she grinned at me. I swooped her up and spun her. "That's awesome! Congrats, Mr. Winters," I called over her head.

"Thanks, son," he said, smiling.

"The spin hug is a nice touch. You're really selling this," Grace said low enough that only I could hear her.

"That wasn't a show," I answered. "I'm just happy for you guys."

Her big grin softened into a different kind of smile for a second—an almost intimate one—before she stepped out of my arms and went to help her mom distribute donuts.

Brooke had us over for game night the following week, and I found that Thursday nights and Saturday mornings were becoming my favorite parts of the whole week. There was no point in lying to myself about how much I liked Grace when every nerve-ending in my body lit up when she was around.

But for the sake of our friendship, I kept it to myself, and I didn't get into it with Brooke, either. Every now and then at lunch, she'd ask how the fake dating thing was going, but I dodged the question like I was in a heavyweight boxing match.

The next game night turned out to be another exercise in Brooke's version of "subtlety."

"Hey," she said, ushering me into the living room where Grace was already curled up on the sofa with a bowl of popcorn in her lap. I plunked down on the other end of the sofa and stole the bowl from her.

"Hey!" she objected.

"Should've eaten faster," I said around a mouthful of popcorn. "Wait, is this my recipe?"

"Yeah. And I might have told it to Tabitha, so you can look forward to it being on the Food Channel someday."

"You stole my secret family recipe. We're in a blood feud now," I informed her.

She gave me a lazy kick. "Gimme back the popcorn."

"Shots fired," I said. "Now you're going to have to wait in terror for a surprise revenge noogie."

"A noogie?" Brooke asked with disgust. "Are you five?"

"No, but Evie is, and I spend a lot of time on her level. What are we playing tonight?" I asked.

"A movie," she said.

"Tired of losing all the time?" Grace asked.

Brooke glowered at her. "I do not lose all the time."

Grace glanced over at me. "Doesn't she, though?"

I pretended to think about it. "She won one game of Scrabble, one time. Maybe we should give her a break from losing?"

"I won Trivial Pursuit," she objected.

"I have no memory of that," I said. "You remember that happening, Grace?"

"I don't. Sounds like alternative facts to me."

"Y'all suck," Brooke whined.

"So what's the movie?" Grace asked, unmoved.

"*What Happens in Vegas*," Brooke said.

Grace stared at her.

"What? It's a good movie. Cameron Diaz. Ashton Kutcher. It's funny." But Brooke acted way too innocent as she fumbled with the TV remote.

"You're having us watch a movie about a couple who is pretending to be in a relationship but then falls in love for real?" Grace asked. "Do I have that right?"

"It's a good movie," Brooke repeated.

"How do we feel about this, Noah?"

"Sounds dumb," I said. "Let's watch a sports movie about underdogs who win. Or a war movie. With bombs. Lots of bombs."

"Maybe some sci-fi," Grace said. "Like with aliens. And explosions. Lots of explosions."

"You guys can always do a movie night and watch those together on your own time," Brooke said sweetly. "My house, my movie. Shut up and watch."

"Is your middle name 'the worst'?" Grace asked.

Brooke ignored her and started the movie, then

turned off all the lights and settled into her arm-chair.

I leaned over to Grace. "So, heckle?" I whispered.

"Definitely heckle."

We did, mercilessly. It was the most fun I'd had since the last time I'd hung out with Grace. Around the midpoint, I got interested in spite of myself and forgot to heckle, stretching my feet out on the coffee table. I liked that Brooke was the kind of host who made me feel totally comfortable doing that. And maybe Grace did too, because she settled back into the couch and stretched her legs out, but when her feet didn't reach, she settled them on top of mine. The backs of her ankles fit the top of my shin like we'd been carved in those places exactly to fit each other.

Maybe I was spending too much time wood-working on this booth project?

But it felt right. It just did. And when I shifted them up to rest on my thighs where they fit just as well, she didn't mind. And when I wrapped my hand around one of her ankles to see how small it was in my palm, she scooted down a little further, like she liked the way it felt when I touched her.

When I feathered my thumb lightly over that ankle, she drew in a sharp breath and went still. I paused to see what she would do. When she didn't move, I kept it up, liking how soft her skin felt against the pad of my thumb.

But when the movie ended and we got up to help Brooke clean up the snacks, Grace made a point of keeping Brooke between us at all times.

"You excited for Ian to come home?" Grace asked.

"Can't wait," Brooke said. "Two weeks! He'll only be here for two days, but still. I haven't seen him in two months. I can't wait for training to be over. Hey, you should come over for Thanksgiving at Gran's, Noah. She'd love to meet Paige and Evie."

"Thanks, but we've got plans."

"What are you doing?"

I shot a glance at Grace, trying to decide if I wanted to dig this hole for us.

She sighed. "He's coming over to our house. Tabitha can't make it home for Thanksgiving, so I thought it would be a good distraction for my parents."

"And?" I prompted her.

"Oh, right, and Noah is the best company ever, so of course that's also why."

"That didn't feel sincere," I complained.

"But that's perfect," Brooke said. "You should all come over on Thanksgiving. Gran does a big spread. It's relaxed and the food is so good. Say yes."

"No," Grace said. "You're bossy. But also,

184

thanks for the invitation. But we're set for Thanksgiving, I promise. You don't have to worry about us."

"Ugh, fine," Brooke said.

I definitely should have known that wasn't going to be the end of it.

CHAPTER SEVENTEEN
GRACE

I didn't normally love Saturdays because we were always so busy at the store with about twenty percent of the customers being dudes old enough to be my dad who didn't listen to me when I told them what they needed for their home improvement projects. Fifty percent of those same guys would be back in the afternoon to return the wrong thing they'd insisted on buying, and the other half would come back to get the right part but be cranky with me for being right about it.

But Saturdays were becoming my favorite now. It was so fun to work with the team on the booth, watching my dad returning to his old self, listening to the boys talk good-natured trash to each other. And then there was Noah.

I'd be lying if I tried to pretend he wasn't one of the best parts of Saturdays. Or that it wasn't fun trying to figure out how to flirt with him before I crossed a line that had his eyes narrowing at me, like he was thinking about how to pay me back. Usually, it involved him coming up with a reason to throw me over his shoulder and move me somewhere else.

No doubt it made me a bad feminist, but I liked it when he did that. A lot.

And I owed him major payback for his stunt at movie night with the ankle stroking and the . . . the . . . the *sexiness* of that. It had become a game between us, seeing how far one of us could push it before the other called them on it.

So far, neither of us had.

I didn't have a set plan for what I would do this Saturday, but I'd know the opportunity when I saw it.

Luckily, the opportunity came up right away. When Noah arrived, he unloaded Evie from the car with an apologetic look at me. Tears streaked her face, and she did the shudder-sob that kids do at the end of a big cry.

"We had a rough morning," Noah said. "Evie wasn't wanting to leave the apartment, but she'll be fine when she gets all set up at her workbench and remembers how fun it is."

I wasn't convinced by his cheerful tone, and the look on Evie's face said she wasn't either.

"Evie needs a new project to work on today," I said. "Let me go grab some things from the house, and I'll be right back."

I rummaged through my mom's office until I found what I needed and returned with a stack of large coffee filters and two pairs of scissors. "We need to make snowflakes for the booth decoration, Evie. It's a pretty big job, and I need you to be in charge of it. Can you handle that?"

Evie sniffled but settled onto her seat at her

workbench. "I don't know how to make snow-flakes."

"Oh, but your Uncle Noah does, and he's going to show you how to do it, right, Noah?"

"Um, yes?" He looked confused.

"Watch his hands while he explains what he's doing." This made Evie look even more interested, but Noah looked even more confused.

I set a few coffee filters in front of Evie along with the blunt scissors, took some for myself, and went to stand behind Noah who still looked baffled. I tucked the scissors and all but one coffee filter into my toolbelt and slid my arms around his waist. His abs tensed for a minute against my forearms.

I would really, really love to know if those abs looked as good as they felt.

I folded the coffee filter into fourths and whispered, "You narrate the directions."

He caught on and clasped his hands behind his back, so now my hands were "his" hands. For some reason, he decided to use a high-pitched lady voice.

"The first thing you're going to do is fold your round paper once, and then fold it again."

Evie giggled.

"Is that supposed to be me?" I whispered.

"Trust me, I'm nailing this impersonation."

I stopped folding long enough to pinch his side. There wasn't much to grab onto. How was that possible with the sheer number of snacks he consumed at game nights?

He cleared his throat and continued, "Then you put the paper on your head like a silly hat."

I stuck the paper on his head, and Evie laughed. I snatched it off and stuck it in his mouth, which forced Noah to narrate around the paper.

"Ren oo ut it in oo mouf."

"Yucky, Unc!" Evie shouted gleefully.

He spat it out. "A little bit yucky." He straightened his arms behind him to put pressure on my arms, demonstrating his displeasure.

But this was too much fun, standing there with my arms around his waist, my front almost touching his back, so close I could feel the heat from his body and smell his soap.

I plucked at the neckline of his T-shirt and tucked a coffee filter into it.

"Then you need to put one of these papers in your shirt to warm it up," he said in his Grace voice. But his hands grabbed at my toolbelt and pulled me against him. It was a warning, but all it did was make me wish I didn't have the toolbelt between us.

I reached up to pluck at the front of his shirt with one hand and dab at his forehead with a filter.

"It's getting kind of hot out here," he said despite it being a crisp November morning.

Yeah, it was.

But the whole thing worked to distract Evie, who settled into making paper snowflakes with Noah while I finished setting up.

Once the boys arrived, we fell into the routine of overseeing their work—today it was painting—while breezing by Evie every few minutes to make sure she was okay. She made about twenty snowflakes before she got bored and switched to using scrap wood as building blocks.

It also meant that Noah and I put on our show for the team, only it felt less and less like a show. His touch was becoming so familiar as he would put his hand at the small of my back to follow me into the workshop or give my hand a quick squeeze as he passed by. It was the kind of PDA that was totally appropriate in front of high school boys, and it never felt like enough.

And just like every Saturday, when it was time for the boys to pack up so I could head over to the store, I wished we could work for another hour to see what kind of flirting Noah would try next.

Even going into the store wasn't a big deal on Saturdays anymore. Noah would take Evie out to lunch and a park to keep her busy for the last two hours of Paige's shift, then drive them home. The last couple of weeks, I hadn't felt like I had to hit the ground running anymore when I walked in on Saturdays. Paige made everything run so much more smoothly.

She'd not only stepped up our display game,

but she was also a whiz on the register and learned very quickly. When she didn't know what someone needed to fix a problem, she'd get me or Gary, listen to the explanation, and then she'd know the next time someone asked for the same thing.

Today when I walked in, Paige looked up from the endcap display of antifreeze she was rearranging and smiled. "Thank goodness you're here. Today is Stump Paige day and I'm losing, big-time."

"Go ahead and run the register," I told her. "I've got it from here."

I was organizing a section of drawer pulls when someone cleared her throat behind me softly, and I turned to find Lily Greene standing there. "Hey, Miss Lily. What can I help you with today?"

"Thanksgiving, actually." She smiled like that was all I needed to know.

"Sure. Do you need a deep fryer for the turkey, or maybe a smoker? We have one left of each."

She waved her hand. "No, no. I mean that Brooke told me you declined her invitation to come for Thanksgiving, so I'm here to extend it again so you'll know you're truly welcome. I would love to see the whole Winters clan there. I hear that means Noah and his sister and niece too?"

"That's so nice of you, Miss Lily, but we wouldn't want to put you out."

She looked almost offended. "Put me out? Have you not heard of the legendary Greene Thanksgiving spread? We could add fifty people for dinner and still have leftovers. And if we couldn't, we'd find a longer table and cook more."

"I appreciate that, Miss Lily, but I can't change plans on Noah like that."

She mulled that for a moment. "I understand. But consider the invitation open, even if you wake up Thanksgiving morning and realize you can't bear the idea of cooking a turkey. Promise?"

"I promise."

"Good girl. Now, tell me what you're thinking about for the spring garden season."

We talked through the seeds I was planning to order, and it gave me a small twinge to realize I wouldn't be here when she came to pick them up. My dad would be here instead because he was better, and that made it okay. Better than okay.

On the last game night before Thanksgiving, Noah and I showed up at Brooke's house prepared to do battle over Yahtzee, but Brooke walked us into a snack-free living room.

"Where's the snacks?" Noah and I asked at the same time, then grinned at each other.

"Sit, because we're fixing to have company."

"Who?" I asked as a knock sounded on the front door.

"Be right back," Brooke said, and she was, with Miss Lily. "Gran wants to talk to you."

"I invited Grace the other day myself, but she was worried about changing plans on you, Noah, so I'm here to ask you myself. I would like you both to come to Thanksgiving, and your families too," Miss Lily said. "My Thanksgivings are never as big as they used to be. These grand-children of mine have grown up but they're taking too long to pull themselves together and start families—" she darted a glare at Brooke who rolled her eyes—"and I need more people in my place. Noah, surely your niece would love to come over and run all around my property while you and Paige take a break."

Noah looked at me, and I shrugged. Why was Miss Lily being so adamant about this? Knowing her, she was up to something, but what?

He looked at Brooke, who only smiled. "Well, if your parents won't mind . . ." he said to me.

"They won't." My dad's endurance improved every week, but he'd probably welcome the idea of having Thanksgiving at Miss Lily's house so he and my mom could excuse themselves when he got tired rather than waiting for Noah and Paige to leave. I would double check with her about all of this, but I had a feeling it would come as a relief.

"Sounds like a plan," he said.

"Good." Miss Lily rose. "It's settled, then. We'll have a big table full of food and people, just as it should be. I'll see you next week."

Brooke walked her to the door, and I could hear Miss Lily reassuring her that she could make it next door to her own house without any help.

Brooke came back in and studied us curiously. "So how are you going to feel about having to keep up the dating act all day?"

"We don't have to. My parents know, remember?"

"But Gran doesn't," Brooke said. "And she invited Dr. Boone."

Noah winced. I studied Brooke like she studied her microscope slides. Miss Lily was definitely up to something.

"Brooke, did you tell Miss Lily about our fake dating plan?"

Her eyes widened slightly. "Why would I do that?"

"That's not a no," I said.

"You're being paranoid. Anyway, trust me, you're going to love Gran's Thanksgiving. Give me a minute to get the snacks."

She *still* hadn't said no.

"Oh," Brooke said, pausing at the kitchen doorway. "Gran has an excellent BS detector, so you'll need to really sell it if you want to fool her. Otherwise, she's likely to ask an uncomfortable question at the worst possible moment." She disappeared into the kitchen.

"She's up to something," I told Noah.

"Isn't she always?" He didn't look concerned. "It'll be fine."

"That's a lot of eyes," I told him. "Miss Lily and Dr. Boone, plus all the other guests. You sure you're up for it?"

He reached over and hauled me into his lap, nuzzling his face into my neck. "I think we've got this," he said.

It was an act to make a point, but it startled me how right it felt to be nestled against him, his breath against my neck. It broke out goosebumps on my arm, and I decided to seize back control by running my fingers through his hair and nipping at his earlobe. He froze as my teeth scraped softly against his skin, but I only looked up at Brooke and smiled, as if the faint saltiness of his skin hadn't just slayed me.

"I think we do too. What do you think, Brooke? Convincing?"

Her eyes narrowed. "Very convincing."

I slid off Noah's lap, and I could feel a reluctance in his hold, like he didn't want to let me slip away, but he did, his fingers grazing my hip as I escaped to my side of the couch.

"Now, what am I whipping you two at tonight?" I asked.

Brooke's face had questions written all over it, but she didn't ask any of them, which was for the best because chances were, I had the same questions and no answers.

CHAPTER EIGHTEEN
NOAH

I'd told the boys we'd take off the Saturdays before and after Thanksgiving. We needed that time to work on the booth, but we'd made it to regional finals, and they needed to practice even more.

It meant less of Grace though. And that felt like a bad trade. Paige drove herself out to the store the Saturday before Thanksgiving, and her car worked both ways so there'd been no need for me to go and fetch her and no reason to pop into the store and say hi to Grace.

On Thanksgiving Day, Brooke had told us we should come around 4:00, drink some cocktails, and prepare to eat ourselves into a stupor starting at 5:00. Grace and I had agreed to meet there, and I pulled into Miss Lily's driveway as Grace climbed out of her car, which was parked behind her parents. She wore boots and a simple cream-colored dress made of sweater material, but it skimmed her curves in a way that reminded me how well I'd gotten to see them in the garden that first night, right next to this house. Dang, but that girl had a backside it was hard to look away from.

"Hey," she said, as Paige and I got out. "Is it

weird eating Thanksgiving with your boss?" she asked Paige.

"Not unless you make it weird, which I'm sure you will with your whole, uh . . ." Paige dropped her voice and looked around to make sure no one else was outside to hear us. "Fake dating thing, you idiots."

"Don't call your boss an idiot," I told Paige.

"We're off the clock and out of the store," she said. "So I'm calling it like it is."

"She might not be wrong," Grace said, looking unbothered.

I walked up to join her at the foot of the steps to Miss Lily's porch while Paige unbuckled Evie from the car.

"Time to get on our game faces." I took her hand, liking how small and strong hers felt in mine.

She looked up, her face serious. "Dr. Boone won't have any reason to doubt us."

Izzy, Brooke's sister-in-law, answered the door and greeted us with smiles and directions on where to leave our coats.

"Welcome, Winters and Redmonds," Miss Lily said as we walked into a giant room where several people had already gathered. "So good to see you all. Ian—" She glanced over to her grandson who sat on a loveseat with Brooke tucked tightly against his side. "Never mind. Landon, get up and see what everyone would like to drink. Miss

Evie, you should run to the kitchen. I believe my cook has something delicious waiting for you, if it's okay with your mom."

Paige nodded, and Evie ran off in the direction of the kitchen as Miss Lily pointed out the way.

While Landon got everyone's drinks, I took a minute to study the room. I'd only been here once for the wedding dinner, but that had been hosted entirely outside on the terrace. It was my first time seeing the interior, and it reflected Miss Lily perfectly. Light, soft fabrics, splashes of color from flower bouquets, well-made furniture, and throw pillows a touch too much on the fussy side for me filled the space, but they did make the sofas and armchairs look inviting.

Izzy curled up in one of the armchairs facing the sweeping windows that overlooked the grounds. She looked as if her mind were off in other places.

Grace nodded toward an attractive couple in their late fifties. "You probably recognize Ian's parents from the wedding." His dad looked as if he were about to give a distinguished lecture in an oak-paneled university auditorium, and his mom wore a cream pantsuit that communicated extreme competence. The Greenes were talking to each other with easy smiles, but Mrs. Greene's eyes kept darting toward her daughter.

I knew how that look felt. That was what it was

like being Paige's older brother: always watchful, always worried. Izzy looked okay, though. Just daydreamy.

Grace's hand was still in mine, and she tugged on it lightly until I leaned down. "This is going to be a long day," she whispered, her eyes on Dr. Boone.

Maybe, but I had no objections to putting on a performance.

We took a seat beside her parents on one of the sofas and settled in for drinks and conversation as everyone began to catch up on town business, their polite way to describe gossiping.

Mostly, the conversation flowed among Miss Lily, the Greenes, the Winters, and the Boones. After a few minutes, I asked Grace in a low voice, "Do you feel like the rest of us should be sitting at the kids' table right now?"

She smiled. "Maybe a little."

Brooke and Ian didn't seem to mind, speaking to each other in quiet tones, their faces glowing, even Ian's. I wasn't sure they even noticed the rest of us were there.

"They are one hair shy of being nauseating," Grace said. "I shouldn't like it, but it's pretty cute."

Paige and Landon had fallen into conversation, Landon talking with his hands, Paige listening intently and asking questions.

For a minute, a pang rippled through my

chest as I felt the absence of my parents. Our Thanksgivings had always been small and simple, nothing as fancy as this one in Miss Lily's house already felt. But there had been something about coming together around our kitchen table, dressed in church clothes, to eat a meal in our plain kitchen that had elevated Thanksgiving every year anyway.

"You okay?" Grace asked, looking up at me.

"Yeah, great."

"You seem far away."

I gave a small shake of my head. "Just remembering some old Thanksgivings."

She slipped her hand into mine and looked up at me, her eyes soft. "Are they making you sad?"

"Yes and no," I said. "I'm happy to be here, but I'm missing the small dinners we used to do with our family."

"I'm sorry." She gave my hand a gentle squeeze. "Can I do anything?"

"Normally, I try to distract myself but today, I don't want to. I want to feel it. Is that weird?"

She smiled. "No. I get it. Do you think it would help to go walk through Miss Lily's gardens while there's still some daylight? It'll be quiet out there."

I glanced at the pockets of people around us, the parents, Miss Lily's canasta friends, her pastor. I wasn't ready to merge into the stream of easy conversation and leave my past Thanksgiving memories behind. Soon, but not yet. For the moment, I wanted to wallow.

"That sounds good."

"Go ahead," she said, letting go of my hand. "I'll run interference with Miss Lily."

I took her hand back. "I want you to come with me."

Her mouth parted the tiniest bit, like she'd given a gasp of surprise so soft I couldn't hear it. But she nodded and stood, turning toward Miss Lily.

"Miss Lily, would it be all right with you if Noah and I walk around the grounds? We want to sneak a peek at your garden before it gets dark."

"Of course, honey," Miss Lily said. "Go right ahead. I'll send one of the boys to get you when it's time to eat."

We thanked her, and I followed Grace through the French doors, stepping out onto the flagstone terrace and into the chill of the late November as dusk began to mute the early sunset. She let me lead, and I drifted east in the direction of Brooke's house, Grace staying close beside me. That led us to the garden that Brooke and Miss Lily worked together.

Two rows of dried-up cornstalks stood next to a couple of rows of empty bean stakes. But next to them, the whole left side of the garden was full of squash vines, their big, green leaves almost hiding the soil completely.

"Five bucks if you can guess what one of our sides will be tonight," Grace teased.

"I'd love some squash," I said as I almost tripped over one. "Too bad it's so hard to find."

"Brooke sure loves working out here," she said.

"The kids love the community garden at school too. They had to do a lottery system to see who would get to take stuff home from the harvest on Friday. Luckily, there was a lot of squash, and a lot of winners."

We fell into quiet and kept walking, drifting around the front of the house with its manicured shrubs to the other side where a path wound toward the bridal garden.

"Returning to the scene of our first date, where we got to second base before I even saw your face," Grace said.

I snorted. "I refuse to let you count that as a date. If I took you on a date, you'd know." I stopped and considered that. "Maybe you wouldn't. Brooke and I went out to dinner once, and neither of us used the word 'date' but it kind of felt like we were on one. It was so weird and awkward that we decided it wasn't a date, that it would never be a date, and then it just turned into a good dinner."

"Wow, you're really selling me on the magic of Noah Redmond here," she teased.

"Would you let me?" I wasn't sure what prompted the question. "If I said I wanted to

202

convince you that we should date for real, what would you say?" I reached out and touched a strand of her hair, and when she didn't pull away, I picked it up and rubbed it between my fingers, feeling its silky slide, while she tried not to meet my eyes. "Grace."

She finally met my gaze straight on at the quiet sound of her name. "Noah."

I let go of her hair and grazed my fingers down her cheek, sliding them beneath her chin to cup her jaw. I stroked my thumb softly over her lips. "What if this were real?"

She blinked slowly, her eyes not leaving mine, and pressed her lips in a kiss against the pad of my thumb. I stilled, her touch scorching through me. Slowly, watching me the whole time, she closed her lips around the tip of my thumb and bit it gently before letting it go.

"Grace." I drew her toward me. I'd been dying to taste her, and there was no holding back now. My head dipped toward hers, and just as our lips touched, a voice from the terrace called, "Dinner, y'all."

Landon.

I'd liked him the few times we'd met, but as I lifted my head, I wanted to break him into small pieces with my bare hands.

I held up a hand to let him know we'd heard him, and he turned and disappeared. I looked down at Grace, ready to continue what she'd started, but she blinked again, and I bit back a curse. It was the kind of blink you did when you were waking up. Or coming back to your senses.

"Grace, I—"

"We should get back," she said. "Brooke said dinner will be amazing."

This time Grace set the pace, keeping a polite distance as we headed back, a distance that wouldn't hint to anyone that she'd just lit my nerve endings on fire in the vegetable garden.

When we walked back into the great room, Miss Lily rose and clapped her hands twice. "Wonderful. This way to the dining room, please. Evie, would you do me the honor of escorting me there?" When Evie looked at her in confusion, Miss Lily smiled. "It means hold my hand and make sure I get there safely."

Evie skipped forward to take Miss Lily's hand, and we followed them into the dining room.

The long table wouldn't have even fit into my apartment, but it easily accommodated all of us plus the pastor, his wife, and her card friends for a total of seventeen guests. "Now boys, you and Izzy go help Mary bring out the food."

The rest of us found the correct place cards and took our seats. A minute later, the cook appeared bearing a good-looking roast turkey on a platter which she set in front of Miss Lily to do the carving honors while everyone applauded.

"That's a gorgeous bird," Grace said. "And

I would know because Tabitha spent four years in high school trying to perfect Thanksgiving turkey."

Each of the Greene grandchildren appeared with a dish in each hand, and soon an assortment of rolls and sides graced the tables. Grace and I grinned at each other when the platter of cinnamon and pecan roasted butternut squash ended up in front of us. Miss Lily carved the turkey with surgical precision, and the dishes began to circulate, one incredible side after another passing beneath our noses.

The cook, Mary, refused Miss Lily's invitation to join us, taking off to be with her own family.

"She does this every year," Miss Lily said with both a smile and a sigh. "She prepares the most incredible meal and then leaves instead of eating it. Says she doesn't trust anyone else to make it correctly, and that once it gets to the table, the best part of her day is leaving and knowing she doesn't have to clean up."

Mrs. Winters held up her wine glass. "To Mary, who is doing it exactly right."

The rest of the table joined the toast. "To Mary!"

The food was amazing. "I may have only caught a passing glimpse of her when she brought in the turkey then disappeared," I told Grace after a bite of the bird, "but I'm pretty sure Miss Lily's cook is the new love of my life."

"I'll fight you for her," Grace said.

When the clink of forks against china slowed then dwindled, Miss Lily said, "Let's adjourn to the great room to relax and digest so we have space for pie and all the other delicious goodies you brought."

We'd each been asked to contribute one dessert per household. "Pumpkin dump cake which is a million times tastier than it sounds," said Grace.

"Pumpkin cheesecake. From scratch," I said.

"Oooh, nice. I like a man who can cook."

Dr. Boone and her husband were sitting across from us, so I took the opportunity to lean close to Grace's ear and whisper intimately, "Pumpkin cheesecake" again. "Also, Dr. Boone is watching."

Grace reached up to caress my cheek, then turned her head slightly to whisper, "Do you have any idea how much I'm going to make you pay at the next game night?"

"Looking forward to that."

I straightened and caught the pleased look on Dr. Boone's face, like she was enjoying this exhibition of young love.

Mr. Greene got to his feet first. "Everyone under forty needs to clear the table. Except Evie, who I would like to come play a game of checkers with me. Would you like that, Evie?"

Her face brightened. "And don't do dishes?"

"And don't do dishes," he confirmed.

"Heck, yes."

That made all the adults laugh, but Evie ignored us as she took Mr. Greene's outstretched hand and skipped beside him into the other room, the other adults filing after them.

When they were done, the rest of us carried dishes into the kitchen where Brooke assigned everyone jobs to scrape, wash, rinse, or dry while she handled packaging up the leftovers in meal portions.

I watched her, slightly awed. "I will never be grownup enough to think about doing stuff like that."

"Me, either. This is Miss Lily's idea. She makes up what amounts to a full plate of food with a sample of everything to send home to people in foil muffin tins. She did it last year and I thought it was brilliant."

"Because it's brilliant," Grace said.

"You two go clear the crumbs off the tablecloth then start bringing out the desserts," Brooke ordered.

"Yes, ma'am," I said.

"Landon, you'll handle the decorative updates?"

He flashed her a grin. "Absolutely."

Grace and I went back into the dining room armed with butter knives that Brooke said we should use the dull side of to scrape off crumbs.

"I think the bossiness is payback," Grace said. "Because of all the bossing I did when we were working on her renovations."

"As a proud feminist, I need to tell you that I object to characterizing initiative as bossiness just because you're women," I said in a fake-pious voice. "You guys are both just strong leaders."

Grace punched me in the stomach with about enough force to knock over a dandelion.

We got the dining room table in good shape and made several trips to bring out desserts, plates, and flatware. By the time we were done, the dishes team had finished, and Brooke and Paige had the leftovers squared away in the fridge, packaged and ready to send home with guests.

Brooke herded us all into the great room. She and Ian claimed the love seat again, but this time when Grace and I sat on the sofa, Brooke darted a meaningful look from us to Dr. Boone and back, making an exaggerated show of snuggling into Ian.

"Is she for real?" Grace grumbled.

"We better obey. Women with strong leadership skills scare me." I put my arm around her and pulled her into my side. She came without any resistance, even drawing up her legs so that her knees rested on my left thigh. "That a girl," I whispered.

"Shut up," she said, and laid her head on my shoulder.

"If you'll indulge me, my John and I had a yearly tradition of each person sharing what they're thankful for," Miss Lily said. "I love it even more than dessert, and I love dessert like Paula Deen loves butter."

Everyone laughed, and she smiled. "I'll begin. I'm thankful for seeing my grandson married. Greatest joy of my life. Greatest. Joy. Of. My. Life. Did I mention it's the greatest—"

"We heard, Gran," Landon said.

"Loud and clear." That was Izzy, sounding the exact opposite of loud and clear.

Ian pretended to slick his hair back in a sleazeball cool guy move. "Still got favored grandchild status."

"How about if we continue clockwise?" Miss Lily said, managing the room like the veteran English teacher she was.

"This was one of my favorite parts of Thanksgiving with my family too," I said to Grace in a low voice.

"Same." She pressed her knees against my leg as if to underscore the shared feeling.

Most people gave simple answers like gratitude for family or their jobs, but when Mrs. Winters gave thanks for her husband's health and he gave thanks for Grace, Grace sniffled a tiny bit. And Evie had everyone smothering laughs when she gave thanks for getting a loose tooth before "mean Kylie B because Kylie thinks she's the best one but she's not the best one at getting a loose tooth."

When it got to me, I gave my answer almost on reflex. "I'm thankful for good friends and family," I said.

Mr. Boone made a "yikes" face, and Miss Lily's eyebrows shot up. I realized my mistake immediately.

"Oops," Brooke said.

"And Grace," I added.

Landon gave a smothered laugh. "Bro."

"I can't believe I'm an afterthought," Grace said.

I gave her shoulder a slight squeeze. I hoped she understood it to mean, "I cannot believe you threw me under the bus but watch out because payback sucks."

It was possible she wasn't going to get all that from a single shoulder squeeze. But the tiny twitch at the corner of her mouth said she was getting at least some of the message.

"I'm sorry, babe," I said. "You're never an afterthought."

"It'll take quite a bit more convincing than that," Miss Lily said. "Good thing Landon got the mistletoe up. We don't usually count Christmas as starting until after we've eaten all the dessert, but we'll make an exception."

Some people might have said that her eyes twinkled at that moment, as if she were a little white-haired elf bent on mischief. But it looked a whole lot more like a glint to me. A wicked, scheming glint.

"You can apologize properly and initiate it for the season," she continued, gesturing toward a sprig I hadn't noticed in the doorway.

"Oh, it's all right," Grace said, tensing ever-so-slightly against my side. "I know where we stand."

Looked like payback was coming even sooner than I hoped. "No, she's right, Grace." I rose from the sofa and tugged lightly on her hand. If I thought for two seconds that she didn't want to do this, I would let her go, but my gut said she would see it as a dare she couldn't refuse.

"Mistletoe, mistletoe," Evie chanted. Landon took it up too, but when Brooke and Ian joined in, Grace shot them a look that said she would have killed them dead on the spot if she could have, I was pretty sure. It only made Ian look more like he was trying not to laugh.

She followed me to the doorway to the sound of cheers, and I pretended to take great care to position us under the sprig, settling her into place, then backing up, holding up my hands to view her through a square, repositioning her, and checking the sprig again.

Our audience loved it, and Landon let out a wolf whistle.

"Don't make her wait, dude," Paige called. Troublemaker.

Grace was still the whole time, but it felt like a watchful stillness, not a stressed one. She had to know she could trust me by now, didn't she?

I joined her beneath the mistletoe and slid my hands beneath her hair, pressing lightly on the back of her head to draw her toward me, but slowly, so she had all the time in the world to escape. Besides, I wanted to draw this out and sell it to Dr. Boone. I lowered my head slowly, keeping my eyes steady on hers in what was turning out to be the sexiest game of "chicken" I'd ever played.

Paige did a catcall which made Ian laugh, but it barely registered as I watched the tiny changes in Grace's eyes, trying to fathom what she was thinking. I thought I'd seen flashes of desire in them before, but they'd gone as fast as they appeared, like she'd clamped down on any pull she felt for me. But now they grew unfocused, her eyelids growing heavy, and I could feel her want wrapping around me like a second skin.

Our lips were so close that her eyes drifted shut, but at the last possible second, when I could feel her breath against my skin, I pressed a soft kiss against the corner of her mouth and straightened. Her eyes fluttered open to reveal confusion.

"Grace isn't big into excessive PDA," I said to everyone as Paige gave a good-natured groan. "I won't put her on the spot like that."

"I don't know." Miss Lily's tone was full of doubt. "I don't think that's nearly enough to get you off the hook, but I guess Grace should have the final say on that. What do you think, Grace? Was that good enough to get Noah off the hook?"

Grace's eyes cleared as she realized I'd set her up, and then they narrowed. "Not even close yet."

"Kiss the girl," the pastor's wife cried, and that won several cheers. "A good one!"

I hadn't stepped away, my hand still resting against her neck. She reached up and clasped a fistful of shirt with a sudden tug that caught me off guard and brought my head down to hers again. She leaned up and pressed a kiss against my lips, warm and soft, and her free hand slid around my neck, holding me like I was holding her.

I didn't know where to focus because I felt all of her at once, her arm pressed between us as she held onto my shirt, her mouth, the heat of her hand on my neck.

I wanted more. I slid my other arm around and drew her closer, her lips parting in surprise, and it was all I needed as an invitation, slipping inside the warmth of her mouth, pressing her even closer as she tightened her hold like she wanted more too.

I didn't know how far that kiss would have gone if a laughing "Whoa!" from Ian hadn't penetrated the thick haze we were in. I drew away and blinked into her stunned eyes, running my finger across her bottom lip while I tried to process what had just happened.

213

"Ew, Unc," Evie said.

"I think we all believe you now," Miss Lily said.

She looked pleased, the reverend looked amused, Mr. Winters looked slightly grumpy, and Brooke looked like the cat who ate all the cream.

I rested my forehead against Grace's. "What the—"

"I don't know," she said, softly. "I don't know."

CHAPTER NINETEEN
GRACE

What even was that?!

The question played over and over again in my mind as I woke up and went into the store early to meet Paige and get ready for the Black Friday madness. I wished I was working with my dad, but only because he wouldn't pry about Noah and that kiss, and I had no idea if Paige would bring it up or not.

Worse, I had no idea what to say if she did, because I didn't know what to think about it.

Except that it had been the freaking hottest kiss I'd ever experienced.

Which was a problem.

A big one.

Because you know what you don't want to do right on the cusp of leaving a town behind forever minus Christmas visits?

Find a guy in it who twists your insides into lustful knots.

"You suck, universe." I paused as I got out of my car behind the store and stared at the sky like it was going to answer. It didn't, but when I turned to go into the back entrance, I tripped over a piece of loose asphalt and ended up bonking into the door instead of opening it.

"I don't take it back," I informed the sky.

An acorn flew out of nowhere and thumped my window.

Fine. I would stop taunting the universe, but I wasn't happy about the situation.

I vented my frustration by using the pricing gun with unnecessary violence for a half hour before Paige arrived, slapping price reductions on jugs of antifreeze like they'd insulted my honor.

When Paige came in, she got right to work. Morning would be craziest as people came in for the Black Friday sales we'd advertised. That included leaf blowers, grills, and smokers, which Paige had suggested adorning with big red bows since people often bought them as Christmas presents. She'd made a window display themed around "What to Buy a Handy Dad," which was brilliant for the wordplay on the store name and because it had already generated presales.

Luckily, she had no comment on Noah and me kissing. She did spend a minute with me reliving the glory of the food, but that was it before she wandered off to make sure we had enough extension cords stocked for everyone coming in to get started on their Christmas light displays today.

The morning flew by. Gary joined us shortly before noon and Dad came in so Paige could leave and get time with Evie before her dinner shift at the diner and so I could take my lunch.

When I came out after scarfing down the leftovers Brooke had sent me home with, I joined my dad back out on the floor.

"It looks great in here, honey. I ran a sales report, and we're already outperforming last year."

"Yeah, but this year, you're here, and it's going to get even better." Last year, he'd been so ill that he hadn't even gotten out of bed on Thanksgiving.

"I think a lot of it has to do with Paige's window," he said. "She's got a good head on her shoulders. Like her brother."

That was as big of a hint as he would ever drop trying to get a feel for what lay between Noah and I, but since I had no answers, I ignored that part.

"Paige is the best employee we've ever hired," I said. "You should consider keeping her on when I leave."

"How soon will that be?" he asked.

"Right after the New Year," I said. "Things are looking good for getting on with a new team at Boeing."

He nodded and looked as if he were mulling it for a moment. Then he mustered a smile. "I'm proud of you, honey. I'd be lying if I said we could have made it through all this without you here, and I'll miss you like crazy when you go. But I'll be happy to see you putting that degree I paid for to work doing something besides selling nuts and bolts to grumpy old men."

"I don't even do that much because they don't listen to me," I joked. Except not really.

As if to prove my point, a man in his seventies approached us and looked at my dad. "I'm looking for a welding torch to do some minor patches. You got anything in stock?"

"That's Grace here's area of expertise," my dad said, gesturing to me.

The customer ran an eye over me, and whether it was because of my age or my boobs, he sniffed and turned to my dad. "You can just show me."

I could see my dad getting ready to insist that the customer let me help him, but I gave a small shake of my head. This had been happening literally since the first day I'd ever worked in the store, never mind that I'd grown up in it. I was done trying to change the minds of men who'd already made them up about what I might know. I wouldn't miss this part at all. AT ALL.

If my dad decided to hire Paige on full-time and she accepted, I'd have to make sure I gave her a customized name tag: Expert Despite My Boobs.

Well. Maybe "I Promise I Can Help You."

The day kept racing along as we served the holiday traffic and bargain seekers, but a text from Noah brought it to a screeching halt.

Noah: Can we talk when you're done with work today?

There was no question what he wanted to talk about. That delicious, infuriating kiss that had hijacked my train of thought every three minutes today.

I wanted to say no. I still didn't know what to think about it. But there would be no avoiding Noah, and Brooke was going to pin me down for a conversation on the subject soon anyway.

But I tapped out a reply.

Grace: Sounds good. Come over to my place @7:00.
Noah: Should I bring dinner?
Grace: No. Planning to live on Miss Lily's leftovers forever.
Noah: Smart.

For the rest of the afternoon, even though we stayed busy all day, time dragged instead of flew, not because I was dreading seeing Noah but because I wanted to see him badly.

Which, again . . . problem.

My dad sent me home at six when the store closed and promised he could lock up without help.

"What are you doing here?" my mom asked when I walked into the house ten minutes later.

"I'm done with work."

"But you need to close up."

"Dad's closing up."

"Grace!"

"What," I said, but it wasn't a question. I knew what was bothering her.

"He's not ready for that. He still needs to recover."

"Mom, he was fine. I promise. I wouldn't have left if he wasn't."

"He pushes himself too hard. It's the worst thing he can do. He'll set himself back."

"He's not going to give himself cancer again if he exerts himself, Mom. I promise. Pretty sure the science backs me up."

"But he can give himself all kinds of new problems from overexertion." She rubbed her temples.

"Did you know he's been taking three mile walks every day for a week?"

She froze and looked at me. "What?"

"Yeah. He didn't do it yesterday, obviously, but every day when you leave for the office, he goes out for a walk to build up his endurance. It totally paid off in the store today. He looked a tiny bit tired when he flipped the open light off, but nothing like he looked even last month when he walked down to the mailbox to get the mail."

"I want you back in Charleston as soon as

possible, but not at the expense of your dad's health."

"He's doing great, Mom. I know it's hard to trust that, but he is." I wasn't going to get anywhere with her, so I changed the subject. "I need to go take a quick shower. Noah is coming, so don't be surprised if you see his car in the driveway."

"What's going on there? For a fake situation, that was a convincing mistletoe kiss."

"It was just a show for Dr. Boone, Mom. It was nothing."

"It didn't look like nothing, Grace. Noah seems like a great guy, but you can't get sidetracked right now. He's as rooted as you can get here, so unless you want to keep working at the store forever, cut bait and run from him and those eyes he can't keep off you."

"Mom . . ."

"Don't 'mom' me. I've been there. I know. You'll have way more options when you go back to Charleston. Don't take your eye off the ball."

I dropped it because I hated any hint that she wasn't happy with her life in Creekville. I knew she loved my dad, and he was still smitten with her after thirty years, so it sucked to know there was a big part of her who would take it all back and do it differently if she could.

"You're worrying too much, Mom. I'm going to take a shower."

Noah hadn't ever been up to my apartment, but he knew where the stairs were from our Saturday booth-building, so I texted him to just come straight up to my place when he got here.

I stood beneath the pounding shower water and tried to think about what I wanted from our conversation. I still didn't have any answers when I hopped out ten minutes later.

At least, not answers that I could say out loud. Maybe most guys would go for, "Hey, I'm definitely leaving Creekville forever in a month, but want to make out constantly until then?"

Noah wouldn't. He was a roots kind of guy, one who had been hurt in his past. He'd glossed over it a couple of times, but something had made him . . . skittish, almost? It was an insulting way to describe him, but I couldn't think of how else to put it.

I'd watched it again last night when we'd broken off our kiss and his eyes had been fever-bright with wanting. But as reality set in and Evie's "ew" had broken the spell, he'd retreated for the rest of the night. He'd still put on a show for the Boones, but I could feel the difference; a slight hesitation each time he touched me, all of the subtext in our unspoken game gone.

I was at a loss, and I had no idea of what he was coming here to say. For as many ways as I'd gotten to know Noah so well—from his sense of

222

humor to his sense of duty to his work ethic—there were still layers I didn't understand.

I pulled my hair into a messy bun and slipped into pajama pants and a Virginia Tech shirt. Whatever was coming next, I was going to be as comfortable as possible for it. I made some hot cocoa while I waited, and when Noah knocked right on time, I opened the door and waved him toward the sofa in the small living room.

He took a seat on one end, and I set a mug down in front of him then settled onto the other end. I had no good ideas to break the silence.

Stupidly, the only thing I could think about was how much I wanted to kiss him again. Like, crawl over, curl into his lap, and lay one on him until he forgot about even having a conversation.

Yeah. That was exactly what I wanted. So how to make it happen? "Tell me about your last girlfriend."

He looked as surprised as I felt by my question. "Uh, what?"

I shrugged. "I don't know much about you. Not as much as I usually know about my friends by now. You've hinted that there was a rough breakup, and now I want to know the details."

His forehead furrowed. "Why?"

"So I can submit it to the front page of the *Creekville Courier*, obviously. Does it matter why?"

"I guess not."

"Start with a name."

"Lauren," he said.

"And how'd you meet her?"

"High school. Or maybe college, depending on how you look at it. She was two years behind me at Granger, but we didn't get to know each other until my senior year of college when my mom asked me if I'd give her a ride home from UVA for Christmas. Our moms worked together as tellers at the same bank."

"Was she trying to set you up? My mom used to do that to me all the time."

He shook his head. "No. But we hit it off anyway. Ended up dating for a year and got engaged. We were going to get married after she graduated. Seemed pretty perfect. I moved back to Granger to save money and commuted to my first teaching job in Charlottesville. By then, Paige had come back home, and I was helping with Evie. Lauren and I still saw each other a lot but not as much as when I was living right there in town. Then she started skipping some weekends, staying at school instead of coming home. And a month before we were supposed to get married, she told me she wanted to call it off."

I called her a rude name, which made him laugh.

"Yeah, that's one way to put it. It turned out that she'd started seeing a guy in law school. So those weekends she didn't come home, she was hanging out with him. She said that in her mind she wasn't cheating because she kept telling herself they were only friends."

"That's bull," I said.

He didn't agree. His expression turned thoughtful. "Maybe."

"Definitely."

"She said when the first RSVP for our wedding came in, she realized people were planning to show up and eat the food we'd picked and dance to the music we'd chosen, and it became real, and she couldn't do it."

"I don't like this girl," I said.

He gave a short laugh, his eyes crinkling the tiniest bit. "You and Paige both. When Lauren called off the wedding, Evie had been begging Paige for months to let her wear her flower girl dress. She said it was princess-fancy, and Paige wouldn't let her. But the day I told her, she put Evie in the dress, took her to the park, let her play in the sand and mud as much as she wanted, then shoved it in a grocery bag and mailed it back to Lauren."

"Brutal," I said, grinning. "I like Paige's style."

"Yeah, well, she didn't love Lauren's reasons. She took them personally."

"What does that mean?"

He looked as if he were debating whether he wanted to explain, tugging at his earlobe a few times before he settled in favor of answering. "Lauren said she'd realized she wanted more than what our life together was going to offer her. She didn't want to be married to a high school teacher, not even one who would eventually become a principal. She wanted someone with more ambition, someone who wanted bigger things than Mineral or even Charlottesville."

"And why did Paige take that personally?"

"Paige thinks she's the reason I won't leave. She felt like Lauren was punishing me for trying to be a good guy." He ruffled his hair, the tips of his ears going pink. "I sound like I'm trying to be the hero of one of those lame Nicholas Sparks movies she's always making me watch. I'm not."

"Maybe you're not *trying* to be but you're that good of a guy anyway." Noah was good to his bones.

"Look who's talking, woman who came home to take care of a sick dad."

"Yep, we're amazing," I said lazily to make him laugh. It worked.

"Anyway, Lauren just got married to the law school guy," he said, still smiling. "But that's part of why I wanted to move out of Mineral. It was so small, and I was so tired of running into people who asked me questions about it, or just looked at me with pity. It made me feel even crappier. Paige needed a new start too."

"Was Brooke's wedding hard for you?"

"It would have been if you hadn't flashed me your panties then entertained me the next day."

"We're having a nice moment. Please don't make me feel like murdering you."

"Fine," he said with a small smile. "I expected the wedding to be rough. Moments were hard, but the more time goes by, the more my perspective changes. Like just now, talking to you, I had one of those moments."

"Which was . . . ?" I liked the idea of being a perspective-changer.

"You said it was bull that Lauren didn't figure out she felt more than friendship for law school guy, and I thought that too. But now I understand what it feels like to hang out with someone as a friend and get blindsided by your feelings for them."

Oh, good. We were going the super awkward route.

Except . . .

It felt . . . not awkward to hear him say that? He was naming thoughts and emotions I'd had since our mistletoe kiss.

"Grace?" He said my name softly, and my name sounded like the prayer my mom had always meant it to be.

"Noah?"

"What is this?"

"You're asking the hardest question." I tried to

227

give him a jokey smile, but his expression didn't waver.

"I'm serious. I thought I understood it. We're friends. We're putting on a stupid show because I panicked when my boss was talking to me last month. You're a good sport. But yesterday, that didn't feel like a show. And for me . . ."

I wanted him to finish that sentence. I also wanted to clap my hand over his mouth so he couldn't. I was a mess, and I did nothing, waiting to see what would happen next, yearning for it and dreading it at the same time.

He rested his elbows on his knees and kept his eyes on his clasped hands before he took a deep breath. "I don't know what's going on, but that kiss was real for me."

The devil made me do it. That was the only explanation for the next words out of my mouth. "We should try it again and see if we can figure it out."

His head whipped around, his eyes wide as he met mine. "What did you say?"

I could back out of this. Laugh it off, lie about what I'd said, change the subject. But I wanted him. "You heard me."

"Try it again?"

"Try it again." It was a dare, and he knew it.

And in case I hadn't been clear, I shifted to my knees and crept toward him on the sofa, not taking my eyes off his.

He settled back into the corner, a small smile playing on his lips as he watched me prowl toward him.

"What do you think you're doing?" he asked, his voice low, as I stopped inches away.

"This." I leaned forward the slightest bit and brushed my mouth against his, my eyes open so I could read his.

His answer was to catch my bottom lip in between his teeth and hold it lightly until I pulled away slowly.

"Do we have to figure out what 'this' is?" I asked softly, my breath a puff against his lips. "What if we let it be its own thing and not pin it under one of Brooke's microscopes?"

His answer was to lean forward and kiss me back with a hunger that would have scandalized Miss Lily's guests. But I welcomed it, giving as good as I got, learning the contours of his lips, exploring the planes of his chest and shoulders with my hands, the soft boundary of his hairline over his collar. Every sense went on high alert, and it was all good. Taste, feel, smell. So good.

His touch was both soft and demanding as he traced light lines along my jaw and down my throat, never breaking the connection of our mouths. He pulled me tighter against him, and I toppled into his lap, exactly where I'd wanted to be.

I pulled away and he murmured a protest, but

I wanted to explore him more, the faint saltiness of his neck, the soft spot behind his ear that prompted his hands to close around my arms tight enough to almost hurt when I kissed it.

"Why is this so good?" I asked, but he didn't answer, just pulled my mouth back to his and explored it more, a soft tangle of tongues and lips, of sliding hands and quickening breath.

I'd never been so lost inside of a kiss, like time stopped but it had never mattered, not like kissing Noah mattered. Not like being kissed by him mattered.

We came up for air eventually, one of our phones buzzing persistently.

Somehow, we'd ended up flat on the sofa, Noah's legs hanging over the arm behind him, throw pillows thrown. He lifted himself onto his elbows and pressed his forehead against mine, eyes closed, taking a few deep breaths, the kind I took when I needed to steady myself.

I'd forgotten what it felt like to disappear into someone so completely that time didn't pass anymore. Maybe it was because I'd never connected with someone like this enough to remember.

I loved that I had done this to him, had scratched beneath the surface of the cheerful PE teacher and game night buddy to discover that Noah Redmond was a stellar makeout.

He straightened and shifted back into his corner

of the couch. I scooched up so my back was against the armrest on my end and tucked my toes beneath his thigh.

"Wow, coach." I smirked at him. I couldn't help it. "I see why they put you in charge of wrestling."

"Grace." This time my name was a half-groan, half-laugh.

"Yeah, coach?"

"I'm twenty-seven. Wasn't I supposed to out-grow making out on my girlfriend's couch with her parents in the other room years ago?"

"One, I'm not your girlfriend. Two, don't worry about it. They're downstairs. They'd have to knock to get in."

He tugged at the neckline of his shirt like it was making him suddenly uncomfortable. "Grace . . ."

I dropped my head back to the sofa arm with a groan.

"What was that for?" he asked.

"Your tone. You're about to say something responsible. I can tell." I lifted my head and scowled. "For a simple guy, you sure like to complicate things."

"No, I like them to be simple. So let's DTR."

"No. Oh, heck no. I haven't done anything to deserve a 'define the relationship' talk. I'm a good person who took care of her cancer daddy, and I shouldn't be punished." I pulled my hands inside my sweatshirt and wrapped them around my knees, then glared at him over the top of them.

"But if we name things, it's not confusing later. No misunderstandings, no miscommunication." He looked at me like he must look at his players when he was expecting them to grow up and do better, a look that said he expected my best.

"Fine," I said, reclaiming my sweatshirt sleeves and sitting up straight like a grown adult. "I define us as make out buddies. We make out when we feel like it—"

"So, like, always?" he interrupted, and it made my belly tingle.

"When we feel like it," I continued, trying not to blush, because how was I blushing when this man now knew my mouth better than my toothbrush did? "And it's fun, and then after New Year's, I leave Creekville, and we'll say to ourselves, 'That was a fun time we had making out,' and it's all simple. See?"

"Is that what we'll say to ourselves?" he repeated, trying not to laugh. "In my head, I'm saying stuff more like, 'Damn, that was hot.' Just me?"

"Possibly not," I conceded, feeling myself go even redder. "But I'm being serious. What if this is a fling? Makeouts only, so things don't get complicated. But I'm all for some excellent making out." I couldn't believe how much I wanted him to go for this ridiculous pitch.

"I'm not a casual relationship guy," he said.

"But this is the perfect situation because it has a built-in expiration date; it's all the fun with none of the commitment, and neither of us will have hard feelings because you're making us define the relationship right now, which I agree now was genius."

It should have been a no-brainer, but not for Noah, apparently.

He got up and scrubbed his hands over his face for a second. "I need to think about it."

It would have stung my ego if I didn't know he was speaking from his "fundamentally decent human being" wiring.

"Noah . . ." And now it was my turn to half-laugh, half-groan his name.

"I know," he grumbled. "I'm positive I'm going to kick myself for being an idiot the second I walk out."

I stood to walk him to the door and tried to fight the impulse to strangle him. Or jump him? I couldn't tell which I wanted to do more.

Jump him. Definitely.

"For what it's worth," he said as he stepped through it, "I wouldn't want to fake date anyone else but you."

"Add 'fake date and real make out with anyone else' and I agree."

He laughed all the way down the stairs and to his car.

CHAPTER TWENTY
NOAH

There was no one dumber in Creekville. Or the state of Virginia. Or on Planet Earth.

I thought about Grace's proposition all the way home, all night while I tossed and turned, and in the morning when I was bleary-eyed and could barely think clearly enough to put on matching sneakers.

I was heading straight back over to her place, but not even to roll around on the sofa again.

"Let's go, Evie," I said, helping her off my sofa. Paige had brought her over a few minutes before so she could work the Saturday breakfast shift at the diner. "Time to go."

She looked at the TV longingly. "Mickey Mouse."

"We're going to see Toodles."

She looked a little more interested. "Building stuff?"

"Not this time." When her face fell, I crouched in front of her. "We're going to surprise Toodles and Mr. Winters with some Christmas magic."

Evie was at the door before I could even click off the TV.

Twenty minutes later, we were at Grace's house, the whole team pulling up in trucks and cars. It was early and they looked sleepy, but I didn't hear a grumble from any of them.

The front door opened and Grace walked out as the team continued trickling into the driveway.

"Boys? What are you doing here? I thought you needed to practice for regionals?"

"We do," Grant said. "But we'll do that later. We thought maybe Mr. Winters could use some help getting your lights up. We always drive by here during Christmas. It's one of our favorite holiday houses, and we missed it last year. We figure it's the least we can do for all the help you and your dad have given us over the years."

Grace's eyes swung to mine. "You didn't have to do this."

I shook my head. "This was all their idea. They wanted to say thank you."

She stared at me for a moment, then swept her eyes over the boys again. I'd heard her talk about giving up her job, her dad being really sick, having to run the store in less-than-ideal circumstances, but this was the first time I'd ever seen her tear up.

She nodded, sniffed, and nodded again. "I'll get him."

A minute later, her parents appeared, both looking stunned.

"Son, what's going on here?" Mr. Winters called.

"I'll let Grant explain," I said, smiling, so Grant did.

Mr. Winters listened then cleared his throat. Then cleared it again, then one more time before he spoke. "Well, I'll be much obliged. Wasn't sure quite how to get it done."

The Christmas-ifying was in full swing by nine o'clock. Mrs. Winters had brought Evie inside to help her test light strands, which Evie would run out to us when they passed muster. Mr. Winters worked on the lawn display while directing the boys on where to hang lights.

Grace had run out a while before and returned with several boxes of donuts. "I can't thank you enough for this," she said, setting them on the hood of my car.

"It's not a big deal."

"It's a huge deal," she said. "This is amazing, and I have to go open the store right now, but this is going to keep me smiling all day." She reached up for a hug, and when I closed my arms around her, she whispered, "Too bad I can't thank you with a makeout. Maybe you should rethink that."

Then she walked to her car and drove off to work without a backward glance.

I swung by Bixby's Café on the way to school Monday morning, in need of stronger coffee than my usual morning brew. I'd been losing sleep over Grace, resisting the urge for the last two nights to drop by or call her to come over.

"Morning, coach." Taylor, the owner and chief barista, seemed to learn everyone's name the first time she heard it. "What can I get for you?"

"Strongest caffeine you got. I don't care what's in it." I was reaching for my wallet when I noticed her bakery case. "And an apple cider donut." Might as well sample what we'd be selling in the booth. It seemed like a baked good I should have had in my life long before now.

"Coming right up." I wandered off to the side and studied the bulletin board bristling with flyers and community announcements. A lost dog. A babysitter looking for work. Business cards for local businesses. Creekville had the vibe of Mineral except I didn't have to keep running into people I knew giving me pitying looks or trying to set me up because they thought I was pathetic.

"Coach Redmond," Taylor called, and I gratefully went to get my espresso. "Strongest I got."

"Perfect."

"Hey, I've been meaning to thank you," she said, as she handed me my donut. "It was really decent of you to give up the apple cider donuts this year. I was so overwhelmed trying to organize the whole thing that I didn't have the bandwidth to figure out what else to sell."

"Sure, no problem," I said, taking a sip of the espresso. It was bitter and strong, like she'd mixed caffeine with water. It was perfect. I waved at her and headed back to my Honda, but as my foot hit the running board, the caffeine hit my system, and the brain fog cleared.

Wait, what had she said? Give up the apple cider donuts this year?

Hold on.

I walked back into Bixby's and waited until she was done with her next customer.

"Taylor?"

"Your drink okay? I can add a shot of cream if you need to cut it."

"The coffee's fine. Did you thank me for giving up the apple cider donuts?"

She smiled but it faded when she saw my face. "Yeah. Because the email I sent?"

"What email?"

"I sent it last month, explaining that I was completely overwhelmed with taking over Christmas Town from Glynnis. I'm so busy trying to figure out how to coordinate the booths that I don't have it in me to figure out what to sell that will be a surefire hit. But my apple cider donuts sell well here, and people love that booth, so I said I'd like to call dibs on those this year, and if it was a problem to let me know." She looked as anxious as if she'd downed twelve shots of her own espresso.

"I didn't see the email," I said. "You're sure you sent it? I stay on top of emails pretty well."

"I'm sure." She pulled her phone from her apron pocket. "I assumed when you didn't email back that it was fine. Maybe that was my subconscious trying to talk me into believing it was no big deal because I needed it to be no big deal." She sounded on the verge of tears as she scrolled on her phone. "I should have followed up with you when I didn't hear back. Here."

She handed me the phone which was open to an email from her "sent" folder. The subject line read, "Change requested to your booth." I scanned it, and she had indeed asked about selling apple cider donuts. But I could see the problem.

"You misspelled my email address. The domain is right, but you put Noah.Redmond. It's just N.Redmond."

"Oh, no." A stricken look crossed her face, chased by panic. "I should have called over to the school when I didn't get a direct answer to the email." She took a deep breath. "It's okay. It's okay." I thought she might be reassuring herself, not me. "I can switch it up. I'll find something else to make. The important thing is to have apple cider donuts, and you'll have those covered."

I couldn't stand it when people cried, and there were definitely tears gathering in her thickening voice. No doubt she'd let them fall the second I walked back out.

"No, don't worry about it," I said against all common sense. "I can figure something else out. I have a whole football team to help me."

In a normal circumstance, Taylor Bixby seemed like the kind of woman who would have insisted on us keeping the apple cider donuts while she planned something else. But right now, Taylor Bixby seemed like a woman on the verge of a nervous breakdown, so instead she gave me a shaky smile.

"Are you sure?"

I hadn't been, but that almost-watery smile clinched it. "I'm sure. Do the apple cider donuts. We'll come up with something."

"Thanks, coach. This whole thing has been . . ." Her eyes went unfocused, like she was imagining horrors I couldn't understand.

"No biggie, I promise. Just promise that there's no problem with our Cat in the Hat theme and I'll survive."

"No, no problem there. I saw it on your booth application, and I think it's great."

"Cool. I'll brainstorm with the boys and figure out what to serve instead."

I gave her a small salute and walked back out to my car feeling slightly shell-shocked. As I started it up, my own panic set in. I was decent in the kitchen, but I didn't know how to bake stuff on a massive scale. I'd been planning to follow the same old ASB playbook. I'd already used their recipe and previous order invoices to order the ingredients for this year.

But my playbook had just been stolen, ripped up, and thrown to the winds. So what was I supposed to do now?

I called Grace on my lunch break. "We have a problem," I said when she picked up.

"Uh, hey?"

"Hey. We have a problem. Or I do, anyway."

"Is this about making out?"

I smiled. "Do you think of anything else?"

"Not lately."

I sucked in a breath. Did she know how sexy she was? "This is not about that."

She sighed. "Fine. Hit me."

I explained the problem with Taylor and the apple cider donuts. "So basically, I have more bags of flour and sugar than I know what to do with, not to mention gallons of apple cider."

"Okay. That sucks, but we can figure this out. There must be other recipes out there we can make."

"It's not that easy. We need time to test recipes and find one that we can scale up and make sure it's good enough for people to want to buy five hundred of them." I didn't panic easily, but my stress climbed as I imagined making well under what the ASB usually brought in. It would only prove to Dr. Boone that I wasn't ready to run the football program if I couldn't pull the Christmas Town booth together. "This is a disaster."

"Hold on," she said. "We have a lot of roads to go down before we can call it a disaster. And this isn't all your problem to solve. Get the boys involved. Make them work on this."

I took a calming breath. "You're right. They pull through when it matters."

"Also, you're dealing with scope creep. This happens a lot when we're working on engineering projects. Solve the problem at hand, not all the ones that may or may not be coming. This is about what to bake. Get that figured out, then you can tackle what may or may not happen after that."

She never talked about her engineering work. It was easy to see why her parents had wanted her home to step in and run things. She sounded unflappable.

"I mean this as the deepest possible compliment: you sound like a computer right now, solving things logically."

"I'm taking it as a compliment," she said. "That's what engineering brains do. Slow down, think it through, then solve. We've got a bunch of stuff we can try before it's time to panic."

It was weird how much I liked hearing her say "we," like it was her problem too.

It was weird how sexy it sounded to get a glimpse into the Boeing badass side of her.

I really needed to make it not weird with whatever I said next.

I cleared my throat. "What if you dropped by after practice today? We can brainstorm with the boys and come up with a solution."

"Maybe," she said. "I'll see if my dad can come in and close up."

"No, don't do that. I'll figure it out with the boys."

"He'll love that I asked," she reassured me. "He's getting more and more of his energy back. I'll let you know if I can make it. And after all the help with the decorations, he'll be stoked to repay the favor."

We hung up, and I almost headed over to Brooke's classroom to ask her advice for the booth. Then I realized she was going to be all over me about the mistletoe kiss, and I hid in my office instead.

She texted me ten minutes before lunch ended: "Chicken."

Absolutely. Brooke would have questions that I didn't have answers to. I couldn't avoid figuring out what was going on between Grace and me forever, but I could definitely put it off for one more day until I solved the booth problem.

Grace texted that she'd be off at five, and I was waiting for her in the gym with the boys.

"Fellas," I said, "we've got a small problem with the booth."

"Did it break?" DeShawn asked.

"We gotta build more?" J.J. asked.

I made the "settle down" gesture. "No, I don't think so. But we're not going to be able to do apple cider donuts." I explained the problem and got the grumbling I expected.

"Maybe that's okay," Grant said. "I could never figure out what apple cider donuts had to do with *Cat in the Hat*."

Grace glanced over to me with a small smile, her eyebrows raised.

"Fair point," I said. "So let's tie whatever we're going to do in with our theme."

"How do we do that?" DeShawn asked.

"I don't know. That's for you boys to figure it out. This is raising funds for your program, so you should have a say in it. Right now, I'm turning our game board into a problem-solving board." I erased the Xs and Os from the play we'd been practicing today and wrote "Brainstorm" across the top. "We've got twenty pounds of flour, gallons of apple cider, pounds of butter and sugar, plus all this stuff." I wrote the additional spices and ingredients. "Pull out your phones and google to see what else we can do."

Rustling and murmurs sounded as they pulled out their phones and set to work.

"Well done, coach," Grace said, joining me

to study the whiteboard. "You should probably also know that if all else fails, I have a secret weapon."

"What's that?"

"My sister, the celebrity chef. She might be falling down right now in the family department, but she never fails in the baking department. She'll have an idea."

"How did I forget you have a celebrity chef practically in your pocket?"

She shrugged. "Because she's rarely actually helpful, but maybe this time she can do some good."

I lowered my voice. "I talk a good game about having faith in these boys, but I'm going to feel a lot better if we have a Plan B."

"You've got a Plan B," she said. "I promise."

"I got something," Grant said. "What about apple turnovers?"

"My mom makes turnovers that are the bomb," DeShawn said. "But what's that got to do with *Cat in the Hat*?"

"I don't know," Grant said, sounding irritated. "Maybe because of how those Things turn over everything in the house?"

"Oh, dang," J.J. said. "That's good."

"That *is* good," DeShawn said. "Okay, okay, what about . . ."

They were off and running, ideas pouring out. I tried to keep up with them on the board as they googled more recipes and connections to the theme.

Twenty minutes later, we'd narrowed it down to three ideas: apple turnovers (because the Cat in the Hat turned the house upside down), apple hand pies (because it seemed like the kind of pies little kids would make), or apple tacos (where the taco shell was a pancake because "that's the kind of messed up thing that cat would make").

"Feeling better?" Grace asked as the boys argued among the three options.

"A little. I like how they connected each of these to the theme. But there's still a lot of experimenting to do to make sure we can consistently make a good turnover or whatever we decide on. And there's no promise it'll sell as much as we need it to."

"That's where my sister can help. Mind if I run it past the boys?"

I held out my hand to indicate the floor was all hers.

"Boys," she called. They were still bickering. She rolled her eyes and gave a short, piercing whistle. They shut up and looked her way. "Do I have your attention?"

"Yes, Miss Grace," J.J. said.

"My sister is a celebrity chef. She even has a show on cable. How would you feel about me getting her on Facetime, and she can give you some professional advice about each of these three options so you can make an informed choice?"

"That's dope," DeShawn said. "My mom watches her show."

"Let me see if she's around."

"Hey," Tabitha said, her face appearing in the screen. She had dark hair like Grace's, but hers had curl like their mom's.

"Hey. You got a minute?" Grace asked.

"A couple, yeah. What's up?"

"I'm with some friends right now, and we're trying to solve a problem I think you can help with. Meet this year's Lincoln Bulldogs football team." Grace flipped the camera and panned over the bleachers, where the boys hooted and waved. "Here's the problem." She summed it up in a nutshell while her sister listened and nodded. "So in short, we can figure out how to tie all these in with *The Cat in the Hat*, but we want to know which one would make the best dessert and if you have any good recipes."

"Hand pies," her sister said without hesitation. "They're a huge food trend right now."

The player who'd suggested it whooped and shouted, "In your face!"

"But with a twist," her sister said.

"This is Tabitha's specialty," Grace explained. "Messing with stuff to bring her own style to it."

"It goes best with your theme because it has the most 'child-like' feel to it," Tabitha continued. "Kids love to make them, and everyone else loves to eat them. Plus, you can mull the cider you got in a crockpot with some spices and serve that on the side for extra money."

"I'm liking that," I said.

"Then you top it off by tying it to football. Hand pies kind of look like empanadas."

"Empa-whats?" That was J.J.

"Think of a potsticker dumpling like Mrs. Li makes at the Dragon House, but bigger, and baked, not steamed."

"That's my auntie," the kicker said.

"Those dumplings are super grub," another player said, and they all agreed.

"Tell your auntie that I haven't found more delicious potstickers, even in New York," Tabitha said.

The kicker beamed. "I will!"

"Anyway, so imagine those, edges all crimped, baked golden brown. Make it a cream cheese apple filling and you'll slay them."

"Oooh, dang," said one of the biggest guys on the team. Definitely had to be an offensive lineman. "I'll buy ten by myself."

"But here's the final touch," Tabitha said. "It would be easy to make the design of football laces on the side because that half-circle shape is football-ish."

"That's dope," DeShawn said over the excited hoots and whistles of the other boys.

"Sounds like we have a winner," I said. "Boys, say thank you to Chef Tabitha."

A chorus of thank yous met her. "I'll call you later," Grace said over the noise and Tabitha nodded and ended the call.

"My work here is done." Grace smiled at me. "Christmas Town is saved. Now they have to work on their costumes, and you're all set."

"I'll walk you out." Raising my voice, I called to the boys, "Figure out whose parents can help with the costumes and report to me when I get back."

I walked her to the gym door. "Thanks again. At some point, I'll even the score."

We'd stopped in the doorway so I could keep an ear out for the boys, but she stepped out of their view.

"I already told you how you can make it up to me." Her smile was . . . saucy. There was no other word for it.

I glanced over my shoulder and lowered my voice even though there was no chance the boys would hear us. "Here's a thing I figured out, Grace. You are literally irresistible, so you better make sure you understand what you're asking for."

Her jaw dropped a tiny bit, and it was hard not to take it as an invitation to pick up where we'd left off on Friday.

I finally had the upper hand. I gave her a slow smile. "I'll stop by after work, Grace."

She swallowed. Hard.

I grinned and watched her scurry away until she was out of sight.

CHAPTER TWENTY-ONE
GRACE

Whew. Was it hot out here or was that just Noah?

I escaped the gym and headed to the grocery store to pick up some fixings for an easy stir-fry. Noah had looked at me like he was planning to make me the main course, but I should probably feed him some real dinner before moving on to . . . dessert.

This whole situation was so ridiculous. I was seventeen again with my first crush. Giddy. Untethered. Wibbly-wobbly like a helium balloon.

I called Tabitha to distract myself from dwelling too much on Noah coming over.

"Hey, thanks for helping out," I said when she answered.

"No problem. You caught me at a good time. How did Thanksgiving go, anyway?"

"It was fine. Miss Lily put on a beautiful spread and the company was good."

"Mom says you have a new man?"

That was interesting. Tabitha dodged my mom's calls more than she and I even tried to dodge each other's.

"Uh, long story."

"I have time."

I rolled my eyes. "We're only pretending to date. It was Noah's dumb idea because he wants to convince his boss he has roots here, and he thinks dating a local girl will do that."

"You're dumb for agreeing to it."

"Not really. Turns out Noah and I like making out."

"So you're real dating?"

"No."

There was a long silence. "Uh, do you do entertainment-type things together and also kiss each other?"

"Yes, but those are two separate things. We do game nights with Brooke, and those are not dates."

"But you make out?"

"Yes, but dating is for if you have long-term relationship plans. We don't."

"Why not? Is he ugly?"

"Like that's the most important thing."

"It's not the least important thing," she said, and it made me laugh.

"Fine. He's not ugly. He's very cute. But also very much staying here, and I'm not." I'd been sitting on a secret since this morning, and the need to tell someone my news bubbled up. Tabitha used to be the person I told everything to until she'd made it clear I needed to give up my career to come back to Creekville because she wouldn't. She'd made it seem like I was replaceable, and she wasn't. She thanked me for running the store every time we talked, but it still bothered me that she hadn't thought my job mattered.

Today . . . today I was missing her being my person. Maybe it was because I had a possible moving date on my calendar now, or maybe it was because she'd helped the football team with no notice, but I felt less resentment toward her than I had in ages. And I wanted to tell *someone* my news, so I did.

"I got an offer from Boeing this morning," I said. "They want me to start in January." That met with silence, and all the resentment flooded back in. "You're supposed to say congratulations."

"Congratulations," she said dutifully. "But what about the store?"

"Dad's fine. Getting stronger every week."

"That's not what Mom says."

"That's because Mom is a worrier. I hear all the same reports she does, and the oncologist is optimistic. Dad said the doctor even grinned, actually." I imagined oncologists didn't have many chances to do that in their work.

"But being cancer-free doesn't necessarily equate to being ready to take back over the business."

I took a deep breath. "I'm trying hard not to get offended, Tab. But I'm the one who's here every day. I see what's going on. I work with him more than even Mom does. I know what it takes to run the store, and I'm a better judge than you are."

"But . . ."

"But what?" I asked through gritted teeth.

"Could your opinion be colored by the fact that you want to get out of Creekville?"

"After I've given up everything to be here and take care of him and the store, you think I'd take off before he's ready?" This micromanaging had made her an executive producer of her own show and the youngest host on her network. But I hated it when she cast me as the know-nothing little sister. I'd never been flighty, and I didn't deserve this. "When you've put in the time and done your share, maybe then you'll have some standing to make those judgments, but you haven't. So don't."

She sucked in a sharp breath. "You think I've done nothing through all of this?"

"Trust me, you haven't lived until you've cleaned out his vomit basin at two in the morning while Mom cries."

"I did what I could." Her voice was tight.

"Yeah, I'm sure your phone calls pulled him through." It was mean, but so was her refusal to acknowledge how much I'd sacrificed to be here. I wouldn't have traded my last sixteen months here for anything. But I'd still like a freaking acknowledgment.

"You want to know why I've been busting my

butt this whole time to make sure my cookbook launches well? His medical bills."

I wrinkled my forehead. "What?"

"Grace, who do you think has been paying all the medical bills?"

I'd assumed my parents were. "Dad never said anything."

"Because he doesn't know! He would hate it, and Mom and I thought the stress would be bad for his recovery. She tells him that her insurance through her real estate office covers it, but she doesn't even get insurance through them."

Guilt gnawed on my insides. "I didn't know."

"The bills are huge. And you know how I can afford that? Booking myself onto so many shows and appearances that I earned a cookbook deal with a big enough advance to cover the chemo. And you know how I'll keep paying for it? Making the bestseller list."

My gut twisted at the hurt and frustration in her voice. "I'm sorry." I hadn't been fair to her at all through all of this. "I really had no idea, but I should have known you were doing everything you could."

She didn't answer for a beat. "It's not your fault you didn't know. I didn't want to tell you, because if Dad ever does find out, the more people who know, the worse he's going to feel." She sighed. "I know it hasn't been easy for you to hold everything together. I feel guilty that I can't do it, and having you there is the only thing that makes me feel less guilty. If you're leaving, I have to feel guilty again. So I guess I'm being selfish when it comes right down to it. Trying to buy myself out of responsibility."

There had never been a more untrue statement about Tabitha. "Sounds to me like the opposite. Like you're taking more than your share of the responsibility."

She was quiet, but I could almost feel her thinking.

"Are you beating yourself up for not being able to pay enormous bills *and* take care of Dad yourself?"

There was a soft huff on her end. "I'm not *not* doing that."

"We probably need to stop playing the martyr Olympics here." I let out a long, slow breath, trying to rein us both back in. "I get why it's hard for you to take my word for it, but I promise Dad is fine. Mom is being neurotic, but he's in a good place. And I'm working on getting him more help for the store so he'll have backup."

"Okay," she said, her voice subdued. "You're right. You've always had a good head on your shoulders. I don't know why I've been so uptight about all this."

"Because you love Dad?"

She gave a small laugh. "Right. I guess it comes down to that."

"And because Mom makes everything sound like a worst-case scenario."

She gave an even bigger laugh. "Definitely that."

"So we're good?"

"Yeah. Except I need to make this up to you. I'm going to text you every single day to thank you for being there. I'll stop questioning you about whether Dad is getting better. And I'll talk Mom down when she's freaking out. But what else can I do to make it up to you? Name it."

I was about to say, "Nothing." Sisters fought sometimes. And we were fighting because we loved our parents. But then I thought of something. "You're coming home for Christmas, right?"

"Right. I didn't book any appearances until the twenty-seventh."

"When do you get in?"

"The twenty-third. Around noon, I think."

"So you'll be here for Christmas Town?"

"Yes . . ." She drew it out like she could hear the trap I was about to spring.

"Help us with the football booth. If we can advertise that we have everyone's hometown favorite celebrity chef, they'll line up for a mile whether they want hand pies or not."

"Graaaace . . ." It was a whine.

"Sixteen months, Tab. Vomit basins."

She made a retching noise of her own. "Fine. I'll do it. But that was stone cold manipulative."

"Got to make my fake boyfriend look good. That way, the principal will be so impressed with him that she won't care when we fake break up. Now tell me how to make a great stir-fry." It felt so good to have a conversation with her stripped of the subtext and resentment that had been thrumming between us for months.

When Noah texted that he was on the way twenty minutes later, I had dinner ready to serve by the time he knocked on my door.

"Hey," he said, walking inside and grabbing me around the waist. I had no objections as he hauled me against him to deliver a knee-melting hello kiss.

"Mmm," I said, sliding away from him. "Save that for when I tell you what I pulled off today."

His eyebrows went up. "Sounds intriguing, but I literally need no bribes to want to kiss you."

I grinned at him. "Just wait. But eat first." I served up the stir-fry and accepted his compliments as we ate it at my tiny table and caught up on our days.

"So what's the big news?" he asked as he gathered up our plates and took them to the sink to wash.

My heart stuttered for a second, thinking he meant the job news. But of course he wouldn't know about that.

I cleared my throat. "How would you feel about having a celebrity chef in the booth?"

He half-spun to look at me with wide eyes. "Your sister would do that?"

"She already committed."

He did a fist pump that dripped water all over the floor. "You are the best. And your sister is the fourth best."

"Who are second and third?"

"Evie and Paige."

"Right.

He dried his hands, his movements deliberate and methodical, all the while studying me.

"What?" I asked.

"Come here."

"You can't boss me in my own house." A flutter of desire rippled through my abdomen.

"Come here," he repeated. "Unless you're scared."

Certified fighting words. I walked over and stopped an arm's length away.

A small smile played over his lips. "Grace?"

"Yeah?" It came out a tiny bit croaky.

"Come here." This time the words were soft, and I took the last step toward him as he reached out to pull me in.

His lips were soft as they settled on mine, a kiss hello. At first. A kiss of *welcome* and *it's good to see you*. I rested my hands against his chest to settle into the kiss, but that first contact with those hard planes and angles reminded me of how much I liked exploring them. It took no time at all for Noah to deepen the kiss as he turned and backed me against the counter. Hello became hunger, and once again, my senses flared into high alert, all of them honed on him.

I could drink him in forever, every breath and touch of his sending my temperature rising.

When the edges of reality grew fuzzy, he drew back and rested his forehead against mine, his breaths raspy. We stayed that way for a long time, my hand over his heart so I could feel it thumping against my palm, the way he had to moderate his breathing to bring his heart rate down.

I had done that to him. I turned my lips up to his to do it again, but he moved his head back. It was a tiny movement, but it was more than enough to make me freeze.

"Grace . . ."

I didn't like the tone of his voice. There were traces of an apology in it.

"No."

"You don't even know what I'm going to say."

"I know I'm not going to like it."

"Grace," he said again, softly, but this time on a sigh. He took a step back.

"See? I knew I wasn't going to like it."

"I've never liked kissing anyone as much as I like kissing you."

That would have made my insides all warm and melty if I couldn't sense the "but" coming. "But . . ."

"I don't know about this whole noncommittal friends-with-benefits thing. I'm not wired that way."

I pushed past him to the sofa and plopped down, the very opposite of grace, but I didn't care. "We went over this."

"*You* did," he said. "You set these terms."

"You agreed."

"I thought I did." He sat on the coffee table in front of me, his elbows on his knees, hands clasped.

"That's your 'I'm serious' pose. It means you're thinking through a problem. Am I a problem, Noah?" I didn't like feeling like I was one more thing he had to manage.

"The fact that you know me well enough to recognize my thinking face but don't want us to date is the problem."

I stared at him blankly.

"Grace, I can't sort you into a neat box labeled 'break in case you need a makeout.' I don't put *some* of me into anything. I put *all* of me into everything. I can't draw the kind of lines you're asking for."

I wanted to throttle him. Not to death. Just until I felt better about the fact that he was sitting right there in front of my face, a guy I shared more chemistry with than I had ever shared with anyone, a guy who could make my last month in Creekville so fun and for whom

I could do the same, and he had to go and be exceedingly . . .

Decent.

It spoke to my core. Because until this proposal to Noah, I had never been a friends-with-benefits kind of girl either. Noncommittal wasn't me. Makeout buddies wasn't me. But what else could we be? We were two roads diverging.

"I hate Robert Frost," I muttered.

He gave me a confused look. "Like . . . the poet? Why?"

"Never mind." I sighed. "I'm leaving, Noah. This can't go any other way. It's not like we can shift this into a relationship and somehow keep it up long-distance. You're not leaving Paige and Evie. I'm not giving up my job. A relationship doesn't make sense between us."

"Define a 'relationship,' " he said. "I don't mean *our* relationship. I mean *any* relationship. What does that mean to you?"

"You do stuff together. Share deep thoughts. Talk about feelings. Go on dates."

He nodded and leaned forward even more, locking eyes with me. "Has it ever occurred to you that by that definition, we already *are* in a relationship?"

What? No. I could see why he would look at it that way. But no. "We're friends."

"With strong chemistry. Like, flammable levels. Isn't that more than friends?"

"Yes," I said, not trying to keep the frustration out of my voice. "Friends with benefits."

"But how is that different than being in a relationship? It's not like it's even another step forward. It's a baby step. Half a baby step."

Something about him putting a relationship label on us made it hard to breathe and not in the good, sexy way from a few minutes before. I felt like I was groping at the walls of a doorless room, trying to find an exit, and finally seeing a crack that I could pry at. "There's one big difference: one has a future. The other doesn't."

"Why can't we have a future?" he asked softly. "We've been hanging out for six months, Grace. I know almost everything about you. The kinds of movies you like, how you cheat at Monopoly, how you like your popcorn, what makes you laugh, what a bad day at work looks like for you, how your dad is doing on any given day. What's that if not a relationship?"

"That's a friendship. Brooke knows all that too. Except the cheating part. I don't cheat at board games." I totally did.

"Does Brooke know about the sound you make when I do this?" He rose and braced his hands on either side of my head against the back of the couch and leaned down to press a kiss beneath my ear, then trail more along my jaw line. "Does she?" he whispered.

"No," I whispered back even as I couldn't hide

a small shiver. "Because that would be weird."

He laughed and sat back on the coffee table. "Way to ruin a moment, Grace."

Yeah, that had been dumb of me. "Do it again," I said. "I won't ruin it."

He shook his head. "The fact that you want me to just makes my point. Why isn't this already a relationship?"

"Because relationships have futures, and we don't have one."

He was quiet for a long moment. "But couldn't we? I know this feels like a huge leap forward, but the more I think about it, the less I think it is one. Not based on the way I feel."

He met my eyes, sure and steady. He was putting himself out there, and it made me want to kiss him again. Or curl into his warm chest and listen to his heartbeat.

All of which was super problematic. Because I knew exactly what he meant. I'd been feeling the pull between us for weeks too. He'd become a part of my day. If I didn't talk to him, I was still thinking about him, wondering what he was doing, how his day was going. He was a bright spot for me, and the time I spent around him made the day glow brighter and feel sharper, like being around him made my senses clearer.

All except my common sense.

"I'm leaving, Noah. I've been clear about that since we met."

"Would it be so bad if you stayed here? You've got family, friends, a job. Me. Is it so hard to imagine sticking around?"

"It's way too easy because I've watched what happened to my mom."

"You've said that before, but she seems happy to me when she isn't worried about your dad."

I shrugged. "You didn't grow up with her. It makes a difference."

"Help me understand."

I sighed. "She is happy. But she's happy in this one version of her life until she thinks about the one she meant to have before my dad. She lost her parents young, when she was in high school, and her great aunt and uncle raised her. They were kind to her, but they were never close. It made her crave family. My dad was the opposite. He's from a huge family—six siblings— so when she fell in love with him, at least a quarter of that was based on him coming from the kind of family she wanted. She clung to that security."

"You think she regrets that?" he asked.

"She yearns for the other life she could have lived where she finished her masters in art history and went to work as a curator in one of the museums in DC. Maybe the National Gallery. And she lived this more cultured life with dinner parties and the theater."

"It must have been hard to grow up feeling

265

like your mom was always wanting something different," he said.

"She was a great mom," I corrected him. "But after Tabitha left for college, I had twice as much pressure. She tried talking me into going to Georgia Tech or MIT instead of Virginia Tech because it was too close. She worried I wouldn't escape the pull of Creekville. She wanted me orbiting out farther. She didn't let up. Still doesn't," I added with a grumble.

"That must have been hard."

I winced. "She was right to push me out. I don't feel fully myself here. You should see me when I'm on my game at my real-life job. I'm solving problems that keep enormous machines in the air. Some even go to space. Think about that." I leaned forward and squeezed his knees for a second, needing him to get it. "I literally have my fingerprints on the guts of machines in space."

The lines at the corners of his eyes deepened. "So this isn't real life? I'm not real life?"

I wished I could give him a different answer, but this was the time for honesty. "You aren't real life for me. You're the best kind of daydream."

"Except I'm not, Grace. I'm real. I'm right here. And I'm falling for you."

My stomach lurched, first with the giddiness of hearing those words, but it dropped right away. It was the crappiest of all roller coasters. I loved

Creekville, but I'd seen beyond its borders, and the future I wanted was out there, not here.

"Am I the only one feeling this?" he asked quietly.

"I don't know." It was true. I hadn't allowed myself to think in terms of falling because it meant thinking in terms of hurting when we reached our inevitable endpoint.

His face closed and tightened. "I see."

He didn't. Not really. Even I wasn't sure I could explain it.

"Noah . . . leaving isn't a hypothetical. I got a job offer today to go back to Boeing in Charleston. I start in January."

His face softened again. "I see."

We sat in silence. Not the good kind.

Finally, he sighed and stood up. "I wouldn't hold you back from that. I guess I was hoping to get you to rethink even applying, but if you already have a job, that's different. And it's great," he said. "I mean that sincerely. You'll be amazing at anything you decide to do."

He walked to the door, and I followed him halfway there, stopping when he turned. "I'm glad you get to do something you love, Grace. I shouldn't have tried to talk you out of that. Congratulations." Then he slipped out the door and was gone.

CHAPTER TWENTY-TWO
NOAH

Grace was leaving.

I drove home with that mantra in my head. Every time a thought tried to intrude about how I could change her mind or convince her to stay, I pushed it out. "Grace is leaving."

I walked in to find Paige and Evie on the sofa watching my TV because Evie preferred it for watching Pixar movies.

"Hey," Paige said. "How's your ridiculous plan with my boss going?"

"About as well as you predicted it would."

She'd told me no less than a dozen times that I was an idiot for not asking Grace out for real and that this plan would never work.

Paige shot a glance at Evie, who was absorbed in the adventures of Woody and Buzz Lightyear. She turned up the volume slightly and followed me into the kitchen.

"What happened?"

I shook my head. "She got a job offer with Boeing. She's moving to Charleston."

Her forehead furrowed. "When?"

"January."

"You look like you don't feel great about that."

I shrugged. "It's . . . whatever."

"It's more than that, obviously. Say what you want, Noah, but that kiss at Thanksgiving didn't look fake."

I took a beer from the fridge, normally only a weekend or Monday night football indulgence, and popped the cap, not even caring when I missed the trash can with my toss and it clattered to the tile. "We put on a good show."

She called my bluff with a pointed swear.

I sipped and didn't bother denying it. There was nothing to say.

"Why are you being so stubborn about this?" Paige asked. "You guys are perfect for each other."

"I'm not denying it," I said. "I went over there tonight to talk to her about making us official, and she told me she's leaving."

Paige took me by the shoulders and looked into my eyes, hers gentle. Then she shook me hard. "Change. Her. Mind."

I broke her hold. "It's not that easy."

"It's exactly that easy," she countered. "Women want to know they matter enough for you to fight for them."

"Not Grace," I said. "It would feel disrespectful to try to change her mind about this."

"Disrespectful?" she repeated in a tone of disbelief. "Are you kidding?"

"I'm dead serious. I'm not going to ask her to give up a career to deal with customers who talk to her like she doesn't know a bolt cutter from a hole in the ground."

"Then go to Charleston. Convince her to spend her time left here doing this for real, do long distance for five months until school is finished, then move out to Charleston and give it a shot."

I scrubbed my hand over my face. "Paige."

"Noah."

"It's so obvious. You do everything together. You hang out more every week. You're happier when you know you're going to see her. Your chemistry is so hot it's uncomfortable for the rest of us."

I shot her a sharp look.

"None of us is blind, dummy. Make it work."

"I can't pick up my whole life and move to Charleston, and I can't ask her to do the same."

"You're not. She's already here. Her family is here. She has friends and a job."

"This is a bump in the road for her. A temporary side trip. Being here feels like going backwards for her."

She considered that for a minute. "I guess that makes sense. She's the most competent manager I've ever worked under. Sharp. No drama. Fair. But also, I never feel like her heart is in it, even when all her energy is."

It only confirmed what I'd finally begun to understand. "Sounds about right."

She pulled out her phone and tapped it a few times. "Charleston is a seven-hour drive. You make it work for winter semester. You spend long weekends and spring break together. You go out for the summer. And by the end of the summer, you'll know if you should make the leap."

I was shaking my head before she even finished. "Drop it, Paige. I've thought about it as much as I want to think about it tonight."

"Just tell me one more thing: are you staying here because of me?"

It was the biggest reason, yeah. But I wasn't going to say that to her. "It's more complicated than that."

"But I'm a reason?"

"I like being by you and Evie."

Her eyes narrowed. "You think you *have* to be near me and Evie because you don't think I can handle it by myself."

"I think you shouldn't have to."

"I refuse to be the reason you don't try to make it work with Grace."

Paige talked a tough game, but I could feel her real distress beneath the words. "You aren't. It's more than that. Grace doesn't want to explore what's between us enough. It's that simple."

And when it came down to it, it was. I needed to remember that.

"I still think you could change her mind."

"If she felt even a fraction of what I do, I wouldn't have to try."

She shook her head but didn't argue. "Does

that mean the world's dumbest fake dating plan is over?"

Grace and I hadn't even talked about it. "It's probably best if we keep it up at least for Dr. Boone until I pull off the Christmas Town booth, but . . ."

"You're not sure you can?" Paige guessed.

I shrugged. Part of me wanted to because it meant connecting with Grace, but the bigger part of me had no idea how I was going to fake like it was enough anymore.

Paige walked back to the living room. "Come on, sweet pea," she said as she turned off the TV. "We're going to give back Unc's TV and finish watching this on ours."

"Hi, Unc. Bye, Unc." Evie climbed down from the sofa as the screen blinked off. "Love you."

She slipped her hand into Paige's and left with a wave.

There was no need to see Grace on Saturday because the boys lost their regional playoff game on Friday night, and Coach Dean was having the entire team over for a waffle breakfast to commemorate what had turned out to be his last game. All the team had left to do was costumes, and that wasn't Grace's headache anyway.

Paige also drove herself to work. "You're doing enough watching Evie for me, but I promise to call if my car breaks down."

Evie had a good time at the waffle breakfast, but she asked three times why we didn't go to "Toodles' house" so she could use her Evie work-bench. It underscored the need to pull back from Grace.

On Tuesday, I turned down an invitation to Brooke's game night on Thursday, saying I needed to watch Evie. I tried to send a text telling Grace not to worry about the final assembly of the booth, that it was fine if she wanted to let her dad handle it. But I couldn't quite make myself send it, and then Thursday, she texted me first.

Grace: Still planning on Saturday. Still going to put on a show. Don't worry.

A show.

For her, it was still a show. A fun one. One with all the rewards of flirting with none of the risk. It had quit feeling like a show to me.

I knew she felt the electricity between us. I could see it in the flicker of her eyes when we touched. I could make her laugh by looking at her a certain way. We never ran out of things to talk about. I loved the way her brain worked. The way she looked at the world.

The way she looked at me.

I should tell her we could call off the fake dating.

But what if it was my last chance to convince

her that we had something here—something special? Something worth staying for.

Noah: Sounds good. See you Saturday.

Saturday was chilly, a strong bite in the December air. Evie whined about climbing out of the warm car, and Mrs. Winters was waiting on the back patio for us with warm mugs of cocoa.

"Hey, coach. I was thinking maybe Evie might like to hang inside with me and watch TV. I don't know if Saturday morning cartoons are even a thing anymore, but I figured Evie could help me figure out what the kids are watching these days."

I shot her a grateful smile. "Sounds good, Mrs. Winters. Thanks. Evie, what do you think?"

She nodded happily and slipped her hand into Mrs. Winters's outstretched one to follow her into the house.

The door to Grace's apartment opened and she came down the stairs bundled in a fleece sweatshirt and jeans that made me wonder why I'd given up even a single second of opportunity to make out with her—until I saw her face. Her guarded expression reminded me of exactly why. She was shutting me out in all the ways that mattered.

"Hey," she said. "I was thinking maybe today

would be a good day to start dropping hints that there's trouble in Paradise. Not enough that DeShawn will run back to Dr. Boone with it, but so that when she asks you where I am after Christmas, you can tell her we broke up, and then maybe DeShawn will mention he saw the cracks if she asks him about it."

"Yeah, good idea. What can I help with today?" None of this made sense. Maybe Grace had so many people to choose from in dating that she found connections like ours all the time. But she'd asked me to drop it, and I wouldn't push her anymore.

I'd focus on the work.

"Patrol and watch for basic shop safety." She didn't meet my eyes.

The first boys appeared from the driveway, and she hurried to direct them, knowing their strengths from previous weeks. We kept busy supervising our own groups of kids, as good a reason as any to avoid any more awkward inter-actions.

At one point, Mrs. Winters came out with a platter of warm cookies that the boys fell on like starved termites, emptying it in seconds and going back to work with their mouths full.

"Sorry about them," I told her. "Mostly they have manners, but I think playing with power tools triggered their cave man brains."

She smiled. "No problem. It's fun having

young men around here. When Grace and Tabitha were young, this house multiplied with girls like gremlins or tribbles."

"Star Trek," I said, smiling back at the reference to the little furballs that replicated in water.

"Exactly. It's fun to see how the other half lives. Have fun!" She went back inside.

"Noah," Grace called. She sounded slightly annoyed. "Can you go watch the boys putting in the hinges on the back wall?"

She sounded like I did when I was telling kids to quit screwing around during gym.

"It's not a big deal," I called. "Just give me a minute." Was that enough pushback to show friction? Too much? I sucked at pretending.

"They're shooting the nail gun at a stump. So now, please?"

I hurried over to the boys. "Knock it off, dummies."

"Yes, coach."

"You can't call us names, coach," DeShawn said, not even remotely offended.

"When you show the same amount of brains as the dummies on your tackling sled, I can and will make that comparison."

"Fair," said one of the offensive linemen, and the perpetrator doing target practice with the nail gun sheepishly returned to the booth frame.

"Can I speak to you over here, coach?" Grace called from near the shed.

"She called you 'coach,'" J.J. noted. "That means you're in trouble."

I walked over to the shed. I had no idea if this was real or a show, and my stomach clenched while I waited to find out. I didn't like this. At all.

"What's up?" I asked.

She stuck her hands on her hips, and then said in a low voice, "Nothing. I'm just making them think we're having an argument." She stabbed a finger in the air for emphasis.

I crossed my arms, the picture of annoyance. "This is not nearly as fun as pretending we're into each other."

Her cheeks pinked. "That is beside the point," she said, shaking her finger.

"It's the whole point," I said. I darted a glance to the players who were shooting us looks. "But for what it's worth, I think they're buying this."

Grace ran her fingers through her hair in a frustrated gesture. "Good."

I stared down at the ground like I didn't want to meet her eyes. "How long is this fight going to last?"

"I think it can be done now." She crossed her arms too. Our body language was screaming "trouble."

"Good, because this is not my favorite." I scuffed at the concrete.

"Mine either," she said. "I'm going back to supervising now. The booth is looking good."

"Good job," I said, frowning.

"You too," she said frowning back, which made me fight a smile. I won. Barely.

Fake fighting with her was not nearly as fun as fake dating, but it was still more entertaining than ninety percent of anything else I did.

The realization was a splash of cold reality, and I didn't have to force a frown as I walked back to the boys.

I'd rather fake fight with Grace than do real anything with anyone else. But I had to shove that down and let coaching football and taking care of Paige and Evie be enough. It had to be. There wasn't another option.

By the time we had all the hinges installed and did a trial run of the setup, it was nearly lunch time, and I was thoroughly sick of fake fighting. It had been funny at first, but Grace found two or three more opportunities to show she wasn't happy with me.

It didn't feel good. I had to remind myself that I hadn't done anything wrong, any of the times. It was just more playacting. But it was starting to feel real, and I hated the knot it created in my chest.

We finally got the whole booth assembled. It was a good size—ten by ten—and could fit up to eight people working comfortably inside at once.

"Stand back and look at it, boys," I called, and they gathered around me to admire the final product. We'd used the design from Omar, who played right tackle and also took advanced art. He'd used forced perspective to recreate the slightly mad feel of a Dr. Seuss house, and the final product in front of us was a clever combination of color and wood cuts.

"It looks dope," one of the tight ends announced.

That met with exclamations of, "Yeah, it does" and "We're going to win Christmas Town."

"Win Christmas Town?" I repeated.

"Yeah," J.J. explained. "Blue Ribbon for best booth and $250 for the team."

"How did I not know that was part of the competition?" I asked. Maybe it had been for the best. It would have been another thing to stress about.

"I don't know," Grace snapped. "Everyone else knows."

Man, I hated fake fighting.

"Anyway," she continued to the rest of the boys, "now that you know how to assemble it, let's see how quickly you can disassemble it. Then you just have to practice the hand pie recipe, and you'll be set for Christmas Town."

"I'd feel so much better if your sister was here to teach us how to do the hand pies," I said to her in a low voice. "I tried it at home, and it came out okay, but I don't know why anyone would pay five dollars apiece for what I ended up with."

"Were you wearing a striped stovepipe hat or a cool Thing One costume when you made it? Because those things make the pies taste better."

"Is that what I was missing?"

"It's the secret sauce," she confirmed. "But also, Tabitha is going to send a video of how to make them. She's using it as a segment for one of her shows, and she's going to shout out the Bulldogs, but she said she'd send the video over in the next few days so you'd have it by next weekend."

The next weekend was dress rehearsal. We'd practice loading the booth, trucking it over to Reed Williamson's house, then assemble it, just like we would need to do it on Friday, Christmas Town day. Then we'd check out everyone's costumes and practice making the food, disassemble the booth, and figure out the shifts.

This was where having overly involved football parents was a godsend. Moms were sewing hats and ironing on Thing One and Two decals, dads were sourcing a portable deep fryer and running the electricity, and more moms stood ready to supervise the practice baking all day.

I'd expected drama and arguments, which was also a thing with football parents, but the simplicity of the theme had headed off a lot of the bickering that could happen around big events, and that was pure, dumb luck. The lack of drama meant no calls to Dr. Boone from people trying to go over my head, and I looked good because of it.

Between a good season, Coach Dean's recommendation, and a successful Christmas Town event, I was finally optimistic about my chances of getting Coach Dean's job.

And, of course, because of fake dating Grace.

CHAPTER TWENTY-THREE
GRACE

"Everything okay?" my mom asked when I finally came in. We'd put the whole booth back in the work shed, and Noah had left with Evie.

"It's fine, Mom." But it wasn't. This whole morning had been the worst. Even though the fake fighting had been my idea, I'd hated every second of it.

"You seem tense."

"Didn't sleep well. No big deal."

"Is it because this thing with Noah is getting real?" She was trying so hard to sound neutral, but I knew her too well. She might as well hold up a neon sign flashing, "SAY NO."

In most ways that mattered, the answer was yes. We made each other funnier, nearly started fires with our sparks, and we had a million things in common.

But long-term goals . . . we were oil and water. Orange juice and toothpaste. I couldn't stay. He couldn't leave.

I wished I could talk to my mom about any or all of this, but she wouldn't be impartial. She'd probably shove me in the car and drive me straight to Charleston just to make sure I got there.

But she was still waiting for an answer. I had to step carefully here. I didn't want to cast a shadow on Christmas by telling her I was leaving or having her worry about Noah and me. Dad was almost back to his old self and I wanted us to celebrate like we hadn't been able to last year when he'd been so weak and tired. My parents deserved an uncomplicated and happy Christmas, and I'd give it to them.

"Noah and I are same old, same old," I said, avoiding her question. "He's stressed about Christmas Town, and I'm stressed for him, but it'll work out because guess who's coming to help with the booth?"

Her expression perked up. "Who?"

"Tabitha. She's going to work in the booth as our special celebrity chef."

She clapped her hands, her eyes shining. "That's so perfect! When does she get here?"

And just like that, we moved on from the topic of Noah.

But *I* couldn't move on that easily from Noah. And it sucked.

I tried to snap myself out of my mood when I walked into the store, but it followed me like a sad puppy. Luckily, my dad was so preoccupied explaining our entire garden center philosophy to Paige that neither of them noticed my moping.

Maybe I would have done okay if I could have avoided Noah the whole week, but we kept having to text about the booth to make sure everything was on track. The parade would be Friday night, starting at the Episcopal church and heading down Main Street to end at the town square. Everyone spent Friday afternoon assembling their booths. We all knew what the other vendors were selling, but people kept their themes a secret. We wouldn't remove our makeshift screens and drapes until full dusk when the parade began.

Santa's sleigh would be the last float. When he reached the square, he'd climb down and announce, "Madam Mayor, Christmas Town is back!" Then the mayor would flip a switch to turn on all the streetlamps and floodlights while everyone—including the vendors—oohed and aahed at everyone else's booths, awash in warm light and holiday magic.

Christmas Town would go for three hours on Friday night, then from noon until nine the next day. Then Christmas Town went away for another year.

Texts flew all week, with Noah about booth details, with Tabitha about the food. But only one of their names made my heart race every time it appeared in my phone.

I was a grown woman, and I was completely ridiculous.

By Wednesday, as an act of self-preservation and an expensive reminder to get my mind right,

I called my old apartment complex in Charleston and rented a unit from them, paying my security deposit and one month's rent. I'd wanted to give myself some time to upgrade to a townhome, and I was going to crash with a friend for a week or two until I found exactly what I wanted. But what I needed more than anything right now was a concrete reminder that I was leaving after New Year's.

Friday afternoon, I left work early. Dad always kept the store open for people who had last minute hardware emergencies with their booths, but he shooed me out.

"Go help your fella," he said. "I already sent Paige home so she could get Evie from daycare, and then they can come back to catch the parade."

"He's not my fella."

"Oh, right. I meant your *friend*." He rolled his eyes. "Dating ain't what it used to be."

"We're not dating. Not for real." He gave me a long look but said nothing. I sighed. "See you later, Dad."

He'd walk over after closing time, prepared to run back and open up for anyone who had a booth hardware emergency but otherwise ready to enjoy Christmas Town with the rest of Creekville.

I ran home and changed out of my work uniform, wanting to look cute but refusing to acknowledge that it was for Noah's benefit. I pulled on a pair of black jeans and boots, a cream

285

sweater, and some festive red lipstick I swiped from my mom's bathroom.

When Noah knocked on my door exactly fifteen minutes after school let out, I opened it with a flutter in my stomach. No matter how complicated and strange things had gotten, it still made me smile to see him.

"Hey," he said, and he looked uncertain, like he wasn't sure what his welcome would be.

"Hey." I reached up and hugged him. There weren't a lot of these left. I wanted to enjoy all of them. He hesitated then wrapped his arms around me and hugged me back tightly. "Ready for today?"

He shrugged. "Ready as I'll ever be. The team moms have been fine-tuning the hand pies, and I think they're turning out pretty good now. The team is down there loading up the trucks."

"Let's go, then." I grabbed my coat from beside the door. Virginia had temperate winters, up around fifty during the day, but it could drop below freezing when the sun set. I grabbed a knit hat, scarf, and mittens to boot.

Noah led the way down the stairs, and I scowled at the jacket he was wearing because it covered the butt of his jeans. I knew those jeans. He looked good in those jeans.

We supervised the rest of the loading for the booth and added canvas drop cloths on loan from my dad to keep the booth hidden until nightfall. The town square was already bustling with activity when we arrived, and Taylor Bixby, wearing a bright orange snow beanie, stood in the middle of it all, directing people everywhere, looking stressed.

"I'm glad you didn't fight her for the donuts," I told Noah with a nod in Taylor's direction.

"No kidding," he said. "Plan B worked out better anyway."

The football team had signed up for different shifts, and we worked with the six boys who'd volunteered for assembly to get the drop cloths strung up first so no one could sneak a peek at our booth. Then they got the booth itself set up. The practice the previous weekend had helped. They had it up and ready to go within the hour.

It had seemed plenty big when we were designing it to accommodate supplies and workers, but somehow, with Noah and I trying to avoid each other in the space, it shrunk. We kept bumping into each other or brushing past each other to get to where we were needed. Everyone had taken off their coats, plenty warm from all the grunt work, but even through my thick sweater, every time Noah and I made contact, it sent my temperature up another degree.

What I really wanted to do was shove everyone out, sweep everything off a folding table, and throw him down on it to recreate our post-Thanksgiving makeout.

What I actually did was avoid eye contact with him while I busied myself with screws and hinges.

Finally, when the last latches were secured and the tables were set up and ready, Noah dismissed the boys to go home and get in their costumes.

"Just be back by 5:30," he told them. That would give them an hour before the moms would descend to start wrangling all the food into a production line. For now, it sat in bins against the back of the booth.

"See you, coach," they called as they took off.

It was suddenly quiet and only Noah and I were left.

His eyes met mine for the first time since we'd gotten to the town square. Mine wanted to skitter away, but I couldn't break his gaze. We stared at each other for a few seconds. I was dying inside. For something to say, for him to say something.

His lips parted like he was about to speak, then he hesitated and tilted his head like he was listening. He jerked his head to indicate someone beyond the drop cloths.

"Hey, Taylor," a voice called.

"That's Dr. Boone," Noah said.

"Where can I find the Lincoln High booth?" she asked.

Taylor answered with our location.

"Sounds like she's headed this way," I said.

"Yeah."

"Yeah." I wasn't sure what we were supposed to do here, and before my brain could hijack me with overthinking, I crossed the booth to Noah and reached out for his front pockets, pulling him against me. "Guess that means it's show time."

His eyes flashed with surprise, but he rested his hands on my shoulders and studied me, his gaze intense enough to make everything around us fade away. His gaze darkened immediately, the way it did when he was thinking about kissing me. I was trapped inside of it.

No, not trapped. It was exactly where I wanted to be, and as I watched his head lower the tiniest bit, I didn't even notice that someone had rustled through the drop cloths until she cleared her throat.

I'd totally forgotten about Dr. Boone in ten seconds flat.

Noah blinked and dropped his hands. I stepped back.

"Hey, Dr. Boone," he said.

"Sorry to . . . interrupt."

"No interruption," he assured her. I disagreed. "The team moms will be here in about a half-hour to set up the food prep line. Then the boys will be back and ready to cook and serve."

"You've done a good job," she said. "I can't wait until the cloths come down so I can see the full effect."

"It looks good," I promised her. "Noah got great

work out of the team." No harm in selling her on his merits. That was the whole point, after all.

Her lips gave a small twist that let me know my endorsement wasn't at all subtle. "I'll look forward to hearing the sales totals tomorrow," she said. "Enjoy the lull."

My cheeks heated, sensing a double meaning in her words as she slipped out.

Noah released a small breath. "She's always nice, but I don't know when I'll stop being intimidated by her. I keep waiting for her to figure out that I'm not old enough to be in the teacher's lounge."

"I can imagine. I feel like I'm in high school again every time I set foot on campus."

He rested his arms on my shoulders and ran his fingers through my ponytail almost absent-mindedly. "What kind of kid were you in high school?"

"The kind who snuck kisses with her boyfriend whenever the principal's back was turned." I pulled him down for a kiss, and Dr. Boone might have fired him on the spot if she'd seen it. The heat that simmered between us boiled over the second our lips touched, and he was tasting me like I was better than cream cheese apple hand pies.

"Grace." He broke away with a soft groan. "There's no one here to put on a show for."

"I'm not putting on a show." I slid a hand up

his chest to toy with a button on his gray thermal T-shirt. "I'm kissing you because I want to."

He pressed his forehead against mine, his eyes squeezed tight for a second. "But this is all fake."

I stopped fiddling with the button and rested my hand on his chest, right over his heart. "This attraction is real."

He took a step back. "Lust is cheap. This ain't that."

I took a deep breath. "I know."

He opened his mouth like he was going to argue, then snapped it shut and blinked at me. "Wait, what?"

"I know this is more than that," I said with a small smile. "All of it. I don't know what I'm supposed to do about that, but it seems like the bigger fake here would be acting like I don't have feelings for you."

He was quiet for a minute, his gaze moving over my face, studying me. Then he reached out and pulled me into another one of his ridiculous heady kisses, his hands on my cheeks, his lips proving how well they already knew mine.

"So then what?" he asked when he let me go.

"I don't know. We just enjoy these last two weeks and not worry about what happens next?"

But he was already shaking his head. "I'm not built that way, Grace."

"But—" I wasn't even sure what I would have said next, but it didn't matter, because the drop cloth was flung aside to reveal J.J. and his mom. Our conversation would have to wait.

I hadn't actually seen the costumes yet, and J.J.'s hat made me laugh. The seniors had decided to wear jeans, plain black T-shirts, and red bow ties, but as long as the hats were red and white stripes, each player could choose the style of his hat. J.J. had clearly stolen a floppy white sun hat from his mom and spray painted it with red stripes, topping off the look with aviator sunglasses.

DeShawn came in behind him in a Rastafarian-style slouchy beanie. "My Grams made me this. It's dope, huh?"

"It's dope," I agreed.

The first shift continued to trickle in, moms bossing the boys around to get the ingredients set up, every single mother stopping at some point to ask me the same question: "Is it true that Tabitha is coming tomorrow?"

My job had been the booth-building, not booth-*running,* so there wasn't anything here for me to do. I walked over to the store to see if my dad needed a hand and found Paige and Evie there.

"Hey," I said to Paige. "You guys are early for the parade."

"Someone," she jerked her head toward Evie, "couldn't wait. I told her we'd wait here so there would be no way for her to miss it."

I nodded at Evie. "Good play, Evie. Can't be too prepared for things like Santa."

"He really comes?" she asked. "On a sleigh?"

"He really does," I told her. Evie and all the other kids who still believed were the reason Christmas Town was so magical every year. Their excitement over Santa's VIP appearance infected all the adults. But even as an adult, watching everyone in Creekville come together and transform the town square into a fantasy for a day-and-a-half was its own kind of magic.

"Why does he come all the way to Creekville?" she asked. "He could go anywhere."

"That's a very good question," my dad said, emerging from the plumbing aisle. "Have you seen how athletes get ready for games by warming up?"

Evie looked confused.

"Like at Unc's games when the boys stretch and do jumping jacks before they start," Paige said.

Evie's face cleared. "So they can run faster."

"Exactly," my dad said. "It's like that for Santa too, but he likes to practice the Christmas spirit, filling up with it right before the big day. Do you know what the big day is, Evie?"

Her eyes shone. "Christmas Eve!"

"That's right. So every year, Santa checks a special map that shows him where he can find the most Christmas spirit, and every year, guess who has the most Christmas spirit in the whole world?"

Her eyes grew big. "Christmas Town?" she asked, her voice reverent.

"Christmas Town," he confirmed.

"Wow," she breathed.

For the first time since the mistletoe at Thanksgiving, the tingle of Christmas spirit swept over me. I'd been so worried about getting the store through the holiday retail season and lining up my job that I hadn't taken time to soak it in. Creekville was something special at Christmas, and whatever else may happen *after* Christmas, at least for right now, the magic was possible.

We helped my dad restock and take care of the two customers who came in until just before dusk when we heard the distant sound of the high school marching band getting ready.

"That's our signal to head over," my dad said.

Right on cue, my mom walked in, bundled for the cold. "Hey, girls. Paige, honey, I see y'all have warm jackets, but I brought a couple of extra blankets too. It'll be below forty when it gets full dark."

"Thank you, Mrs. Winters," Paige said.

"Call me Lisa."

"Thank you, Miss Lisa," Paige said.

"You're welcome, honey. Now, Evie, why don't you hold my hand so you can show me to the best place to watch this parade?"

Evie slipped her hand into my mom's. "How will I know if it's the best?"

"Are you a good picker?" my mom asked.

"Maybe?" Evie said doubtfully.

"Can you pick the best rocks in a pile? Or the best crayon in a box?" my mom asked.

"Yeah." Evie was firm on this.

"Then you can pick the best parade spot."

Evie gave a firm nod. "Let's go, everybody."

Then she grabbed my dad's hand and led my parents to the door, each of them looking happy to flank her while Paige and I followed behind.

Paige shook her head. "That child wraps everyone around her little finger."

"She's a sweet kid," I said.

"That's because she got more of Noah's temperament than mine." She offered me a wry smile and we headed out. I paused to lock the door then raced to catch up with them. I didn't want to miss a single second of the look on Evie's face as the parade passed.

She turned out to be the very best part. I'd always sort of loved the low-key Creekville parade, the local Brownie troop marching by in an organized line and flashing grins with missing teeth as they waved at the crowd followed by the Cub Scouts in mismatched uniforms, shirts untucked, darting here and there like a pile of puppies.

A horse farm outside of town always showed off a few of their beautiful Thoroughbreds with bells braided through their manes, and the town's only fire truck drove past with firefighters tossing candy canes to the crowds.

Whether it was the sheriff waving from his car, lights flashing without the sirens, or the high school cheer squad bouncing past in Santa hats, Evie loved every bit of it. And when the band struck up "Santa Claus is Coming to Town," she squealed like a teen at a Harry Styles concert. It was the cutest thing I'd ever seen.

"I'm afraid she's going to pass out when she sees the big man himself," I called to Paige over the marching band.

She grinned back. "I highly recommend having a five-year-old for Christmas. It's pretty much the best."

Sure enough, by the time Santa came into view on his sleigh, Evie was vibrating with excitement. I pulled out my phone and recorded it to show to Noah, who'd had to stay with the booth. He shouldn't miss his rosy-cheeked niece, her eyes wide with awe and happiness as Santa came into view.

It was Mr. Groggins in the costume, one of my favorite customers, because he always believed me when I recommended a part or tool for whatever project he was working on. He waved to the crowd and let out hearty "Ho ho hos" to the cheering masses.

My dad scooped Evie up and perched her on his shoulders for a better view, wincing when she grabbed his hair in her excitement, but all with the good-natured expression he'd probably worn when he used to do that for me. It choked me up for a second to see how easily he did it, hefting her into the air like his old self, and I paused to soak in the Christmas miracle of that too.

When Santa reached the edge of the town square, Mayor Derby was waiting for him in a pantsuit and a shiny top hat, which she lifted and waved. "Welcome to Santa Claus and all our Creekville friends and neighbors. Santa, would you do us the honor of opening Christmas Town?"

Then, like every mayor before her, she handed Santa a brass key as large as a trumpet, which he put into the Christmas Town switch. "On three, Mr. Claus," and then everyone counted with her. "One, two, three!"

Santa turned the key and Jeff Brume, the head of the parks department, quietly threw the real switch at the same time to send the streetlights, flood lights, and town Christmas tree lights all blazing to life.

Evie gasped, then clapped so hard that her palms must have stung even through her thick mittens, delight written all over her face.

"Wow," Paige said, looking over it all. "This is amazing."

The crowd surged forward to spread through Christmas Town, and I swept a glance at all the other booths to see how we measured up. Verdict: very well. Our Seuss booth was distinctive while still fitting in with the cozy Christmas vibe. It was easy to see what our theme was too, while with some of the others I'd have to wander closer to be able to tell. Ours was fun and eye-catching, and I thought it had a pretty good chance of winning the blue ribbon.

I was a civilian in all of this until Tabitha got here, so I contented myself to wander with my parents, watching my dad closely for signs of exhaustion since he'd worked all afternoon too. But he didn't flag at all, looking like he'd never been sick a day in his life.

We stopped at booths to sample Christmas pickles and peppermint fudge, admire handmade quilts and hand-thrown pottery, chat with friends and neighbors, and eat way too many cinnamon-toasted almonds.

When we got to the Cat in the Hat booth, my mom wrapped an arm around each of us as we took our spots at the back of a respectable line. "It looks good, Team Winters."

"That was mostly Grace," my dad said. "I'm going to miss you when you're gone, kid."

"I never knew there were so many ways to make red-striped hats," I said. "There's supposed to be two seniors and six other players on every shift, but it looks like they all wanted in on opening night action." In addition to several blue-haired Thing Ones and Twos, a half-dozen red-and-white hats bobbed around inside the booth. There was the sun hat and the Rastafarian beanie, but also a traditional stovepipe, a newsboy cap, and on Noah's head, an absurd cowboy hat, all striped.

Noah looked more keyed up than he regularly did, like he had when he was coaching in the district final and the team had insisted I come to see them play. Focused but happy, running the show but clearly getting a kick out of the kids.

He looked like I felt when I was at work. Not at Handy's. At my real job, working on an intricate engineering problem, running the math and testing the materials to find new solutions. It was Zen even in chaos, and I knew it when I saw it on his face. This is where he was meant to be and what he was meant to be doing.

It was an uncrossable bridge.

The night had grown even colder, the air heavy with the puffs of people's breaths. It had to be closer to thirty degrees than forty, and I shoved my hands deeper into my coat pockets and stepped out of the line.

"I think I'll skip the hand pie tonight. I'm sure I'll get my fill spending all afternoon in the booth with Tab tomorrow. I'm going to head home. It's been a long day."

"You sure, honey?" my mom asked.

"I'm sure." Once we got to the front of that

line, I was going to look like a Victorian London orphan with my nose pressed up against the glass of a bake shop, drooling over what I couldn't have.

But it had nothing to do with pie, and everything to do with Noah.

CHAPTER TWENTY-FOUR
NOAH

Everything about this moment should have been perfect. The booth was doing well, people were complimenting the design and the food, and Dr. Boone had walked past and given a pleased wave.

The boys were working hard and selling pies like crazy, cracking jokes and being their usual dumb selves, one of my favorite parts of my job.

And it *was* perfect when I looked up and spotted Grace in line with her parents.

But a few minutes later, she slipped out, and everything was less fun.

Less warm. Less entertaining. Less magic.

What was I supposed to do about that?

CHAPTER TWENTY-FIVE
GRACE

"Honey, I'm home!"

It was Tabitha, shouting from the front door.

"Tabitha!" My mom jumped up and ran to greet her prodigal eldest daughter.

Well, not prodigal in the sense that Tabitha had been frittering away her life. She was wildly successful by any measure, and I didn't begrudge her that. I just wanted to be able to say the same thing. Soon. I'd be able to say it soon.

"Hey, sis," I said, claiming my hug after my mom finally let her go. "Not to rush you, but we have to get over to Christmas Town in an hour. We've been advertising it in all the local Facebook groups, and we're expecting a big old surge of visitors during your shift."

"No problem," she said. "Let me go put my things up in my room, and then we can run over there."

"Grace, give her two seconds to rest," my mom complained.

"It's fine, Mom." Tabitha was already heading for the stairs and her old room. "I travel all the time. It's better if I stay busy all day. Then I don't have any time to realize I'm tired until I sit down at night."

"Okay," Mom said, her voice reluctant. "But we've hardly had time to catch up."

"We'll have all night plus the next two days," Tabitha reassured her. "And we talk on the phone almost every day anyway. I'm not sure I even have anything new to report."

She disappeared up the stairs and I felt my mom's eyes on me. I turned to meet her slightly accusatory stare. "What, Mom?"

"You hijacked her."

"For a good cause. I'll have her back by seven. I'm going to go get changed." I escaped up to my apartment and switched into black leggings and a black sweater, fastened one of my dad's church bowties around my neck, then picked up the hat one of the moms had made for me. She'd made one for Tabitha too, cute red-striped sun visors. I made my ponytail up higher than usual to give it a more Seuss-ish touch, then went back to meet Tabitha and hand off her visor.

"Cute," she said. "Look what I got the wardrobe girl at the studio to make." She unfurled an apron that looked like the Cat in the Hat's body.

"That's going to be stupid cute on you," I said.

"Right? Let's go do this. Mom, you'll bring Dad over after the store closes?"

"We'll be there," she said.

As we climbed into my car, Tabitha asked, "So do I get to meet the boyfriend?"

I sighed as I pulled my door shut. "Fake boy-friend."

"Small-town. Hot guy. Cute girl. Christmas time. Fake dating. Wait. Are you *living* a Hall-mark Christmas movie? Should I have brought popcorn for this?"

"I'm definitely living the dumbest version of my life right now," I grumbled.

"I can't wait to watch you and fake boyfriend," she said, grinning. "This will be the second most entertaining public appearance I've ever done."

"What was the first?"

"Snoop Dogg and I did a cooking segment on 'Good Morning America,' and he messed up cracking an egg then cursed. It was bleeped on the West coast, but they couldn't do it fast enough on the East coast, so they got that earful live."

"I saw that one. Woke me up better than coffee. But also, there will be no show today. Noah and I are cool. Nothing to see. Move along."

We parked at the store and popped in so Tabitha could say hi to my dad, who smothered her with a giant hug.

As we walked over to the booths, my stomach flipped. And not even because it already had a long line of people waiting for Tabitha. My stomach did this every time I was going to see Noah.

People started calling Tab's name the second

we crossed into the town square, and it took nearly fifteen minutes to navigate all the people wanting to say hello. She proved what a pro she had become when people asked for selfies, telling them to come get a hand pie and she'd do selfies then.

"Way to push the pies," I said.

"That's what I'm here for, right?" she asked, smiling as she waved to her fourth grade teacher. "And also to spy on you and Noah."

"There's nothing to spy on," I said.

"I get to decide that."

I rolled my eyes, and she laughed as we slipped in through the back of the booth.

The two moms on shift immediately cooed over her. Noah turned from the cash register to shoot me a grin. The five boys working all called out some version of, "What's up, Miss Grace!" They gave Tabitha curious glances, but I had no doubt Noah would make sure each one of them thanked her personally before their shift ended.

"How's it going?" I asked, threading through the hustling boys to join Noah at the cash register.

"A little slow, but only because most of this line has been standing here waiting to order until Tabitha gets here. Should get crazy now."

"How can I help?"

"Just stick with your sister and make sure she's

happy. We've got the cooking down, I think."

Tabitha wanted to start by checking their setup and testing their hand pies. I thought DeShawn might split his face grinning when she pronounced his football-shaped hand pie to be "super tasty."

"I'm going to make a slight recommendation," she said. "I think you need to add some grated sharp cheddar to each one. Sounds nuts, but I promise it will work." She pointed to one of the boys. "Can you run over to the market and get every bag of shredded cheddar they have? Let them know Tabitha Winters will stop by later to pay for it."

"Yes, ma'am," he said, and darted out of the booth to go get the cheese.

"Cheddar? Now I'm curious," Noah said. "Nice to meet you, by the way."

I cleared my throat. I would have gotten to the introduction. Eventually. "Noah, this is my sister, Tabitha. Tabitha, this is—"

"Your boyfriend, Noah. Nice to meet you. I've heard so much about you."

She would pay for that. She knew I couldn't correct her with the team listening. Noah's eyebrow arched up for a split second before he smiled and went back to ringing up orders.

Hot, she mouthed at me.

I grabbed her arm and hauled her over to the order window next to Noah, which was not

306

where I wanted to leave her, but it was where she needed to be for her adoring fans. "Behave," I told both of them. They exchanged glances that were a full conversation all by themselves. I was doomed.

"You know what," I said, taking Tabitha's arm again. "Never mind. It'll work better if you stand outside the booth, ready to take pictures with people when they get their orders."

"Scared?" Tabitha taunted, and Noah grinned like an idiot.

"You only think this is funny because you're also an older sibling," I complained.

"I think it's funny because it's funny," he said. "You trying to keep your sister from your boyfriend is premium comedy."

Another stomach swoop at hearing him refer to himself as my boyfriend. Didn't matter that my brain knew it was a show. My stomach would do what it wanted.

I half-dragged Tabitha out of the booth. The people in line began waving as soon as she appeared. I positioned her in front of the booth for the best backdrop, then turned to the line. "When you get your order, you can stand next to Tabitha for a picture. Ask a friend in line to take it for you. She says these hand pies will be even better with cheddar, so you can wait for the cheese to arrive in about fifteen minutes, or you can get a no-cheddar hand pie now. If you want to wait, keep shuffling backward in line until the no-cheese people are up front."

This set off a bunch of dad jokes about "I'm cheesy, moving back" until the line reshuffled and the orders began flying. Within a few minutes, the picture madness had begun.

And by madness, I meant that everyone was nice and cheerful like people in Creekville always are. Tabitha kept the picture line moving while still making each person feel like they'd gotten special attention. Did we even share the same gene pool? She was six inches taller than me, extroverted, and happy working a crowd. I'd rather hide my short self inside the booth and work on the logistics, so after a few minutes, I did, stationing myself at the inside corner nearest her in case she needed me. Then I took over pouring and capping the apple cider cups since the boys kept splashing it everywhere.

Tabitha had been right about the cheddar, of course, and the line grew even longer as people who had bought hand pies last night lined up to try the new version and check out the hometown celebrity.

About an hour into it, a new shift of boys came in, and it stalled the line until we got them all situated. Noah put Grant in charge of the register since he worked as a cashier at the market part-time, then came over to join me serving cider.

"Heads up," he said. "Dr. Boone is about halfway back in line."

I spotted her with her husband. "Show time?"

He nodded. "Yeah. Sorry about that."

I wasn't because it meant he touched me more, and when I needed to get past him for more cups, I put my hands around his waist and moved him out of the way instead of asking politely, my fingers brushing against his taut abs. When he wanted to hand a customer some cider, he stood right behind me, his chest against my back, curving his arm around me to hand it to them instead of waiting for me to move.

I was aware of every breath. I could feel each of his looks like a touch. I could smell his unique scent even beneath the cinnamon and apple.

It was torture. Delicious torture. But torture.

And I didn't want it to end.

Dr. Boone ordered her hand pies and cider and stopped to chat with us at the window while she waited for the food. "Looks good," she told Noah. "I'm impressed, coach."

"Thanks." I could feel him fighting to play it cool. "We're on track for almost twenty-five percent more revenue than last year based on ASB's records."

She gave him a wide smile. "I might have underestimated you. We'll have to talk after winter break."

Noah nodded and said, "Sure thing," laid

back as usual, but he'd grabbed the back of my shirt and was holding on tight, like it would somehow keep the coaching opportunity in his grasp.

Dr. Boone stopped for her picture with Tabitha, who greeted her warmly. "Noah is doing a fantastic job raising money for football, but I'd like to talk to you about making another donation to the school. Specifically, to the home ec program. That's where I got my start."

"That sounds excellent, Miss Winters." Dr. Boone was all smiles.

"Tabitha," my sister corrected her. "And I'll have my assistant reach out in the new year. With hires like Coach Redmond, you clearly have an eye for talent and good program management, so I have no doubt my donation will be well-spent."

I elbowed Noah, and when Dr. Boone got her picture and moved on, Tabitha winked at him and greeted the next customer.

"She just did me a huge solid," Noah said. "Your family is the best."

"Except for when they're being the worst," I said, but there was no bite to it. They drove me batty, but there was no doubt they were pretty great.

"If that's your idea of 'the worst,' I'll trade you Tabitha for Paige who likes to tell me at least three times a week that I'm an idiot. Except I don't want to trade away Evie, so never mind. You have to keep your sister."

"Guess I can deal with that." I smiled as I watched her greet yet another customer but noticed that she gave a slight shiver first. "She's getting cold because the sun is setting. Let's move her in here where it's warmer."

I leaned out of the window and called her in while Noah relocated the cider setup so she could lean through the window for pictures with fans. It would still be a cute picture with her framed in the window.

Even though Dr. Boone had gone, it was like she'd flipped some switch between Noah and me, and we couldn't turn off the flirting. Not that I wanted to. I loved the feel of his hand at the small of my back when he needed to get past me for more napkins. And I might not ever get tired of him reaching around me almost in a hug to hand off cider to a customer at the window.

"Is this your go-to move?" I asked in a low voice the next time he did it, making sure I spoke close enough to his ear that he could feel my breath against his skin.

"Right now it is," he murmured back. "It's currently my favorite move in the whole world."

There was a snort from Tabitha, and I glanced at her to find her eyeing us with the look of someone who was watching a comedy.

I stepped out of the circle of Noah's arms

and busied myself with securing the lids on the cider cups. When Noah zoomed to the back of the booth a few minutes later in search of extra nutmeg, Tabitha leaned over to whisper loudly, "You are an idiot, and you need to just go for that. If what's going on between you is fake, then I'm the pope."

We weren't even Catholic.

But her words chased themselves in my mind. *You need to just go for that.*

I'd been looking at this whole thing like an engineering problem, assessing the available parts and determining I had incompatible pieces, so there was no point in assembling them. But the whole point of engineering was to find efficient, creative solutions to problems. Noah and I fit; there had to be a way to make us work.

I couldn't stop thinking about it for the rest of the night, pieces of a plan coming together. I thought about all the possible obstacles, and when each of them led to us breaking up after Christmas, I shoved them aside, focusing instead on all the possible solutions.

When my parents stopped by at eight o'clock for their hand pie desserts, Tabitha yawned, and I ordered her home, cutting off the line to see her. It took another twenty minutes to get the remaining people through, then I sent her home with my parents.

We served another thirty pies before Christmas Town closed for good, and we began the cleanup. Noah had ordered the whole team to help, so what could have been a very long process only took a half-hour. It still felt like forever as I waited for the last player and his dad to drive off with the booth secured in their truck bed, ready to be reused for the elementary school spring fair in a few months.

"Can I walk you to your car?" Noah asked.

"Sure." Did I sound as nervous as I suddenly felt? The words I'd been waiting to spew all night were fighting to get out, and I wanted him to say yes to them. A big, fat yes to my big, fat crazy idea.

"I like your sister," he said. "I didn't get how big of a deal she is until I saw every female in Creekville who cooks lined up to meet her and gush over her."

"She's pretty all right," I said. "I definitely lucked out compared to, say, Paige."

"Oof." He clutched at his heart, pretending to stagger.

"Ugh, fine. You seem like you're an okay brother."

We fell quiet then and walked that way for another block until we reached the turn to get to my car.

"Thank you again for helping," he said, as we got closer to the parking spaces behind the store.

"There's no way I could have pulled this off without you, and I know it."

We stopped beside my driver's side door.

"Noah?"

"Yeah?"

This was it. The big, fat ask. "Come to Charleston."

His eyes widened in surprise. "Like a visit? When?"

I fought prickles of embarrassment that he hadn't caught on to what I meant right away. "No, not like a visit. Like, to live."

He straightened and went still. "Wait, what?"

It was not the sweep-me-into-his-arms-and-whisper-yes moment I'd imagined. "I mean after the school year. Charleston has a big school system and plenty of smaller suburban ones around it. There's bound to be a job for you out there."

"I have a job. Here." He sounded confused more than anything.

"I know this feels like a one-eighty, but it's not. Not really. I've been thinking about what you said. That we work."

"We don't just work, Grace," he said, his voice soft. "I've never had anything like this with someone else, not even my ex-fiancée. Have you?"

"Had something like this with your ex-fiancée? No."

314

"Grace." It was a low warning growl.

"Okay, no. I haven't. You've convinced me that we should take a chance on us. I can see it. Exploring the city, game nights for two until we make more friends, hanging out, going out. Making out," I said with a grin. He shook his head but smiled. "So come to Charleston. With me." I smiled up at him, but the edges wobbled because he was still not swooning, still not looking thunderstruck with delight at the spontaneity of the offer. He shoved his hand through his hair. "This doesn't make sense."

"What doesn't? Us?" My stomach clenched, and it wasn't because of that third hand pie I should have skipped.

"No, we make perfect sense. Our geography doesn't."

"You're right, and you were also right that we shouldn't let it get in the way. My job isn't portable. Aerospace only has a few main centers, but you can get a teaching job anywhere. I bet if you Googled right now, you'd find a dozen you're qualified for down there."

"Grace . . ."

His tone was a warning that he was about to say something I didn't want to hear.

"I know you're worried about leaving Paige, so don't. She and Evie should come. I get that they're a part of your life. I love that about you." His eyes sharpened and my chest tightened at how close those words were to "I love you," something I'd never said to a guy before. I hurried past the moment. "There's a million more opportunities for Paige out there too. More school choices, more housing choices, more daycare choices. And she can find a better-paying job, too."

"That might all be true, but Evie needs more stability than that." His voice was quiet.

"She'd still have you and Paige." My butterflies were gone, leaving behind a jumpy tangle of knots tied from disappointment and rejection because I knew his answer.

I wanted him. And if this had only been about lust, that would be one thing. But I wanted him in all the ways that count even more. I wanted to see him every day, to do boring and ordinary things together but make each other laugh while we did them. I wanted to have him to look forward to at the end of a long day, and I wanted to hear stories about his crazy students or his sometimes crazier colleagues.

"You're asking me to choose between you and my family."

"No, I'm not. I'm saying I'll take all of you. You, Paige, and Evie. Maybe even especially Evie, and you other two can tag along."

But he didn't smile. "It's not just us. She thrives in routines. Paige isn't going to want to yank her out of kindergarten and her daycare."

"Would you at least talk to Paige about it?" It was an embarrassing, last-ditch plea. Right now, most of all I wanted him to be the guy who wanted me enough not to make me beg. To not have to be talked into this. To be willing to make sacrifices instead of expecting me to give up a career I couldn't have here just to stay with him.

He slowly shook his head.

I opened my car door and stood staring at the steering wheel without seeing it, sick with myself for even asking. I'd wanted to make it work so badly that I'd engaged in magical thinking to convince myself that these were differences we could solve.

He grabbed the top of the door, his hands closing over mine to hold me in place. "Grace. If this was just about Paige, I would ask her. But it's not, and I can't. Please don't ask me to choose."

I wanted to dive into the safety of the car and drive off, leaving this whole scene behind me. But his eyes were soft, pleading for understanding, and I did. I did understand. Instead, I picked up one of his hands, and pressed a kiss against his knuckles. "It's okay, Noah." I let go of his hand and mustered a last wobbly smile. "If we're being real, you've chosen, and I won't make you say your choice out loud again."

I eased into the driver's seat and pulled the door closed as Noah stepped back. Then I lowered the window and smiled at him. "Good job tonight. I think Dr. Boone will also make the right choice. Merry Christmas."

I rolled my window up to cut off the saddest Merry Christmas I'd ever heard in return and drove toward home.

CHAPTER TWENTY-SIX
NOAH

It was late enough when I got home that I knew Evie would be asleep and Paige wouldn't be dropping in.

I almost never minded when she did, but tonight I needed time and space to think.

I was in a relationship. With Grace. I'd known it for a while. Grace knew it too.

We hung out, worked together, discussed life problems and relationships, joked around, spent Thanksgiving with each other, kissed. Like, mind-blowing kisses. I loved her work ethic, her family, her sense of humor, her brain. I'd never had more fun doing nothing with someone than I did with Grace.

So how could everything be so right between us, and it still not work out?

Because . . .

Because I still hadn't told Grace the whole truth. There was more to it than not wanting to leave Paige and Evie or uproot them.

I'd been here before with Lauren. Lauren had needed me to be more and want more than I did. I wasn't the guy who needed to climb a career ladder for the prestige of it. I loved what I did, and Lauren had seen my passion for teaching as lack of ambition.

I loved teaching. I wanted to be a principal eventually. Principals made a comfortable income with good benefits. The downside being, of course, that the job politics were some of the toughest around. But I loved kids. And I'd be walking into administration someday with my eyes wide open, ready to take on the challenge of transforming a school.

The fact that Grace could argue in one breath about how essential her job was to her happiness and then try to convince me to "just do mine anywhere" was the ultimate irony. She didn't understand how I felt about my work any more than Lauren had. It took time and tenure to build the relationships and roots that would lead to administration jobs down the road. If I kept *literally* moving down the road, I couldn't do that.

Grace wasn't Lauren. I knew that. But this similarity was too strong for me to ignore just because my feelings for her were strong too.

I flopped on my couch and stared at the ceiling. Not just strong. Damn near overwhelming. And not just wanting her, although that nearly knocked me flat every time I was around her. It was everything about her: the fact that she'd dropped everything to come home for her family even though she loved her career, her problem-solving mind, her can-do attitude. The way she took life seriously without taking herself seriously.

Everything about her was perfect except her future address.

I couldn't trade pieces of myself for her. But most of all, I couldn't trade Evie and Paige for her, no matter how badly I wanted her.

And I wanted her badly.

I stared at the ceiling as if the dull white surface could give me an answer.

It didn't.

"Noah?"

I blinked awake. I'd fallen asleep on my couch in my clothes. I felt gross, and Paige was smiling down at me.

"Wake up," she said. "And shower. You stink. Text me when you're done."

I pushed up to a sitting position. "What time is it?"

"Eight o'clock. A little after. I'll start some coffee for you. Go shower."

"Is something wrong?"

"No, but I need to talk to you."

I nodded and rose to head for the shower. "See you in a few."

I emerged fifteen minutes later, showered, shaved, and still groggy, but she had coffee ready to pour as promised. I let myself get half of it down so the caffeine could do its work before I texted her.

She popped through my door thirty seconds later.

"Where's Evie?" I asked when she didn't follow.

"Watching The Grinch."

"It doesn't freak her out?"

"No. She says Grinchy is sad and nice."

"Smart girl. I got her a few more things from Santa. Is she ready for tonight?"

"Noah . . ."

"I wanted to. I promise you can eat all the cookies if you don't lecture me about spoiling her."

She smiled and shook her head. "It's Christmas Eve, so I'll let it go."

"It's a Christmas miracle."

"We still need to talk."

I took a sip of my coffee, stalling. Nothing good ever followed that phrase. I wasn't a particularly anxious person, but I felt knots forming in my stomach.

"I was talking to Mike the other day."

"Mike?"

"Mr. Winters."

Oh, right. I forgot sometimes that parent-aged adults had first names.

"Anyway," she continued, "he said he was worried that you and Grace are going to break up. Are you?"

I guessed the show we'd put on for her mom

had done its job of planting that seed. "No. Because we're not together, which he knows."

"Aren't you?"

"You know the situation."

"I do. The question is whether you two do. You get that whatever is going on between you isn't fake, and everyone else can see it, plain as day?"

I didn't answer.

"That's what I thought," she said. "So when is she leaving?"

"Right after New Year's. But she's not telling her parents until after Christmas because she wants them to have a stress-free holiday."

"That's sweet. So where are you moving?"

I wrinkled my forehead. "Nowhere."

"That can't be right. Where is Grace going?"

"Charleston. Boeing."

She whipped out her phone. "That's only a seven-hour drive. Not bad. And I hear Charleston is a cool town."

I shrugged.

"You'll like living there," she pressed.

"Paige. I'm not moving there."

"Sure, you are."

"No, I'm not."

"Why not?" The words sprang out of her, sharp, like she'd snapped a trap closed.

"My life is here."

"Define 'life.' It needs to include the name of the woman you've fallen head-over-heels for or it's an invalid answer." I said nothing. "That's what I thought. So you're moving to Charleston."

I was getting tired of this loop. "Paige."

"Why. Not." It came out as a challenge, not a question.

"Are *you* moving to Charleston?" I asked.

"No."

I shrugged. She had her answer.

She grabbed my wrist and pulled me over to the couch, pushing me until I sat down. Then she sat on the coffee table facing me. "Noah, listen to me. You are the best brother in the world. It's not even close. But Evie and I aren't your responsibility."

I didn't argue because it would only insult her, but the fact remained: they were. She hadn't seen herself the day she showed up at my door, so skinny I barely recognized her, her belly already showing Evie, dark circles under her eyes. There was no one else to be responsible for her. And I hadn't regretted opening the door wide and taking her in for a single second.

She grabbed my shoulders and made me meet her eyes. "Evie and I are *my* responsibility. I can't even begin to thank you for everything you've done for me, and I'll definitely never be able to repay it."

I waved my hand, a sharp, impatient movement. "You don't need to thank me."

"I do. Saving me wasn't your job, and you did

it anyway. But Noah . . ." She paused for a deep breath and sat back. "You're fired."

Fired? "What does that even mean?"

"It means I'm not your job. But I'm here to offer you an early Christmas gift in the form of an amazing severance package."

This was only getting more confusing. "What are you talking about?"

"If you knew that Evie and I would be fine without you—thriving and happy—and that we'd come see you once a quarter plus however often you wanted to come back here, would you feel okay about moving to Charleston?"

I started to answer, but she held up her hand. "No. Don't speak. *Really* think about that. Visualize it. Evie and I, stable, well-adjusted, doing well. And while you think about it, I'm going to grab your present. Be right back."

She darted out of the apartment, and I sat back against the sofa, trying to process the conversation. It was hard to imagine her in a secure enough position to ever be okay with leaving, but I tried. I tried to picture it.

Spending Saturday mornings with Grace trying new running trails or cafes, being tourists, doing nothing, doing . . . everything.

For a second, everything in me felt lighter.

Until I realized how hard it was to picture Paige with the kind of stability it would take for me to have that future with Grace. The split second of hope turned heavy. It felt a hundred times worse than the close loss the Bulldogs had suffered in the regional finals.

A million times worse.

Not even in the same universe kind of disappointment.

Paige walked back in with a box, the kind department stores used to wrap shirts. How would a shirt help anything right now?

"Open it," she said. "It's the best thing I've ever gotten you."

"Better than the RC car when I was eight?"

"Way better, because I earned this gift for you myself."

I unwrapped it, determined to like the shirt no matter how "not me" it was—her crusade to spruce up my style never ended. I braced myself to exclaim over an ugly designer shirt.

Instead, when I parted the tissue paper, I found a stack of papers. "What's this?"

"For Christmas, I got you your life back."

I picked up the top sheet. It was job paperwork. A W-4 and I-9, all filled out with her name and listing Handy Hardware as the employer. I shot her a confused look.

"Look at the position."

I scanned it until I found the right line. "Position: Manager."

"Mike is promoting me. He says I can open every morning, Monday through Friday, and if I take half hour lunches, I can pick Evie up by four-thirty. He says it's so busy, he's losing money by not having another full-time employee." Her eyes shone with excitement, and I didn't have the heart to point out that even that wouldn't be enough for her to make it on her own. "He and Lisa are going to lease me the apartment at their house for the cost of utilities, so I can save money and pay for online school at night. I'm going to major in business."

Whoa. That was huge, and I loved it for her. But it didn't solve everything. "But Evie will have to change schools."

She waved her hand. "She doesn't like her teacher anyway. We checked out Creekville Elementary, and all she needed to see was that they have more swings at their playground, and she was sold. Lisa helped me find this amazing home daycare for a hundred dollars less than the one Evie's in now, and I won't need evening babysitting anymore."

"But your car—"

"Is junk, yes." She grinned like she'd been waiting for every objection. "But we're walking distance from the store if it breaks down, and I've been saving the money from my shifts at Handy's. One of our regular customers owns the auto shop, and he came in when I was trying to start my Chevy the other day. Said he had a good deal for me on an older Honda. It's not too cute, but he says it runs great, and he'll hold on to it for me until I can pay cash. With this raise plus the drop in rent and daycare, it'll only take me two months. If my dumb car breaks down during that time, I can handle it. Plus, you'll still be around for a while. You can't move to Charleston until the school year ends, right?"

"Right." I parroted it, trying to absorb everything she was telling me, and something like hope was flickering to life inside of me.

"So you'll go? Because here's the other thing, Noah." She reached into the box and pulled more papers. "I did some research and found all the school districts in and around Charleston. There are six that are all pretty close, and I found a ton of open positions. Between your credential to teach science and your PE experience, you'll be able to find a job easily. They all use the same portal for applications, so I created an account for you and started applications at the ones that looked good. It won't take much to finish them. I printed them out and highlighted the parts I didn't know. And I called Mr. Beaman—"

"Our old principal?"

"Yes. I wanted to know how school hiring goes, and here's more good news: he said even more jobs open up in the spring when teachers get serious about retiring. You'll have no problem."

I took a deep breath, trying to sort through my feelings. "Okay, but—"

"Wait," she said. "Before you say anything, just think. Close your eyes and imagine yourself in Charleston, teaching, coaching, and seeing Grace as much as you want."

There was no such thing. I could never get enough of Grace.

"Close your eyes," she demanded. I snapped them closed. "Picture it. Evie is happy at her new school. She's in daycare less than two hours a day and with me the rest of the time in a snug little apartment. I have good hours, steady pay, and time to do my schooling. We're happy, Lisa has introduced us to all kinds of young moms and kids at church and school, and we're thriving. And you and Grace are just as happy, going wherever this takes you."

I could picture it. I'd imagined all of that happening here in Creekville, but I could imagine it happening in Charleston as Paige painted the picture. But then I snapped my eyes open.

"And if it doesn't work out? Then I've moved my whole life to Charleston, left behind my job, and for what?"

She leaned forward to take my knees again. "Noah. Come on. Do you really think if you and Grace commit to making this work that by the time you've done the long-distance thing for six months, you won't both be dead certain about you moving there?"

"Grace needs some say in this too." I still wasn't sure the life I wanted for myself would be enough for a woman whose mother had raised her with high ambitions.

"Is she going to say no?" Her inflection said she already knew the answer. "Because watching you fake date Grace is the realest thing I've ever seen."

"She already asked me to move to Charleston," I said, a smile tugging at my lips, more hope exploding inside of me even as I tried to keep the safety brake on.

"Then what the heck are you waiting for?" Paige said with a whoop. "Go get your woman!"

I gave her a sheepish smile. "She may not be up for that. I've possibly definitely made it clear that I expected her to make all the compromises here."

"I work a twelve-step program," she told me. "And we are expert apologizers. I got you, Noah. Let's figure this out."

"Paige?"

"Yeah?"

"You are a total pain, but I love you."

"I love you too, but you'd best be saying that to her. And don't even try to deny it because I know it's true."

It was. It was as true as the laws of physics, the inevitability of Christmas, and the blue of Grace's eyes.

Paige turned over one of the applications to its blank side and plucked a pencil from the cup on my counter.

"All right, big brother. Let's make a plan."

CHAPTER TWENTY-SEVEN
GRACE

Tabitha barreled into my apartment. "We're on a mission, sis."

I looked up from the laptop. "We are?"

"Yes. We need to go pick up Mom's Christmas present."

I turned back to my laptop. "I already got her one."

"Like what? A sweater?"

I glared at her. "She likes sweaters."

She snorted. "Trust me, what we're about to go get for her will make her exceedingly happy and make our lives a little easier for the next twelve to sixteen years."

"We're getting her a giant bottle of tranquilizers?"

"Something better than a drug. Come on. What could you possibly be doing right now that's more important than saving Christmas?"

I didn't have the heart to tell her that for some of us—okay, me—Christmas couldn't be salvaged. It was only the morning of Christmas Eve, and it was already the worst Christmas ever. Which was a bummer since I'd thought that about last Christmas when my dad had been so frail that he'd slept most of the day. This was supposed to be the Christmas to celebrate his return to health.

Instead, I was reading reviews for gyms and restaurants in Charleston to distract myself from how much I would miss Noah when I left. Maybe I could keep myself busy enough to fill up the space he'd taken, and I wouldn't notice how much it hurt. Not that it helped at all so far.

I closed the laptop and got up. "What kind of mission is this? How do I need to dress?"

"You're perfect as is. Drive out to Roanoke. I'll tell you what we're doing on the way."

Roanoke was an hour away. "Tabitha . . ."

"Trust me," she said, grinning. "If I don't have you convinced within five minutes of getting on the road, you can turn around and drive us back home."

I shook my head. "You're such a weirdo. Let's go."

I grabbed my car keys and as we got into the car, she showed me a picture on her cell phone of the cutest puppy I'd ever seen in my life. It was a gray bundle of curls with big, black velvet eyes. "Gimme it."

"Can't. Meet Mom's new child," she said. "Now drive while I explain."

Apparently, Roanoke was the home of Misty Mountaintop, a standard poodle who had won the Westminster Dog Show four years before. The tiny moppet Tabitha had shown me was one of Misty's most recent litter.

"I've been thinking about this ever since I did a celebrity catering gig in the Hamptons this summer. The hostess had a bat infestation in her belfry, and she was totally nuts for her dog. She raises Pomeranians for show, and she built them their own mini-house on her estate. I had this lightbulb moment while I watched her hand feed them Wagyu beef that cost a hundred dollars a pound."

"You're joking."

"I wish. You have no idea how these rich people live."

"Miss Lily isn't like that." The Greenes were the richest people in two counties.

"Miss Lily is salt of the earth," Tabitha said. "Hamptons people are not. I mean, most of them are okay. But then you get people like Pomeranian Lady, and you understand where the stereotypes come from."

"So that's related to us picking up a poodle . . . how? Because Mom isn't hand feeding anyone hundred-dollar beef, much less a dog."

Tabitha smiled. "She'll do her own version of it. Best dog food. Best groomers. Softest dog bed. Obsessively watch dog obedience videos. Can't you see it?"

"She's never wanted a dog."

"Because she's allergic and because she was

too busy with us. But I did some research and poodles are hypoallergenic. They're also the smartest breed, and it will give her something to pour all her focus into. I put a deposit down on a pup from Misty's next litter back in October when I heard the drug trial worked. I bought Mom a compilation DVD of poodle competitions from the AKC and a few books on dog training. So you're going to hide Poodle Pup at your place until tomorrow morning. What do you think?"

I stared in the opposite direction for a few moments to collect myself, looking as far away from her as I could while still keeping my eyes on the road.

"Grace?" She sounded anxious.

"You did this for me, didn't you?"

A long pause. Then, softly, "Yeah. I knew it would make her happy, and you could leave without worrying."

"Thank you." I couldn't say much more or my voice would have thickened with tears.

"Of course," she said. "It's the least I could do."

"No," I said. "It's not. It's incredibly thoughtful, and I'm sorry I spent even a second resenting you."

"It's okay," she said. "I get it. If I could do my show here, I would. But an entire crew depends on its success to earn their living, and I have to live in a major media market so I can do the promotions and networking that keep my audience interested. I wish I could have been here more to help, but I'm so glad you were. It was the only reason I didn't spend the last year plus in a blind panic about Dad's diagnosis."

I sniffed, the tears coming closer, but I blinked rapidly until I banished them. "But he's good now. Perfect, even."

"It makes me so happy," she said. "He's back."

"He's back."

We drove in quiet for a while, soaking in the goodness of it.

After a while, I smiled over at her. "So tell me about the show. What's it like shooting it?"

"No."

I threw her a startled glance. "No?"

"Yeah. No. I don't want to talk about the show. I want to talk about you and Noah. What's going on there?"

"Tab."

"You're stuck with me for another forty-five minutes, and I refuse to talk about anything else until we cover this ground."

I ignored her and stabbed on the radio. Christmas music filled the car. "Feliz Navidad," I sang with Jose Feliciano. "FELIZ NAVIDAD PROSPERO AÑO Y FELICIDAD." I shout-sang with Señor Feliciano for two more minutes.

The next song was Mariah Carey. When she got to the part about wanting only one thing for

Christmas, Tabitha turned it off and pronounced, "Noah."

"You want Noah for Christmas? You've only spent one afternoon with him, but I can see if he'd be into it."

She punched my arm. "All *you* want for Christmas is Noah. Don't try to deny it."

I reached for the radio again, but she batted my hand away.

"Just admit you like him."

"That's not headline news, Tab. Of course I like him."

"A lot?" she pressed.

I nodded.

"How much?"

I shrugged. "I don't really have the words."

"Wow." She fell quiet, and I could feel her eyes on me. I ignored her and kept my eyes on the road. "Grace."

"What."

"Is the word 'love'?"

The tears sprang to my eyes before I could stop them this time.

"Oh, Grace." Her voice was full of understanding and compassion that I couldn't take right now, or I'd come undone completely.

"Yeah, that's the word." Her sympathy was warranted.

"So tell him."

I drew a deep breath to steady my voice. "I

asked him to move to Charleston. He said no, and I get it. My life is there, and his is here. If I moved back permanently, I'd resent him over the long run, and I won't do the same to him."

"Also, Mom would kill you."

"Also that." I watched the road for a bit. "Paige and Evie need him. It sucks, but the situation is what it is."

"What does that even mean? 'It is what it is.' I never understood that phrase."

"It means this was shaping up to be another crappy Christmas, but picking up a puppy makes it feel better. It means I'm going to find my Christmas spirit by tomorrow. Maybe Santa will leave it under the tree for me. Then I'll give Mom enough time to fall in love with Coal and then I can break the news that I'm leaving in a few days." I sighed. "Why does she push me so hard to leave when she's going to bawl like a baby when I do?"

"Hold on, back up," she said. "Cole? Like your eighth-grade boyfriend?"

"No, c-o-a-l, like what Santa leaves under the tree at Christmas. What else are you going to call a charcoal gray dog you give on Christmas Day?"

"Ha, ha," she said.

She dropped the subject of Noah and entertained me with stories from her set until we reached the breeder's where we were immediately smitten by the poodle puppy Tabitha would *not* let me call

Coal. He preoccupied us all the way home as he sat in her lap, and she cooed over every single puppy snuffle and blink.

I kept watch while she snuck him up to my place. Then I played with him for the rest of the afternoon. When my mom texted for me to come down for our Christmas Eve tradition of watching *Holiday Inn* and drinking cocoa with homemade marshmallows, I pled a headache so I could stay with the puppy in case he started crying and gave himself away before morning.

Dad came to investigate and grinned when he saw Tabitha's gift, leaving with a promise to run interference for me with my mom.

Puppy and I curled up and watched *The Holiday*. Or rather, I lay on the sofa with my laptop, and he curled up on my chest.

I could totally see the value of an emotional support animal. Maybe I should get a dog but from the pound. Something scruffy and loyal, who wanted to live with me in Charleston or wherever I might go, no matter what, because dogs were better than humans.

Puppy didn't convince me that I didn't actually want Noah. But his snuggles helped more than chocolate did. And if I went to bed sadder on Christmas Eve than I ever had, at least I had the reminder that good things like puppies still existed in the world, and maybe one day, I wouldn't feel a giant hole where Noah should be.

• • •

"What in the world?"

Normally, we ate breakfast together first on Christmas morning. My parents had taught us since we were little that presents were the least important part of the day, and that we should always start it by spending time together first. It had been torturous as a kid, eating a big breakfast while a pile of brightly wrapped presents from Santa waited for us. As an adult, I loved it.

But Tabitha and I had switched it up this year, and now my mom was sitting in her favorite armchair, looking baffled that we wouldn't let her follow her nose to the kitchen where Tabitha had been cooking up something delicious-smelling since early this morning.

"Sorry, Mom, but this present can't wait," Tabitha explained. "Grace?"

I went to the garage door and brought in the box I'd set there just before stepping into the house. Tabitha had slid an ottoman in front of my mom, and I set the box on top, careful not to startle its occupant.

My mom's eyes narrowed. "Why does that box have airholes?"

"Open it," Tabitha urged.

Mom lifted the lid, and her eyes widened. "Oh, my goodness, who are you?" she said into the box.

"He's yours," I told her. "Tabitha thought you should finally get your boy."

"What's his name?" she asked, reaching in to pick up the sleepy puppy blinking up at her.

"That's for you to decide," Tabitha said. "But there are some things you should know about this little dude." She listed the selling points she'd given me on our drive, but from the second she mentioned "hypoallergenic," Mom was only half-listening as she held him right up to her face to rub noses and coo.

Tabitha and I grinned at each other. "I think she likes him," I said.

"I'll call you Smokey," my mom said. "No, Pepper. Maybe Sergeant Pepper? Or Flint." She was trying out more names when the doorbell rang.

"Who rings the doorbell on Christmas morning?" I glanced in the direction of the door, confused.

"The Redmonds," my mom said, like it wasn't the one answer guaranteed to stop my heart for a full second.

"Why?" This wasn't how I wanted to spend my day, trying to avoid Noah and pretend everything was okay. "Christmas is for family."

"Grace," my mom said, finally looking up from her puppy. She made my name a scolding. "That's exactly why I invited them."

"Evie and I have adopted each other," my dad said, heading for the door.

"I made enough food for everyone," Tabitha said. I shot her a frustrated look. Traitor. She

341

smiled like there wasn't a thing wrong in the world.

Dad came back a minute later with Evie, Paige, and Noah in tow. "Do you see that pink pile of presents, honey?" he asked, crouching so he was on Evie's level.

She looked over at it and her eyes grew big. "Yes."

"There's a card on top with your name on it. You should go check it out."

I hadn't even noticed the pile. It hadn't been there yesterday, but I could barely concentrate on anything because I was working so hard to keep my face pleasant as I smiled at Paige and Noah.

Evie ran toward the pile and plucked the card from the top. "To: Evie, From: Santa." Her mouth fell open and she stared at Paige who looked unsurprised by all of this.

"I guess he left them here since there's more room," she said.

"Better open them," my mom said.

"Those aren't the rules," Tabitha objected, laughing.

"It's different for grandkids," my dad said firmly, and it felt like a knife twisting in my gut, and I failed utterly to resist a look at Noah.

He was watching me with an expression I couldn't read. It was nervous, maybe, like he wasn't sure of his welcome. I mustered a smile for him. "Hey."

"Hey," he said back. "Merry Christmas."

"How about this one first," my dad said, handing Evie a package the size of a shoebox.

She plopped on the floor and ripped the paper off to reveal a toolbox.

"Look inside," my dad said.

She opened the lid and pulled out a hammer, her face lighting up. "Purple! It's all purple tools! That's my favorite color!" She held up one after the other, exclaiming over each of them. "We can build something so super, Papa Dub."

Papa Dub? I glanced at my mom, not understanding.

"It's short for Papa W. That's what she calls him because she says 'W' takes too long to say."

When had this "adoption" taken place? How had I missed it?

"We take turns opening gifts," my mom said to the Redmonds. "I've got mine." She held up her puppy, which drew Evie's notice and caused her to immediately abandon her toolbox to investigate. "Someone else's turn. Tabitha, do you want to handle distribution?"

Tabitha walked over to the tree. "Here's one for you from me, Dad."

He opened a jar of spices. "That's the secret steak rub that Chef Antonio uses on his steaks at La Carne, the highest rated steakhouse in Manhattan. He doesn't sell it, only gifts it to friends at Christmas, and he gave me this for you."

"I can't wait to grill with this," he said. "I love it, honey."

I tried to pay attention, but it was hard when I kept feeling the weight of stares from Tabitha, my parents, even Paige.

And Noah. Every time I looked at him, he was watching me with that same look, and I still couldn't decode it.

But as my dad opened his bottle of spices to smell them, I traded a thankful smile with Tabitha over how different this part of Christmas was compared to last year. Over how good it felt to have our dad back.

"Here's one to Paige from my mom and dad." Tabitha handed her a present, which Paige opened to reveal a pretty green wool coat.

"I confess Lisa picked it out," my dad said, his eyes twinkling.

"I love it," Paige said, getting up to drop a kiss on each of their cheeks.

Not that I wasn't happy to see them get along so well, but again, when had *that* happened?

"Oh, and here's one from Noah to Grace."

My eyes flew to his. "You didn't have to do that," I told him. His eyes sparked with a different kind of energy now. Nerves, still. But what else was I seeing in there? Focus, like I was the only other person in the room.

"I wanted to," he said, his voice quiet. "Open it. Please?"

I hesitated, but his eyes were pleading. I removed the wrapping paper, neatly and methodically, the way I had ever since I was a kid. It had the added bonus of letting me stall as I tried to plan a reaction to whatever it was. It was the size of a sweater box. Sweaters were good. I liked sweaters. With any luck, Paige had helped him pick it out.

But when I lifted the lid, it was just some papers. I glanced up in confusion.

"Read it," he said softly.

I picked up the first one. "It's a print out of a hotel reservation."

He nodded. "For Charleston over President's Day weekend. And several more reservations for every long weekend and holiday between now and the end of the school year."

Twin feelings of hope and disappointment mingled in my chest. It produced the odd feeling of hope rising only to turn into acid reflux as it went. I cleared my throat. "That's great." Seeing him on holiday weekends when we couldn't close the gap was only going to make things harder, but I knew I wouldn't say no.

"There's more," he said. "Keep going."

I shuffled through a few more reservations until I got to a map. I turned it around and showed it to him, my eyebrow raised.

"The best route to Charleston by car," he said.

It was another papercut to the heart. "Nice," I

said, forcing the word around a growing lump in my throat.

"Keep going," he urged again, his voice soft.

The next paper was another printout. I skimmed it, not understanding at first, then I froze, went back to the top, and re-read the title. "Application for Certificated Employment, Charleston School District."

"Is this for real?" My eyes shot to his, which crinkled now at their edges with a smile. He nodded. "But you can't. Paige and Evie." I waved at them, more than confused than ever.

"Well," Noah started.

But my dad cut in. "I fixed that," he said, grinning. "I've been trying to figure out something special I could do for you, and I decided giving you peace of mind was pretty good, so here you go: Paige here has turned out to be the finest assistant manager I've ever had."

"Hey," I objected.

"You know your stuff, kid, but Paige loves being in the store."

She flashed me her own grin. "It's true. I do."

"And she's accepted a full-time job as the store manager."

My mom jumped in. "She and Evie are going to take over your apartment."

"And Evie can't wait to start at Creekville Elementary," Paige said. "She met the principal and her new class on Friday."

"I keeped it a secret, Toodles!" Evie announced, clearly proud of herself.

"That's a good secret, Evie," I said, but my eyes were on Noah, searching his face.

"I just found out yesterday," he told me.

"There's more," my mom said. She rose and cleared her throat. "I'm pleased to announce that Paige and Evie have agreed to adopt us *both* as Evie's honorary grandparents." She and my dad could not have looked more pleased.

"Noah?" I turned back to him.

"They were the only reasons to stay," he said. "And now they've both threatened to disown me if I do, so if you're willing, I'm applying for teaching jobs in Charleston and moving this summer."

"Noah . . ." I didn't know what to say.

"I know teaching doesn't seem like the most ambitious profession, Grace." He looked so earnest that I wanted to reach out and hug him. "But I promise you, I have big goals. I love being in the classroom right now, but eventually I want to get my admin credential and run an entire school. I promise that I love pushing myself as much as you do."

"You think I have a problem with you being a teacher?" It was so far from what I was feeling that I almost laughed.

"You don't?"

"Not at all. I love that about you." There it was again, the almost-confession.

"You said she would say yes, Mama," Evie said, looking up at her mom. "Why don't you say something, Toodles?"

I met Noah's eyes and hoped he could see everything I felt shining from them. "How do you find the words to describe the feeling of a dream come true?"

His forehead smoothed, a relieved smile spreading across his face. He walked over to me, his hands out, and pulled me to my feet. "This next part needs to happen over here."

He led me to a sprig of mistletoe over the doorway—not one of our usual decorations. I shot a look at my mom who only grinned.

Excited whispers sounded behind us, but they barely registered as Noah drew me beneath the mistletoe, his eyes reflecting his hopeful smile.

"Grace Winters, I love you like crazy." My heart did harder flips than I'd ever done in cheer. "That didn't start under Miss Lily's mistletoe," he said. "I think it happened when you wobbled away from me at Brooke and Ian's party. But that first kiss sealed it. Will you give me the chance to come to Charleston and prove to you that you'll be my first, last, and everything for the rest of our lives?"

I smiled up at him, and let everything I was feeling show on my face. "I love you too, Noah. And I can't wait to show you Charleston."

The rest of the room erupted in cheers, but I heard Evie's clear voice piping over everyone's.

"Unc! Kiss the girl!"

And he did.

EPILOGUE
GRACE

"Hurry up, Evie! We don't want to miss Santa!"

"Coming, Toodles! I just need to make sure Jinx is okay!"

I smiled at my honorary niece. She and Paige had been living upstairs in my old apartment for a year, but she'd made herself right at home in my parents' house too.

Noah and I had driven in from Charleston yesterday, arriving at almost the exact same time as Tabitha and her fiancé did from New York.

We'd spent an evening of happy chaos in my parents' living room, talking so loudly no one could hear *Elf* playing—the movie we were all supposedly watching—except for when we all yelled along with the lines we knew and then went back to talking.

Today we'd spent decorating the Christmas tree and making Danish ebelskiver under Tabitha's supervision in the kitchen where she drove all of us crazy except for Evie, who, in Tabitha's book, could apparently do no wrong.

"I think I'm going to like Christmas Town more as a civilian," Noah said, coming up behind me to slide his arms around my waist.

I leaned back against his chest. "Oh, I don't know. It was pretty great working on the booth with you last year."

He gave a murmur of agreement. "Still, I think I'd rather walk around holding mittens with you and not worrying about a single thing except what to eat first."

"Ready," Evie announced. "Let's get Mama."

Tabitha was already at the parade route holding spots for us, so we just needed to meet up with my parents and Paige at the store and walk over to wait for Santa.

We found Tabitha right next to the dais where the mayor and Santa would throw the switch to light Christmas Town. Normally, we took our places a block further down. "Why so close this year?" I asked.

"Just wanted an extra good view, that's all."

"Yeah, because—" Evie started to say something, but Paige cut her off by wrapping a scarf around her neck. "You need to make sure you stay warm, Evie. It's cold tonight."

I smiled as the marching band approached. They were winding down "Rudolph the Red-Nosed Reindeer," and Evie was already jittering impatiently in place. As a second-year Christmas Town veteran, she knew their next song would be the anthem announcing the main event.

"It's almost time," she practically shouted up at Noah who was nearly as antsy as Evie, peering down Main Street to watch the band.

A roar went up from the parade crowd when the opening notes of "Santa Claus Is Coming to Town" sounded, and I grinned as my family cheered along with everyone else. An extra bit of magic wove through this year, a fullness warming my insides more than thick sweaters and hot cocoa ever could. I sniffed when the happiness threatened to leak out as tears, and Noah looked down at me.

"Everything okay?" he asked.

"It's perfect."

"Almost," he said, smiling. "Just wait until Santa gets here."

The band reached us a minute later, the horns uncomfortably loud, the thump of the bass drum filling my chest, the snap of the snares adding a crackle to the anticipation in the air. Then everyone stopped playing except the drummers, who kept beating out a rhythm for them as they marched around the dais to the green itself, clearing a path on the road. It ended with a drumroll followed by a cymbal crash, and in the silence, we all heard it. The jingle of sleigh bells. Another cheer rose from the crowd.

Santa appeared at the end of Main Street, the reindeer pulling him at a gentle but steady pace toward the town green, two elves who looked a lot like Mrs. Li's youngest daughters perched on the sleigh and tossing candy to the crowd as they passed.

When they reached the mayor, Santa handed his reins to a waiting parks employee and stepped from his sleigh to the dais.

"Welcome to Santa Claus and all our Creekville friends and neighbors. Santa, would you do us the honor of opening Christmas Town?"

"Of course," he chuckled with a mellow "ho, ho, ho" for good measure.

"Madam Mayor," he said as he did every year, "Christmas Town is back!"

She handed Santa the oversized brass key and waited as he slotted it into the switch. "On three, Mr. Claus," and then everyone counted with her. "One, two, three!"

A collective gasp followed by murmurs of confusion rippled through the crowd. The Christmas Town lights hadn't turned on. Instead, only a single spotlight shone, falling on Santa's hand, which now clutched a Christmas stocking, a red one with a furry white top.

"I nearly forgot, Madam Mayor," he said. "I have a special early delivery for someone in the crowd." The spotlight widened so we could see all of him. He pretended to adjust his reading glasses as he examined the tag. "Who was this for? Oh, yes, Gracie Winters."

Evie looked up at me, her eyes wide. "That's you, Toodles. Better go see Santa."

"What?" I asked. I'd understood the words everyone had just said. I wasn't processing the situation.

"Santa's asking for you," my mom said. "Go."

My dad took my hand and drew me over to the steps. "Up you go, my girl."

I threw a look at Noah who was only grinning. "You should go see what's going on."

I climbed the stairs and crossed to Mr. Groggins, whose eyes twinkled behind his glasses.

"I believe this belongs to you, my dear." He handed me the stocking.

Whatever was in it was very light. I looked at him questioningly. He smiled and waved at me to get on with it. I reached into the stocking and . . .

"There's nothing in here." What was going on? We were by the mic and a murmur ran through the audience as it broadcast my confusion.

"Oh, silly me," Santa said. "I get so forgetful with all these pre-Christmas details crowding my brain. I believe I need a helper for this. Do I have a volunteer?"

Noah vaulted himself onto the stage. I paused to note how sexy that move was. A year of dating, and I wasn't even close to being tired of him. If anything, he made my butterflies more fluttery, my knees even weaker, and my heart beat faster. What a man.

"I'll help, Santa," he said. "I think I know which gift you're looking for. It's right here." And with that, he pulled a red velvet ring box from his pocket and dropped to one knee.

My hands flew to my mouth, and for a few seconds, the spotlight narrowed again to shine on the ring nestled in the box, a simple solitaire on a delicate gold band.

I couldn't believe that he'd set all of this up without me having the faintest clue. I'd thought I could read him like a book, but it appeared I still had depths yet to discover in this man of mine.

"Grace Winters," he said, apparently the cue for the lighting guy to open the spotlight again as it grew to cover both of us. "You've given me the best year of my life. Playing, laughing, and growing with you has made me far happier than I ever dreamed I could be. I love everything about you with everything that I am. Grace, would you do me the great honor of letting me be your husband?"

I smiled down on him, knowing every ounce of my love and happiness shone in that smile.

Santa cleared his throat. "I believe we'd all like the answer to that, young lady."

"Oh," I said, my eyes opening wide. "Yes, Noah. Yes, I'll marry you!" I pulled him to his feet, and he wrapped his arms around me to sweep me into a kiss as the crowd cheered.

"I kept the secret, Toodles!" Evie called above the noise. Noah smiled against my lips as he heard her.

"Ho ho ho," Santa chuckled. "What a *marry* Christmas indeed! Madam Mayor, I believe that's as good an opening to Christmas Town as we've ever had!" And with a nod in the direction of the parks manager, he and Mayor Derby flipped the switch to flood the scene behind us with light and warmth.

The rest of the town surged into the green to discover what magic the vendors had created this year, but Noah and I stayed put for a long time, creating our own.

ABOUT THE AUTHOR

Melanie Bennett Jacobson is an avid reader, amateur cook, and champion shopper. She lives in Southern California with her husband and children, a series of doomed houseplants, and a naughty miniature schnauzer. She substitutes high school English classes for fun and holds a Masters in Writing for Children and Young Adults from the Vermont College of Fine Arts. She is a four-time Whitney Award winner for contemporary romance and a *USA Today* best-seller.

Center Point Large Print
600 Brooks Road / PO Box 1
Thorndike, ME 04986-0001 USA

(207) 568-3717

US & Canada:
1 800 929-9108
www.centerpointlargeprint.com